When Darkness Falls:

The First Vampire Redemption Story

by Ellen Chauvet

When Darkness Falls: The First Vampire Redemption Story

By Ellen Chauvet

We are always happy to make corrections, updates or include missing sources or information. You may contact us at books@relentlesslycreative.com

ISBN- 978-1-942790-05-1

Author's Website: http://ellenchauvet.com

Author's Blog: http://ellenchauvet.wordpress.com

Twitter: @ChauvetEllen

Published by Relentlessly Creative Books

Publisher's Website: http://relentlesslycreativebooks.com/

773-831-4944

Dedication

This book is dedicated to my husband, Michi.
Thank you for always being a demand for me to be all that I can be.
I miss you.

Contents

Chapter 1
Lexie Miles

Lexie Miles sat waiting for her best friend Emma Gunther to join her at their favorite French bistro, the *Boeuf sur le Toit,* off the Champs Élysées. Emma had been away for two weeks and Lexie was looking forward to their reunion.

Her thoughts drifted to the latest vampire novel Emma had given her to read. It contained hot, juicy sex scenes. Her gaze settled on a handsome man who had entered the restaurant. His wool coat outlined broad shoulders and chest, and tapered to a slim waist and hips. Dark eyes caught hers for a moment before shifting on. He sauntered to a single table radiating sex and passion. Lexie's imagination took over. In her fantasy he was a vampire and she was his lover. She undressed him and heat rose in her groin as she pictured him naked. Lost in her fantasy, she jumped when a hand touched her shoulder.

"Earth to Lexie," Emma's familiar voice intruded.

"Shit you scared the be-jesus out of me." Lexie rose and hugged her friend, then stood back. "Darlin' I'm so happy you're back," she said slipping comfortably into her native Atlanta drawl. The accent she had to clip when speaking French or the Parisian's would look at her with disdain.

"It's good to be back," Emma said, removing her coat before sitting at their table. Emma was tall, had long brown hair which she pulled back in a severe bun and thick glasses. They worked together as translators for the United Nations and their friendship had flourished over the past three years. Emma was the science translator as well as a chemist and math whizz. They were a

1

strange combination: a pretty Southern belle from Georgia and a stodgy but brilliant German fraulein, but the friendship worked. Rather than going home to Atlanta, Lexie had spent summer vacations at the Gunther's cottage in the Taunus Mountains, and Christmas holidays with Emma and her father in Frankfurt.

Too cold in late November to sit outside, Lexie and Emma enjoyed the warmth and coziness of the restaurant as they waited for their meals.

"What were you thinking about when I came in?" Emma said. "You were a million miles away."

Lexie felt her cheeks redden and dipped her head to avoid Emma's stare. "I was thinkin' about some stuff at work. How was your trip?" Lexie steered the conversation to a safer topic.

"It was good. Saw some friends from university and had a good visit with my father."

Lexie noticed that Emma's response was vague, and wondered what she wasn't saying. Before she could ask, the waiter arrived with their food. They ate in silence, the awkwardness between them increasing.

Puzzled by her friend's reticence, Lexie leaned back and said, "How come the subject of men and vampires hasn't come up yet?"

"You always make fun of me when I talk about vampires," Emma replied. "And as for men…" she left the statement hanging. Lexie did think that Emma's fascination with the undead was odd so she steered the conversation toward men.

Lexie felt a twinge of remorse that Emma was reluctant to mention vampires around her, so she chose to bring a bit of humor to the conversation.

"We're not spring chickens anymore," Lexie said.

"Don't be silly, we're only 29." Emma replied. "Besides, you tried a committed relationship, and we both know how that went."

"Don't remind me," Lexie said as Justin's handsome face flashed through her mind. "I still get my panties in a wad when I think of findin' him with that bitch. That still hurts."

"Ach, let's not rehash that one again." Just like Lexie's drawl, Emma's German accent was always more evident when it was just the two of them.

"At least I have one to rehash. How much longer are you gonna to pine over Tom?"

"That's not fair."

Lexie could see the hurt in her friend's eyes. "I'm sorry. I just get frustrated that you waste your time longin' for our unapproachable boss." The truth was Lexie also had a little crush on their brawny, Daniel Craig-like English boss. But of the two of them, she had the role of being the one who was worldly about men, and she enjoyed that. Since the disaster with Justin, she had shied away from any long term relationships. One night stands were exciting and safe. Never mind that they left her feeling empty and lonely.

Emma smiled at her. "I know you worry about me. Maybe my destiny is to find a 'good' vampire like in the books we've been reading. Then I could live a life of adventure and hot, juicy, passionate sex." Emma purred.

"Girl they are just myths. Besides, I don't believe in good and evil." Lexie usually saw Emma's eyes twinkling in amusement through her thick glasses at their ongoing debate.

But this time Emma's eyes held no sparkle and she said with a serious tone. "All myths have some truth in the background."

"I guess everyone needs to believe in somethin'." Lexie said. *Especially when you're a mousy nerd.* She experienced a twinge of guilt at her unkind thought. Lexie loved Emma like a sister and her attempts to improve her appearance came from a place of caring.

"Hon you are barkin' up the wrong tree if you think I'll ever believe vampires are real. There isn't any 'truth' in the background. Although I must admit, I enjoy the erotica. The

3

scenes give me wonderful ideas for my own flings." She winked at her friend. "C'mon let's get out of here and go for a walk."

Even Lexie noticed that male heads turned to ogle her as she exited. She and Emma walked the Champs Élysées, wandering in and out of the fashionable stores that were still open.

"This would look wonderful on you," Lexie said. She held up a deep purple sweater for Emma's approval. Lexie felt it was her mission in life to break Em out of her dowdy wardrobe.

"It would look better on you." Emma replied. "This is more my style." She held up a mustard yellow sweater and Lexie cringed at the sight.

"The color is awful. It makes you look dead. Will you at least try this purple one on?"

Emma took the sweater and slipped it over her head. Lexie smiled. It was stunning and brought out Em's chocolate brown eyes.

It's too....bright," Emma said and yanked the sweater off.

"I love it on you."

Emma regarded the sweater and Lexie could sense that she wavered.

"Won't you at least give it a try?"

"I don't know...I have plenty of clothes."

"C'mon hon, it's sexy."

"I never think of myself that way."

Lexie grabbed Emma's arm and pulled her in front one of the store mirrors. "Hold it up in front of you."

"Does it really make me look sexy?" Lexie could tell the idea of sexy appealed to her.

"Absofrigginlutely, you have to have it." Lexie smiled to herself as Emma walked to the cashier and paid for the item.

Will wonders never cease?

They stepped back out on the boulevard and Lexie linked arms with Emma as they walked. In soft whispers they commented on the men that they passed on the street. It was their usual game of imagining whether or not certain ones could be good vampires or bad vampires and then laughed at their silliness.

Lexie pointed to a couple approaching. "Now he's someone I could take to bed in a heartbeat," she whispered into Emma's ear.

They were passing the Cartier store and Emma grabbed her arm and pulled.

"Look at that diamond necklace. Isn't that the most beautiful thing you've ever seen?"

"I guess so." Lexie stumbled after her.

Startled by Emma's sudden interest in the incredibly expensive item in the window, Lexie started to say something when Emma tensed holding her arm so tight it hurt.

"Em, you're hurtin' me." She tugged at her friend's grip but Emma held on tighter. "What's going on with you? The necklace is gorgeous, and way out of our price range."

Lexie felt a presence behind her. Her scalp prickled and her heart rate accelerated. She scratched her head wondering if she'd picked up lice. The scratching didn't help.

"Oui, that is a most delightful piece," said a tinkling female voice with a heavy French accent. "It would look stunning on you."

Lexie turned and the petite young woman who had spoken was too gorgeous for words. Her hair was blond almost white in the soft light of the Cartier window. Blue eyes twinkled from her heart shaped face. Her skin was translucent and flawless. The woman extended her hand and as Lexie shook it she noticed delicate blue veins on the back.

"My name is Marielle," she said. "And this is my husband François."

Lexie looked up into eyes so dark brown they appeared black. High cheekbones that any model would kill for were framed by lustrous brown hair. His broad chest and shoulders filled out the suede jacket he wore, and tight fitting designer jeans revealed a slim waist and long legs.

So young to be married.

"Enchanté" Lexie replied taking the man's outstretched hand. "Je m'apelle Lexie." Again her scalp prickled. It was annoying.

She looked at Emma who still clutched her arm. Emma stared at the couple in a way that was not friendly but as if she knew these strangers.

"Do y'all know each other?" Lexie asked puzzled by Emma's demeanor.

"Ah no, mademoiselle." François spoke for the first time and reached out his hand toward Emma.

Emma released the death grip she had on Lexie's arm. In slow motion Emma raised her hand and when Lexie looked into her eyes the pupils were dilated and fixed. Her mouth opened but no sound came out. Lexie could see that François had captured Emma's eyes with his own and the intensity of his gaze reminded Lexie of a hypnotist.

How odd.

"This is my friend Emma." Lexie was pleased to introduce her friend but for the first time felt the male attention was being stolen by Emma.

François raised Emma's hand to his lips and kissed the back of it. When he released it, it hung in the air like some disembodied prosthetic. Before Lexie could say anything, François turned to Lexie.

"We were just passing by and noticed you admiring the necklace. We were both struck by your good looks and Marielle couldn't resist saying hello. Are you perhaps a fashion model?"

"Oh, well it's nice to meet you both and no, I am not a fashion model. But thank you kindly for the compliment," Lexie replied, her ego soothed.

"C'mon, we need to go," Emma said. "It's getting late and I have a lot to do tomorrow."

Rude much? "It was nice meeting you both," Lexie said.

"It was our pleasure mademoiselle," François replied. "Perhaps we will bump into each other again soon." He smiled at Emma and Lexie noticed that the smile never reached his eyes.

"I would enjoy that," Emma responded and then blushed to her roots. "We need to go." Emma hustled Lexie to the curb. She waved her arm to hail a cab.

"Em, what are you doing? You just live a few blocks away, and I can take the train to Montmartre." Emma didn't respond, and as a cab pulled alongside, she jerked open the door and climbed in.

"Get in," she demanded. Lexie hesitated. Emma reached out and yanked Lexie's arm and she stumbled into the cab.

"Em, what's wrong with you? You're acting very strange."

"There was just something about that couple that I didn't trust. Especially the woman. They just - how do you say it in English 'bugged me.'"

"But, honey, what's with the cab? Aren't we going to the Bus Palladium for dancing?"

"I'm too tired to go dancing tonight." Emma replied. "Besides I want to make sure that you get home safe."

Still puzzled at her friend's strange behavior, Lexie sat quietly for several minutes hoping she would explain further. When she didn't, she decided to change the topic.

"Are we getting together tomorrow?"

"Not tomorrow," Emma replied.

"We could go shopping at the Gallerie Lafayette and Printemps. Have a late lunch at Café du Margot and finalize our plans for Christmas. It'll be here before you know it."

"I have some things I need to take care of. But I will call you on Sunday morning and we can get together then, okay?"

"Sounds good. Don't forget my Mom arrives in the afternoon." Lexie said wondering what things Emma needed to take care of. On occasion her friend could be aloof.

"I haven't forgotten. I'm looking forward to meeting her." The cab pulled up in front of Lexie's apartment. She was surprised when Emma leaned over and grabbed her arm.

"Be careful, Paris is not as safe as you think. Lock your door and check your windows."

"I promise I'll be careful," Lexie replied. "Are you sure you're okay?"

"I'm fine. I'll talk to you Sunday."

Lexie waved as the taxi pulled away from the curb. Emma's eyes stared at her, but she didn't wave back. *So strange.* She entered her apartment unable to shake off the sense of unease brought on by Emma's behavior.

Large by Paris standards, Lexie's home reflected her eclectic taste. Deep red drapes covered the French doors that led to her balcony, and the pieces of furniture she'd acquired were ultra-modern in design. She took a moment to review her to do list in preparation for her mother's visit. Most of them were ticked off. She would clean the next day.

In contrast to the rest of the apartment, her bedroom was romantic with wooden shutters painted a robin's egg blue, a bedspread to match and big fluffy pillows tossed casually about. Her bed was wrought iron with gauzy soft blue drapes. Lexie changed into her pajamas and her eyes locked on to the most recent vampire book she was reading. Her thoughts turned to Emma and the discomfort she'd experienced earlier returned. She picked up the phone to call her then smiled at her concern. *I'll worry about that tomorrow.*

Chapter 2
Emma's Meeting

Emma slumped against the back seat as the taxi pulled away from Lexie's apartment. Heart still pounding, she focused on breathing deeply to quiet her nerves. She couldn't remember ever being as unraveled as she had been when she had seen François and Marielle on the Champs Élysées. They had recognized Lexie and that boded trouble.

She stepped down from the taxi in front of her apartment. "Please wait for me. I won't be long," she said to the driver handing him twenty Euros.

He smiled, happy she was not just another cheap foreigner trying to get a free ride.

After she locked and bolted her front door behind her, she felt relieved, but she no longer knew if she was safe anywhere. She wondered if François and Marielle were watching or had followed her home. Her thoughts lingered on François. She had fallen hard and fast and now her hopes and dreams centered on him. The last time they had met alone François had promised her many things. To leave Marielle and be with her, heal the rift with his father and leave the dark side. She touched her lips where the memory of his last kiss lingered. She still couldn't believe he wanted her. She knew the risks – vampires are not to be trusted – especially the dark ones. She had promised François she would tell no one and kept her promise. Tonight it had taken everything she had not to blurt out her secret to Lexie. She hated lying and worried Lexie was now vulnerable.

Everything the Society had worked for and stood for was in danger now that François and Marielle knew of the precious antiserum and its formula. When they had first approached her several weeks prior, François had done most of the talking. His good looks and smooth compliments had turned her head. He had compelled her and the only thing that had saved her from falling completely under his will was the human serum mixed with verveine she took daily. But it had not prevented her from falling in love with him.

Despite her strong feelings for François, she had managed to keep her wits. Instead of giving him what he wanted she devised an elaborate plan to conceal the authentic antiserum and formula. As she reviewed the details she felt confident the life-saving items would be safe. She was playing with fire, surviving the night was uncertain.

Tonight she was meeting François in the Jardin de Tuillieries to give him the fake antiserum and formula. It was a test to make sure he would be true to his word. She could only hope he loved her. He assured her he did.

She surveyed her Provence-style decor with its hues of orange, red and sunflower yellow. She loved her place with its treasures from home - the small antique carriage clock that had belonged to her grandmother, and the beautiful old steamer trunk that she used as a coffee table. They were her Dad's loving contribution to her apartment.

The vial of clear liquid and formula caught her eye. She opened a small *Printemps* shopping bag, placed each item inside, and stuffed it in her purse.

Would she ever see her home again?

She shrugged off her sudden departure into sadness, and ran down the stairs freeing her hair from its customary bun. François preferred it loose and flowing. Besides, it made her feel sexier. She gave the taxi driver the address of a small Internet café near the Jardin de Tuilleries.

Emma sat at one of the computers going over and over her e-mail to Étienne and Tom. She gathered her courage, entered the next day's date and pushed the send later button. She left the café, turning right toward the Tuilleries, and pulled the collar of her jacket close. The night was cold and clear. She entered the garden, and paused, listening for any strange noise before proceeding along the path. The full moon and soft white lights strung in the surrounding trees showed her the way.

"*Bonne nuit, chérie,*" a silky male voice whispered in her ear.

Emma's heart almost stopped. The first rush of carnal heat moved through her body. He surprised her.

"*Bonne nuit,*" she replied, turning to face him. François' handsome face was lost in shadow. His wintry blue eyes were all she could see. Delicious and dangerous. "Come into the trees," he said taking her hand. She followed him into the underbrush glancing over her shoulder.

"Have you kept your promise?"

"I told no one, not even Lexie. and I made sure no one was following me. I would never disobey your instructions. Your trust means everything to me."

"Do you have the package?"

"I have what you asked for."

"That is good *chérie.*" He stroked her face with his hand.

She shivered at his touch and fought to keep a cool head.

"Give them to me," he said.

"In a moment. Have you thought about your promises?"

"We can talk about that later. We are together and alone," he said. "That's more important."

Emma took a step back. She needed a little distance to think. "By the way, why did you and Marielle approach my friend and me tonight? It was awkward."

11

"We were out for a stroll and noticed you admiring the necklace. Marielle insisted on meeting her." François stroked her cheek again.

"I was afraid you wouldn't be able to get away from her tonight." Emma said.

"Don't worry about her. *Elle est une musaraigne.*"

Emma couldn't help but smile at his use of the word shrew.

"After five hundred years I am sick of her nagging and jealous fits." He reached to take her in his arms.

Emma clutched her purse closer, still hesitant to give in too soon. "I've missed you." The beating of her heart sounded like thunder in her ears.

"But chérie, it's only been a few hours since we last met." Once more he caressed her cheek.

Emma shivered at his touch. "It's seems like an eternity and you were with Marielle."

"Perhaps I have been a little too *délicat* with you." His silky voice turned her insides to mush. He raised her chin and gazed into her eyes. Emma felt a pulling sensation. "Maybe you want a little walk on the wild side, *n'est-ce pas*? Let me have my way with you and I will leave Marielle and come to your light side." He grazed her cheek with his lips.

"Don't tease me," Emma whispered. "You know how I feel about you." She reached for him.

He took her in his arms his cool lips brushing against her eyelids and cheeks. She threw her arms around his neck and pulled him close. He hardened against her body and moist heat flooded between her legs.

Her efforts to stay focused faltered in the wave of lust that washed over her. She wanted to believe he loved her. He thrust his tongue between her lips until she felt the tips of his fangs. Titillation overpowered fear and she tightened her grip.

He pulled away from her. "Wait *chérie*," he said, removing his coat. He spread it on the ground. Impressed by his act of chivalry, Emma relaxed into him. He eased her down.

"I want you," he said against her ear.

Before she could respond, he ripped her blouse open and shoved her bra away. The gentleness was gone. He pinched her nipples and despite the pain, they turned into hard nuggets. François captured her mouth with his and reaching under her skirt, he traced the inside of her leg. He pressed his hand against her wet mound and rubbed almost sending her over the edge. She arched against him wanting more. He was hard. Ready. With one quick movement, he ripped her panties, his fingers rough as he fingered her clit. Emma whimpered in pain. She tried to pull his hand away. His smile was cruel as he squeezed harder.

"You're hurting me."

"I'm just getting started." He raked her most intimate parts with his tongue, biting and fondling. "You're so juicy and you taste…," he said as he lapped at her opening. His fangs hurt as they scraped against her.

Emma was mortified that her body was still responding to his violence. "Please stop," she said pushing at his shoulders.

His response was biting her nipple so hard she cried out. She could feel blood running down her side. She began hitting him and he laughed at her efforts. He took both arms in one hand and held them over her head. She'd never felt so helpless.

"Relax chérie," he said. He licked the spot where she was bleeding, his tongue gentle and soothing. "Sometimes I get carried away. You're safe with me." He kissed her and desire overruled her fear.

She rubbed against him the need for release making her reckless. She heard the soft whish of his zipper and his cock caressed her inner thigh. He nudged against her vulva and she felt the head of his penis slip between her labia. He grunted and thrust hard.

Emma moaned as pain and pleasure washed over her. "Be gentle *liebe*, this is our first time and it has been a very long time for me."

13

"I will make sure it is pleasurable for one of us," he purred. He pounded into her and Emma could tell he had no intention of making it pleasurable.

"Stop, you're hurting me," she cried pushing against his shoulders, struggling beneath him.

"Too late for that *chérie*," he growled.

The thrusting intensified. Emma screamed in pain as he rubbed her raw.

Emma heard a twig snap and a familiar voice shrieked, "François".

His head snapped to the side.

"*Enfoiré, que faites-vous?*" Marielle cried. She grabbed François by the hair and catapulted him toward a nearby tree. He slammed into it and Emma could hear a crack as his head connected with the trunk. "Did you think I wouldn't know? I can read your thoughts from miles away. Sex was not part of the plan! I should castrate you for this."

François lay dazed and disoriented. Marielle turned to Emma who was trying to cover her nakedness as she scrambled to her feet.

The beautiful woman's hair shone pale and ethereal in the moonlight. Her gleaming red eyes gave off fiery sparks as she advanced toward Emma. "And you are a mate-stealing *poutain*," she said. "I should kill you!"

"Wait *chérie*," François said approaching the two women and laying a hand on Marielle's shoulder. "I do not have the antiserum and formula yet."

"You should learn to keep that thing in your pants," she retorted. "It gets in the way of your brain." She turned and looked at Emma intently.

"Give it to me. Give me the antiserum." Marielle demanded.

Emma took a step back.

"It is not meant for you. It's meant for François."

"You can give it to her." François said. His eyes bored into Emma's.

"How do I know she won't kill me as soon as I give it to her?"

"You don't," Marielle sneered as she inched closer. "But we will surely kill you if you deceive us."

Emma stepped sideways so she could eyeball them both. "You will probably do that anyway. Your kind lies."

"What has happened to your compelling?" Marielle asked François.

"She's probably been taking verveine to counteract the effects," François said. "It doesn't matter. I'm sure she has the package. She is in love with me."

Moving faster than Emma's eyes could follow, Marielle jerked the purse from her shoulder and dumped the contents on the path. Marielle's laughter pealed in the night air as she pounced on the *Printemps* bag. She reached inside and withdrew the bottle of liquid and the paper with the formula on it.

She waved them in front of François' face. "We have them."

"Wait *chérie*," François cautioned. "We must be sure."

He grabbed the bottle from her and took a swig of the liquid.

"*Sacre bleu*," he wheezed. "The bitch has laced this with verveine and poisoned me." He began coughing violently, spitting it out.

"In love with you, bah," Marielle caught him as he fell. "*Merde*," she exclaimed. "This can't be happening. François how could you be so stupid? All these centuries and you're still an *idiot pathétique*."

Emma turned and ran toward the lighted path. She'd been so certain that François loved her, certain he would leave Marielle and come to the light side. It had all been a trap.

"Where do you think you're going?" Marielle asked, moving so fast she was a blur. She grabbed Emma's arm and twisted hard.

Emma cried out in pain as Marielle dragged her back toward François. She summoned every bit of strength she could and wrenched her arm free, throwing the tiny woman off balance. Emma delivered a devastating round house kick to her head. Marielle went down and Emma stomped on her throat intent on killing her. Marielle lay clutching her throat her mouth moving in silence. Emma pressed harder.

The verveine had made François sick but not weak. Emma realized it too late.

"You bitch, you'll pay for deceiving us," François said, grabbing Emma's hair. He pulled her back into the shadows, ignored Marielle and threw Emma to the ground. "You said you love me and you have lied and tricked me. We had a deal."

"I do love you but I couldn't trust you," Emma said, getting to her feet. "If you promise to leave Marielle and enter the light I will tell you where the real antiserum and formula are."

"Why should I trust you now?" François asked. "It may be more of your treachery. If I could be certain you really love me I would leave her and join you."

"You would betray me for this piece of shit?" Marielle said quite recovered. Marielle lunged at him, fangs bared.

"In a heartbeat," François said drawing a stake from his jacket. He stood his ground.

"I will have your heart for a snack," she snarled.

He plunged the stake into her chest. She fell clutching the stake trying to pull it from her body. "You bastard, *vous m'avez tuée.*"

"Emma I've killed her for you, does that prove my love and my intention?" He took her hand and pulled her deeper into the bushes, his arms encircling her.

Still conflicted, Emma gazed up at him. She wanted to believe that this vampire, the culmination of all her passionate dreams, desired her, but reason prevailed. Even if he was rough she craved his touch, wanted him, loved him. But her years working with the Society had trained her well. She couldn't trust him.

"I've hidden it at the Society in Grignon," she replied. "It's in a small lock box in the tack room of the stables." Her heart tripped at her lie.

"I hope you're telling me the truth. Our future together depends on it." He kissed her, running his hands through her hair. For a moment Emma forgot everything.

"Finally you've done something right," Marielle said coming up behind them. The stake had not pierced her heart and she was healing.

"What do we do now?" François asked.

Emma was unsure who he was speaking to.

Marielle grabbed Emma and twisted her head, snapping her neck. Emma was dead before she hit the ground.

"We kill her," Marielle said.

"*Sacre bleu*, idiot," François exclaimed. "She was our only link. What if she lied about where she hid it?"

"Do not fret *ma cher*," Marielle said. "We still have our source on the inside. We will not fail. I promise."

"I hope you're right *chérie*" François said. "We've come a long way and I hate failure."

"So do I," Marielle said. "By the way you were very convincing. You really played her. But I didn't expect you to go so far. You were having a little too much pleasure."

"Tu *est stupide*," he replied. "She was a cow. She did nothing for me. She was an easy lay. You know I love you. After all these years you shouldn't doubt me."

"Hmmph, I'm just thankful your aim was so accurate to miss my heart. What should we do with her?"

He dropped to his knees and lifted Emma's head to expose her neck. "Perhaps it is time to drive our point home."

He began to feed.

"You pig, save some for me," Marielle said. She shoved his head aside and found her own spot.

In no time they had drained Emma. Her neck a gaping wound.

"Occasionally you have a good idea. That was very tasty," Marielle said. She stood wiping the blood from her mouth.

"It felt good to kill the treacherous bitch. We'll leave her here and inform our source of the possible location of the prize." François wiped the blood from his mouth and burped.

"Disgusting," Marielle said. "You are so gross."

"I was born a man. It's in my nature." He retrieved the bottle and formula, placing them in his breast pocket.

They disappeared into the darkness leaving Emma Gunter's broken blood spattered body lying where she had died.

Chapter 3
Lexie's Story

Lexie was running, running fast – panting, her heart threatening to burst from her chest. She was running from something she couldn't quite see. Sharp brambles like clawed fingers grabbed at her clothing. She was scared, so scared. She glanced down at her slippery and wet hands, red with blood. Is this my blood?

There was no pain, but where had the blood come from? Did I hurt someone else?

She pushed through the dense undergrowth stumbling upon a body she recognized immediately. "Daddy, Daddy are you hurt?"

She bent down gasping in horror at his ravaged throat.

Danger, I'm in danger.

But she couldn't remember why. She just knew she had to keep running. Her legs struggled to flee from the gruesome vision of her father.

There was no light, only dense, sticky darkness. She stumbled and fell. Falling endlessly into nothingness. She screamed but there was no one to hear her; only a bottomless black void.

Lexie woke with a start, the scream in her nightmare echoing in her ears. Her bedding was soaked with sweat. Hugging her knees to her chest, she fought to calm her pulse. The nightmare replayed. Flashes of her father's face and blood, so much blood she was drowning in it.

"Shit, that was too real." It was the recurring dream she'd had off and on since she was ten, and although she'd seen doctors over the years, it remained a mystery.

She stayed huddled for a few moments, waiting for her racing heart and breathing to return to normal. When she felt she could stand without passing out, she unfolded her body and stood, trembling as if she'd run a marathon. She made her way to the kitchen, poured a glass of water, and plopped into one of the kitchen chairs. The horror of the nightmare receded as she sipped. *My Dad is always in the dream. And he's always bloody.*" Dad had died of a heart attack when she was ten.

She still remembered his infectious laugh and how he had entertained her with stories from his travels. He had been her hero. Her Mom had insisted on a closed casket and never let Lexie see him though she knew most funerals had open caskets. She assumed her Mom hadn't wanted her to freak out, yet a resentment lingered she didn't understand. Maybe she needed to see him to let go. Maybe that's what the dreams meant.

The clock on the stove showed 3:00 A.M. She stumbled back to the bedroom, punched her pillow a couple of times in frustration, and fell asleep.

Saturday morning as the aroma from her automatic coffee machine tickled her awake, Lexie's first thought was of Emma and her strange behavior with 'Mr. and Mrs. High fashion.' *They were almost too beautiful.* She remembered when she touched the woman's hand her scalp itched like she had a bad case of lice, and her heart rate accelerated.

She yawned. *Wonder what that was about?* And her nightmare, first one she'd had in months. She shivered remembering her terror. *Coffee, I need coffee.*

She sipped a cup of the strong French Roast, Legal le Gout Café des Chefs, and paused in front of the doors to her balcony. She mused how she had fulfilled her childhood dream of living and working in Paris. She was blessed with Emma, who was more a sister than a friend and her boss, Tom Grant, was the best. The fact he was a tall, ruggedly handsome hottie and had that sexy English accent was an added bonus. Even his English tweeds and handmade leather shoes were sexy. She had always had a crush on him, but she had never done anything about it as he was unavailable.

Lexie loved everything about Paris and felt at home as soon as she stepped off the plane. Cassie was another story. She had accompanied Lexie 'to make sure she got settled properly.' For the entire two weeks Cassie fussed about the decadence of French food, all the 'foreigners' on the streets, and that there was no decent Southern Baptist church for her to attend. Lexie tolerated her Mom's down home prejudices as she had all her life, and was relieved Cassie finally left. But now, with her mother due to arrive tomorrow she forgot her resentment and was looking forward to seeing her. A moment of homesickness and nostalgia washed over her.

Crap, I'm gonna be late. She hurried into the bathroom to wash and do something with her hair. As she brushed her hair and pulled it into a pony tail she was relatively satisfied with her reflection. With shoulder length brown hair, large brown eyes, and as Emma had said last night, a good figure, she knew by most standards she could be considered 'a looker'.

Her thoughts turned to having a man in her life. All the men she had dated seemed self-absorbed and shallow. In university, dating had been casual. There had only been one man, Justin Connelly – ah, Justin. *Why did she always go for the bad boys?* She had loved him completely, and his infidelity in her senior year of undergrad school at Emory University had left her gun shy. Even with the sultry temptations of French men she was wary. *There has to be more to life than workin' for the next twenty years and waitin' for a good man to come along.*

You need a purpose, she said aloud to her reflection. Then, she thought of her trainer, Gaétan. *What I really need is a good, sweaty workout.* She jogged the twelve blocks to the gym.

21

"Bonjour Gaétan," she called.

"Bonjour Lexie." Her delicious trainer called back from his stretched out position on the floor. His muscular body caused her heart to flip flop.

"Are you ready for your workout?"

Lexie laughed. "Are you ready to get your butt kicked?"

She reached out her hand to pull him up, marveling at the depth of his smoky brown eyes.

"Mon Dieu, you are in fine form this morning," he said. "Get warmed up and we shall begin."

"I'm already warmed up. Let's get started."

Still grasping his hand, she whirled and threw him over her shoulder. He landed on the floor with a thud. Hanging on to her hand, he used the leverage to twirl around, and deliver a crushing round house kick to her legs, landing her on top of him. He pushed her away, turning to confront her. They danced around each other looking for an opening to strike. It was Gaétan who landed the next punch. He caught her on the shoulder, and as she staggered, he kicked her legs out from under her.

"No sympathy for you today, Lexie. But before we continue, we must put on the gear, *non?*"

He pulled a pair of boxing gloves and helmet from the storage box and threw them to her. He donned his own while waiting for Lexie to finish before sparring with her again. Lexie dodged and weaved, deftly deflecting his punches until she found an opening, and landed a hard right to his jaw. He staggered, scrambling to regain his balance. She pressed in taking advantage of his momentary vulnerability but he spun away avoiding a crushing left. They parried this way until both of them were sweating from the exertion.

"Merde!" Gaétan said, after Lexie delivered a whacking blow to his midriff. He was doubled over gasping for air.

22

"Sorry." She backed off waiting for him to catch his breath. "I thought you were ready for that one."

"You're getting faster and stronger," he said, grinning. "The pupil is surpassing the teacher. I think we can move on to *Jiu Jitsu*." He threw her a towel and wiped his face.

He grabbed her towel, pulled her towards him and wrapped his arms around her, using the weight of his body to force her to the mat.

Lexie gripped his head with her legs. She tingled as his chin rubbed her clit. He never missed a beat as he rolled her around breaking free.

They went through the movements, slowly and sensually. At the end of the hour, she finally had Gaétan pinned and straddled him triumphantly.

"*Mon chérie, votre force est au-delà de la croyance,*" he said, peering up at her from the mat. His praise of her increasing strength made her flush with pride. A lock of hair had fallen rakishly over one eye, and his fathomless eyes drew her into their darkness. His animal attraction had her vagina wet with desire. *Oh man, it just sucks that this guy is gay.*

"You can say that again," she said. "That's the first time I've ever been able to pin you. Come on, let's keep goin'. I'm just gettin' warmed up."

"I think I've had enough for today," he said, grasping her hand. She pulled him to his feet. "I'll see you next Saturday at nine A.M. We'll see how you're progressing."

Although cold and crisp, it was beautiful and sunny for a November day in Paris.

Lexie decided to take advantage of the break from the drizzle that had lately blanketed the city, and do her weekly grocery shop on her way home.

She greeted the shopkeeper gaily at the neighborhood fruit stand. "*Bonjour*, Madame Villaume,"

"What would you like today?" the shopkeeper asked, as Lexie fingered the beautiful melons and tomatoes that were on display.

She made her choices, and headed out to walk the charming old streets of Montmartre. She was, as always, awed by the impressive sight of Sacré Coeur looming over the city. There was something about the basilica that caught her attention and gave her a sense of peace and grace. *Funny that, given how much I hate religion.*

She visited each of her favorite shops for the rest of her groceries, and spent the next hour wandering the streets. Soulful jazz played from an open window. She paused to listen. The smell of fresh baked bread from a nearby *pâtisserie* made her mouth water.

The Montmartre carousel boasted horses of every color and the accompanying accordion music was so typically Parisienne it made her smile. The exquisite boutiques and tourist shops she passed offered everything from expensive designer clothing to popular trinkets made in the images of the City of Lights. Indulging in one of her favorite past times, she sat at the foot of Sacre Coeur before heading home. She was enchanted by the parade of people from different ethnic groups and the different languages she could hear passing by.

Suddenly she stiffened, cocking her head.

"*Mary, mère de Dieu, mon enfant me manque. Ma douleur et la souffrance sont insupportables.*" A mother's prayer to the Virgin Mary mourned the death of her child.

Then she noticed she could hear other people mumbling their prayers as well. But the church was across the street. It was odd. *I don't remember being able to hear prayers before.*

Puzzled, she gathered up her packages and walked the two blocks to her apartment.

She hated cleaning house, but Cassie was arriving and her mother's white glove test was imminent.

She was vacuuming when her intercom buzzer sounded. *That's strange. Em said she was busy today.*

"Who is it?" she said into the speaker, expecting Emma's voice to reply.

"It's Tom. We need to talk."

"Is somethin' wrong?" She couldn't imagine why her boss would drop by on a Saturday. He'd never been to her apartment.

"It's urgent," he answered.

Lexie hurried into the bathroom to run a brush through her hair. She sprayed a dash of her favorite perfume on and added lip gloss. Her doorbell rang.

"Sorry to burst in on you this way," Tom said.

There was a strange man with him, a couple inches shorter than Tom, but the same coloring. "What's so urgent you couldn't call?"

"This is Détective Robert de la Croix, an associate of mine," Tom said.

When Lexie shook his hand, his grip was powerful.

"Détective. What's happened?"

"*Enchanté* Mademoiselle Miles," the detective responded, ignoring her question.

"I'm afraid we have bad news. I think it would be best if you sit down." Tom said leading her to the sofa. "Bollocks, there's no easy or gentle way to tell you."

"Tell me what? Y'all are scarin' me."

"Emma's been murdered."

In a pig's eye. "I'm sorry I don't think I understood you. Something's happened to Em?"

"She's been murdered," Tom repeated.

25

"What are you talkin' about? I was just with her last night and we made plans to see each other tomorrow. We're pickin' Cassie up at the airport. She can't be dead."

Tom took her hand the expression on his face told her more than his words and reflected his sorrow.

"He's telling you the truth," the detective said. "We found her body…"

Lexie's breath caught in her throat as the reality sank in. "If this is some kind of joke, it's not funny." She leapt to her feet and paced the floor. "We were in a taxi last night and Em was goin' straight home. Did someone break into her apartment?"

"No, her body was found in the Jardins de Tuillieries." Tom said. "Her throat had been torn out and …the police think it was an animal attack."

"What was she doin' in the Tuillieries? This is Paris for heaven's sake. There are no wild animals in the city."

"Mademoiselle that is the 'official' story the police have given the media. However, we suspect it was not an animal," Détective de la Croix said. "It was something much more *dangereux*."

"Will somebody please explain what in tarnation is goin' on? Y'all aren't makin' any sense at all and I'm gettin' really pissed. I don't believe that Em is dead."

"Steady on Lex," Tom soothed. "We'll explain everything in good time. The detective needs you to go down to the station and answer a few questions."

"Why? I'm still havin' trouble not thinkin' y'all are pullin' my leg."

"You were the last one to see her alive. Emma may have said something or maybe you noticed something odd in her behavior."

Unwanted tears threatened to spill down her cheeks as she stared at the two men in disbelief. *Shit Em, what the hell?*

"I still don't believe you. I'm gonna call her." Lexie dialed Emma's number. The phone rang several times before going to voice mail. She hit re-dial frustrated that Emma wasn't answering. "Come on Em answer." No answer.

"It's no use Lex, she's not going to answer," Tom said, taking the phone from her hand.

"She's really dead then," Lexie's voice quivered with held back emotion.

"She's really dead." Tom put his arm around her shoulders and she turned toward him. Grateful for his show of tenderness, she let the tears come.

"Have you seen her?" she asked.

"I identified her body."

"Détective, you said it wasn't an animal. If it wasn't an animal, then what or who was it and what happened?"

"All in good time," the detective said. "Please come with us."

The drab police station bustled with activity and Lexie felt like she was trapped in a parallel time warp. The detective led her to an interrogation room and as they approached, a man came toward them. He moved so gracefully he seemed to float. His eyes were fixed on Lexie causing goose bumps to rise on her body. He joined them, nodding to her but said nothing. Despite being numb with grief, Lexie was acutely aware of the handsome stranger walking at her side and the soft swish of silk from his Armani suit.

Tom closed the door behind him. "I'd like you to meet an associate, Étienne de Benoit."

Étienne was a couple of inches taller than Tom, and perhaps a few years younger. High prominent cheekbones framed green eyes. Straight, jet black hair fell to his shoulders, and appeared soft and lustrous. His broad shoulders filled his silk jacket and his silk shirt clung to his body, tapering to a trim waist. She looked into his eyes, and they drew her in.

Étienne took her hand and raised it to his lips. *"Enchanté, Mademoiselle* Miles.*"*

He knows my name.

Lexie struggled to maintain her composure as he continued to stare.

What the?

"The p-pleasure is all m-mine *Monsieur.*"

"I asked Étienne to join us as he has experience in solving murders like Emma's," Tom said.

Lexie barely heard him. Her cheeks burned in embarrassment at her reaction. The back of her hand tingled where Étienne had kissed it and her heart was pounding so hard she was certain they could hear it.

"Please sit down," Détective de la Croix said, interrupting the awkward moment, and motioning to a chair. "I want you to tell us everything that happened during the time you spent with Mademoiselle Emma last night."

Tom's cell phone buzzed. He left the room to answer it leaving Lexie alone.

Lexie settled into the chair and gathered her thoughts.

"We had dinner together at one of our favorite restaurants on the Champs Elyse. We finished around eight o'clock and walked the boulevard window shopping until it was quite late. Em mentioned she was tired and ready to go home. We hailed a cab which dropped me home and then I assumed took her home. She didn't say anything about going to the Tuillieries."

Lexie felt tears and the pain in her heart was unbearable but she continued after a deep breath.

"We had no plans to see each other today. She said she'd call me tomorrow morning. My Mom's arrivin' from Atlanta and we were gonna pick her up at the airport and have dinner together."

Lexie's flimsy composure shattered and she sobbed into a Kleenex. Étienne's hand on her back was warm and to her surprise comforting.

"I'm sorry," she said. She dabbed at her eyes and blew her nose. "This whole thing is overwhelmin'. I can't imagine what Em was doin' in the Tuilleries at that hour of the night. If this is a nightmare, I wanna wake up."

She couldn't sit still and paced the small room. Anger replaced grief and she wanted to hit something.

"I'm sorry for your loss Mademoiselle," the detective said. "I know this must be difficult for you. Is there anything else about last night that you can tell us?"

Lexie sat down.

"Think about it before you answer," Étienne urged, leaning toward her. "Anything at all could be critical to the investigation."

"Wait, there is one thing. After dinner we bumped into a couple who seemed to make Em very uneasy, almost frightened. They introduced themselves to us. Their names were… let me think a minute. I can't quite recall. I think the man's name began with an F."

"Was it perhaps François?" Étienne asked.

"I believe it was. The woman's name began with an M – Martine or Marie, something like that."

"Marielle?"

"That's it, François and Marielle. Em couldn't get away from them fast enough. She insisted on takin' a cab and seein' me home. It seemed odd at the time."

"That's very helpful, mademoiselle," Étienne said laying his hand over hers. "Are you sure their names were François and Marielle?"

She blushed at the intimate gesture. "I'm sure Monsieur Benoit. And, please call me Lexie."

"With pleasure, and you must call me Étienne. Is there anything else?"

"Not really. Just that she became extremely agitated when we ran into François and Marielle." She felt a little twitch of pressure in her brain. Étienne pressed her hand and then let go as Tom entered the room.

Tom entered the room and overheard her statement. "Bloody hell!"

"*Exactement,*" Détective de la Croix commented. "It is what we feared."

"What," she asked. "Was that important?"

"You have no idea," Tom muttered.

"There's something you're not tellin' me."

"I think it's time I filled you in on some of the details."

"Étienne nodded. "She is more likely to believe you than someone she has just met."

Tom took a deep breath. "The first thing you need to know is that my job as head of the translation department is a cover."

"What do you mean it's a cover?"

"For the past fifteen years I have worked for an elite secret Society called *L'Organisme de Fraternité et Solidarité*. Four hundred years ago, the Society was formed and its specialty is investigating bizarre and unexplainable deaths or attacks. My official title is Guardian and I am one of two-hundred men and women tasked with solving these crimes. Emma's death is one such incident."

He paused for a moment running his hand through his blond hair. Lexie took advantage of the pause.

"What's bizarre and unexplainable about Em's death?" This time Étienne answered.

"The blood was drained from her body."

Lexie processed the new detail. "What sicko would do that...?"

"Likely, François and Marielle," Tom said.

"But why, we just met them last night?"

Tom reached over and took her hand. "They're vampires, Lex."

"Give me a friggin' break," she said, leaping to her feet she glared at the three men. "Vampires are a myth. Why would you say such a dumb thing?"

"It's true, mademoiselle," Étienne said.

"No it isn't. And you, what do you have to do with any of this?"

"Étienne is the Chairman of the organization," Tom replied. "He's in Paris to work with Robert and me in investigating Emma's death. She was also working for the Society."

Lexie was speechless. She looked from one man to the other. *What the hell is happenin'!*

"She couldn't have. She would've told me. I would've known." Lexie stopped, her breathing ragged.

"You look ill. Perhaps you should sit down." Étienne said, taking her arm.

She pulled away. "Don't touch me. I feel like I've fallen down the rabbit hole. "

She felt another little tickle in her brain and her eyes met Étienne's. Her heart was pounding and it took effort to pull her eyes from his.

"Let's pretend and I mean 'pretend' that what you're sayin' is true. What do we do now?"

"*We* do nothing," Tom said. "Robert, Étienne and I will continue to investigate the evidence."

"There must be some way I can help. You can't expect me to stand by and do nothin'."

"For now, that is exactly what we expect. It's too dangerous, even for you," Étienne said. "François and Marielle know you were friends with Emma."

"What do you mean even for you?"

31

"All in good time," Étienne replied.

"Do you really think they would come after me?"

"They are unpredictable and capable of anything," he said.

She suddenly remembered Emma's Father, Heinrick Gunter. "Has anyone contacted Em's Dad?"

"I called Heinrick," Tom said. "He's catching the next plane. Since most of Emma's friends are here he wants to have her funeral in Paris. He'll take her body back to Frankfurt."

"He must be devastated. First his wife and now his daughter. I'll try to call him later."

Robert rose and opened the door to the interrogation room. "I think we're finished for now."

"Come on Lex, we'll take you home." Tom said taking her arm and guiding her to the front of the station. She noticed the mysterious Étienne was coming with them.

Étienne and Tom insisted on seeing her to her door. They climbed the stairs in silence.

Lexie was acutely aware of Étienne's magnetism. It irritated her that her body wanted to react in inappropriate ways. They reached the third floor landing, and her door flew open. Cassie Miles enveloped her in a bear hug.

"Cassie, what in the world are you doing here? You weren't supposed to arrive until tomorrow."

"I wanted more time with you," Cassie replied still hugging her. "Where've you been?"

"I've been down at the police station," Lexie said stepping back from her Mom's embrace. "Em's been murdered."

"Oh sweetheart, I know, that's another reason I came early."

"But how?"

Cassie nodded at Tom. "He called me last night after he'd identified the body. I caught the first flight out. I didn't want you to be alone."

Why would he call her? "I still can't believe she's gone. I just saw her last night."

"Do we know what happened?" Cassie asked Tom.

"Her body was found last night in the Jardins de Tuillieries. Her throat was mutilated and all the blood was drained from her body."

Cassie directed her next question to Étienne. "Sweet Jesus, it's starting isn't it?"

Lexie was shocked at the hatred in her eyes. "Sorry, I forgot my manners. This is Étienne de Benoit, one of Tom's, um associates."

"I know who he is," Cassie said. "Come on honey, let's go inside. It's chilly out here."

Étienne moved so fast he was a blur and blocked Cassie's way. "You cannot avoid this."

"Don't tell me what I can and can't do," Cassie said. "I have no use for you and your kind. She doesn't have to do this."

"She must choose."

"What in tarnation are you two talking about? How do you know each other?" Lexie felt she was in at parallel universe and the people there had gone mad.

"Give it a rest you spawn of the devil!" Cassie shouted. "She's just lost her best friend. Now is not the time."

"On the contrary Madam, it must be now. François and Marielle will be coming for her. Her life is in danger. I've brought Charlie's journal. You must tell her tonight."

Lexie noticed that Étienne had captured Cassie's eyes with his. *Daddy's journal?*

"Don't try that hoo doo on me," Cassie said through gritted teeth. "I've been takin' verveine."

"You knew my Dad too?"

Étienne and Cassie were engaged in a staring contest and ignored her.

"If you don't tell her than I will be forced to do so," Étienne persisted. "I don't think you want her to hear this from me."

"Hear what from you?" Lexie asked. "I'm gettin' whiplash watchin' you two go at it."

"You wouldn't dare," Cassie spat at Étienne.

"Don't test me Madam."

Tom stepped in. "Maybe this could wait until tomorrow. Lexie's had enough to deal with for one day."

Cassie and Étienne turned on him.

"Stay out of this," Cassie said. "This is between me and him."

Tom raised his hand in surrender and backed off.

Cassie pulled her sweater around her. "This is not the life I want for her. But I'd much rather she hates you than hate me."

"I have no problem with that. Come Lexie, I have much to tell you." Étienne took Lexie's arm to lead her away.

Cassie grabbed Lexie's arm yanking it away from Étienne. "Wait, you win. I'll tell her everything tonight." Cassie's shoulders slumped and she pulled Lexie close.

Étienne reached in his briefcase and retrieved a worn leather bound book which he handed to Lexie. "It's not about winning. It's about the future."

"I'm goin' inside," Cassie said. She turned and disappeared into the apartment.

Lexie clutched the book to her body and hurried after her. She heard Étienne call out as she closed the door.

"Lock your doors and windows, and do not let ANYONE and I mean ANYONE in."

"What was that all about?" Lexie asked, slamming the apartment door behind her.

Cassie said nothing.

"Don't play dumb with me. You know exactly what I am talkin' about."

"It's a long story. Where do I sleep?"

It was clear her mom was not going to say anything until she was ready. Lexie set the book on the dining room table and wheeled her mom's suitcase into the bedroom.

"What did the police say?" Cassie asked tagging after her.

This is awkward. "The police have no suspects." she said. "They're callin' it an animal attack."

"Animal attack, my ass!" Cassie said. She shrugged. "Probably some kind of a psycho."

"Maybe, the detective hinted it was somethin' much more dangerous. I'm so angry and sad I can hardly think straight."

"I know honey, I know. Why don't we get comfy and then we can talk more?"

Lexie heaved the suitcase onto a chair next to the bed. She opened her chest of drawers and dug out a pair of sweats.

"I'll give you some privacy and change in the bathroom," she said. Cassie had already started unpacking and didn't answer. When she emerged from the bathroom, Cassie was sitting at the dining room table.

"I'll be right there," she called.

Cassie was caressing the cover of the old journal. "Take your time. I'm not goin' anywhere."

"Do you still miss Daddy?"

"Every day," Cassie said.

When her mom didn't elaborate, Lexie didn't push. She grabbed a bottle of Guigal, an excellent Côtes du Rhône from the kitchen cabinet. "I can scrounge up some cheese and crackers and fruit if you're hungry."

"No thanks, darlin', I had a passable dinner on the plane. First class you know."

She sat opposite Cassie and poured the wine she had uncorked. "I still can't believe Em's gone. Why did that have to happen to her? There's this hole in my heart, and at the same time I could spit nails. Please say somethin'!"

"Oh sweetie, there's nothin' I can say to make it any easier. It's unfair and unjust and more than I can say grace over. Keep sayin' your prayers. The Lord always hears. Have the funeral arrangements been made?"

"I didn't ask Tom. Heinrick knows and is on his way. I'm sure he'll take care of everything. Is that really Daddy's journal and why did Étienne have it?"

Cassie stared at the book. "There is so much I need to tell you, I hardly know where to begin."

"The beginnin' is usually a good place."

"When I married your father I thought my life would be easy and fun. Charlie made good money so I never had to work," Cassie began. "When you were conceived, I thought life couldn't get any better. We were so excited. We couldn't wait to tell everyone. I didn't know we were livin' a lie."

Cassie opened the clasp of the book and caressed the worn page. Lexie recognized her father's handwriting scrawled across the page.

"This was supposed to be given to you on your thirtieth birthday. But, in light of Emma's death at the hands of François and Marielle, Étienne insists I share it with you now. Life as you've known it is about to be transformed forever."

Cassie reached out and took Lexie's hand. "Honey, remember you have a choice."

"A choice about what? I don't think I can handle any more surprises."

"You're stronger than you know," Cassie said, flipping through the journal. She looked intently at Lexie. "I think Étienne is using you. If I had my way you would never know about your legacy," She pushed the journal across the table. "Read the first couple of paragraphs."

Lexie's eyes teared up.

> *November 20, 1984*
>
> *Our daughter was born today. She is so beautiful and already I can see that she is a warrior. Her legacy of Vampire Executioner will come naturally, and with Étienne and the Society's guidance she will be the best. We have named her Lexie and as a 'Chosen One' she will take up the fight between good and evil.*
>
> *Although she has a choice I know she will make the right one and take her place in a long line of executioners. Cassie will be her only deterrent. She will do everything she can to keep Lexie safe and away from this life. I guess we'll cross that bridge when we come to it. For now, our joy is unbounded.*

Unable to sit still, Lexie sprang to her feet and paced.

Cassie said nothing for a couple of minutes watching her daughter struggle with this news. "Honey, I know this is a lot for you to process, but please take a deep breath and listen to me."

"This is a nightmare! My best friend has been murdered by *vampires*. At least that's what y'all are tellin' me. And, if that isn't crazy enough, you're tellin' me I'm this, this thing called a vampire executioner. If all that's true, then my whole life has been a lie."

"I never wanted any of this for you. You don't have to become a vampire executioner. You could die horribly. A vampire killed your father and your grandfather. I think you should come home."

"Daddy died of a heart attack. That's what you told me."

"I had to lie to you back then. You were only ten and it was too soon to reveal your legacy. Your Grandfather Jeremy was killed trackin' the same vamp down." Cassie stopped, visibly upset, her brown eyes bright with hatred.

Lexie sank into a chair. "So that's what my dream has been about all these years."

"I thought you'd outgrown that. I've prayed and prayed that you had. It's a bad dream full of evil and destruction. I thought the Lord had finally answered my prayers. You haven't mentioned it in years." Cassie's voice rose in pitch as it always did when her religious zeal rose up.

"You always got so upset I stopped talkin' about it. I had one last night. In the dream I'm running. There's lots of blood. I see Daddy covered in it. I know I'm in danger 'cause someone's chasin' me. I fall and then there's nothingness."

"Honey, you were there when your Dad was killed. He was fleein' with you when the vampire caught up. Your Dad did his ever lovin' best to protect you. He staked its chest but missed the heart. The vampire tore him apart. It was hurt badly enough it fled without taking you. Your grandfather had chased after y'all and when he realized that you were safe, he went after the vampire. Vampires heal fast, and Jeremy died fightin' it. I found you holdin' your father's body. You had blood all over your arms and hands and so traumatized that you blocked the memory. Grandmother Bessie and I decided it was for the best, so we never told you."

"Hog wash, you sound just like Em. She was always sayin' vampires might be real. Do you know how crazy this all sounds?"

"She was tellin' you the truth."

Lexie stared at Cassie speechless. "Are there other vampire executioners?"

"A few, but I've never met one," Cassie replied. "Honey there's more. Your friendship with Emma was no accident."

"Tom told me she was working with the Society as well. Did you know that?"

Cassie nodded. "When you took the job in Paris, Bessie and I contacted Tom. We knew that Emma was workin' with him as a cover for her work with the Society. We wanted the two of you to become friends. I always thought she was too enamored with the whole vamp thing. I've often said if you lie down with pigs you'll get up with mud. I'm not surprised she was killed by one. All vamps are evil and against the teachings of good Christians."

"How dare you say that about Em? It wasn't her fault. Maybe, just maybe this is your fault. If I had known all this sooner, given I'm supposed to be this super being, I might've saved her."

"I'm just sayin' she meddled in things she had no business meddlin' in. Besides I would never have allowed you to risk your life to save hers. The thought of losing you to a vamp was more than I could bear."

"Tom and Étienne have known all along?"

"Étienne came to Atlanta with your grandfather shortly after your father and I announced the news that I was pregnant. Tom has known since he joined the Society. He was the one who made sure you got hired at the UN."

Lexie resumed pacing. "Thunder crap, I feel like y'all have been peein' down my back and tellin' me it's rainin'. I'm thirty years old for friggin' sake. Supposedly, I'm this super power vampire executioner and y'all expect me to believe that vampires are real. Has the whole world gone mad? Y'all lied to me and kept me in this little cocoon. What gives y'all the right to run my life like that? I'm almost as pissed at Tom and Étienne as I am at you. Not to mention Em."

"Darlin' I know this is a lot to take in all at once," Cassie began.

"Don't interrupt me, I'm on a roll," Lexie said. "I can't believe that y'all let me go through life livin' a complete lie. What if I don't want to be a vampire executioner? What if I just wanna live my life as a translator, meet some nice man and settle down and have kids?"

"Sweetie, you can still do that. In fact I want you to," Cassie said.

"Stop it, Momma. I'm madder than a wet hen, and right now I wish you'd never come. Nothin' you can say can make up for the lies and deceit."

"If push came to shove I'd do it again." Cassie said, tears welling in her eyes.

"Bullshit," Lexie said. "And don't pull that weepin' crap on me. You did it because you didn't have the courage. You just wanted to play your safe little game of Southern girl growin' up the way you wanted her to. This has been an ongoing battle between us. I'm not a Bible-thumper like you are and I never will be. So just get over it and leave me alone."

Cassie blew her nose and took a long swig of her wine. "Oh sweetie, please don't say that."

"Today has been the worst day of my life – except maybe when Daddy died. You should just get some rest."

"Do you want me to go to a hotel?" Cassie's voice quivered with emotion.

"Of course not," Lexie said. "Just go to bed and I'll see you in the mornin'. I want to see Em's body."

"I could go with you."

"Enough Momma, talk to the butt, the head is tired. I'm callin' Tom to go with me."

She watched Cassie walk to the bedroom, shoulders hunched. She was sniffling.

Lexie punched speed dial for Tom's phone.

"Lex, what's up?"

"I want to see Em's body. Will you come with me?"

"Now?"

"Yes, now. If you don't I'm goin' alone."

"Bollocks! I'll pick you up in twenty minutes."

"I'll be downstairs waitin'."

True to his word, Tom's sleek black Mercedes pulled up in front of her apartment twenty minutes later. To her dismay, Étienne got out and opened the back door for her.

"I didn't know you'd come too," she said, her heart speeding up at the sight of him. *He looks so young.*

Étienne's eyes held hers, and that tickle she'd felt earlier in the day returned more strongly. He smiled and took her arm, guiding her into the car. She got goose bumps from his touch. Her cheeks flushed and she ducked into the car to avoid his eyes. Those hypnotic green eyes.

"I couldn't pass up the opportunity to see you again," he said. "I find you fascinating." His silky voice sent shivers through her.

Lexie settled into the back seat with a humph.

"Did your Mum share everything with you?" Tom asked, maneuvering the traffic.

"You mean that I'm some super vampire executioner and how everybody's been lyin' to me for years?"

"It's true," he replied, glancing at her in the rearview mirror. "You are the future so you might as well face it."

"Who says I have to face it? It's taken everything I have to face the fact that Em's dead. And, if, and I do mean 'if' it's true, then I'm as pissed at you two as my momma. What if I just disappeared? It would serve y'all right. All I want right now is to see Em."

"Why do you want to see her body?" It's not a pretty sight and I think it's a bad idea."

"I still can't believe she's dead. I want to see the proof of how she was killed."

"Nothing's been done to hide the mutilation," Étienne said. "You have every right to be angry and distrusting, but I wish you wouldn't put yourself through this."

"Stop tryin' to talk me out of it. My mind's made up."

They pulled up to the morgue.

41

"Are you sure about this?" Tom asked again, reaching over the seat back to take her hand. "You must be sure."

Lexie yanked her hand away and leaped from the car. The two men followed looking uncomfortable.

Once inside Lexie's heels clattered on the bare tiles and she shivered in the cold gloom of the hallway. She dreaded seeing Emma.

She felt nauseous. "These baby-shit green walls are makin' me sick."

Tom knocked on a door, opened by a short, paunchy male intern who peered at them over the top of his glasses.

"*Puis-je vous aider?*" He asked.

Given the hour, Lexie was surprised he offered to help them.

"*Bonne nuit, M'sieu, nous voudrions voir le corps d'Emma Gunther.*" Étienne said, telling the intern they wanted to view Emma's body. Étienne held the man's eyes with his own.

"*Nous sommes fermés pour la journée, revenez demain.*" The man said.

Lexie's heart sank. The morgue was closed and they had to wait until the next day.

"Tomorrow doesn't work. *C'est très important,*" Étienne said, stressing the importance of their visit.

Lexie saw the intern's irises dilate and he looked confused.

"Of course, please come in."

Another starin' contest? Lexie puzzled over the alteration in the intern's attitude.

Lexie had never been in a morgue. Her heart pounded as the odor of formaldehyde assaulted her nostrils. Several tables were lined up in the center of the room, and she could see the outline of bodies under stark white sheets on two of them. She didn't want to think about what lay underneath. A large drain occupied the middle of the floor and she blanched as she realized what would be sluiced into it.

The intern checked a clip board, and led them to a drawer labeled 'Gunther' He pulled it open and rolled out a slab. A sheet covered the body. Lexie snatched it away. *This is a really bad idea.* Emma's bloodless face barely resembled the friend Lexie loved. Emma's cheeks were shrunken and her skin was shriveled and icy. The bones protruded as if they would break through the transparent skin. Skeletal was the word that popped into Lexie's mind.

Lexie was transfixed by her throat. A gaping hole, the size of a baseball, had been cleaned and she could see Emma's spinal column. The edges of the wound were ragged as if something or someone had gnawed through. She dropped the sheet and whirled away.

"Sweet Jesus," she said. She grabbed the closest trash can and threw up.

"Shit, shit, shit," she blurted, wiping her mouth with the back of her hand. She threw the trash can against a cabinet splattering vomit.

"She was almost decapitated!" Tears streamed down her cheeks. Her chest ached and she wanted to punch something.

Tom reached out to comfort her.

"Don't touch me." Lexie batted his hand away. "This is your fault. You and Mr. High and Mighty over there."

She pointed at Étienne. "How could you let this happen to her?"

"Lex we didn't know…" Tom said.

"Just shut up. Nothing you can say is gonna help."

Lexie took Emma's hand. "Oh Em, I'm so sorry this happened to you. Why didn't you talk to me? I might've been able to help." She kissed Emma's cheek and her heart clenched with the painful loss.

There was only one thing left and she knew she had to do it. She gritted her teeth and examined Emma's neck more closely.

"I don't see any puncture marks. How can we be sure it was vampires?"

"They drained her body of blood," Étienne said.

Lexie stroked Emma's hair. "You must have been so scared."

She gently replaced the sheet over Emma's face and turned away swiping at the tears that trickled down her cheeks.

The intern slid the body back in the drawer. "*J'ai découvert quelque chose d'autre quand j'étais en train de faire l'autopsie. Mademoiselle Gunter a été violé,*" he said, telling them that during the autopsy he'd discovered that Emma had been violated.

Lexie picked up the clipboard and flung it at the door. "What do you mean Em was violated?" the grizzly implication horrific.

"She was raped." Étienne said.

"Bloody hell, we didn't know that. We saw her before the autopsy." Tom said.

"Fuck, this just gets worse and worse." Lexie quivered in anger. "Throw me in jail right now! When this butt hole is caught, I'm gonna beat the crap out of him. I'll kill the son-of-a-bitch slowly and watch while he bleeds to death."

Tom smashed his fist in the wall. "You can have whatever's left of him after I get done with him."

Étienne had been oddly silent and Lexie jabbed him in the chest. "What about you?"

"You don't want to know."

"I have to get out of here," Lexie said, walking toward the door of the morgue. "Take me home, I've seen enough."

The ride back to Lexie's apartment was painfully silent. Guilt over Emma's death nibbled at Lexie even though she knew it wasn't her fault. She couldn't seem to stop the tears. When Tom pulled up in front of her building, she jumped from the car and waving goodbye slammed the door behind her.

There was no sign of Cassie when Lexie got home but she could hear deep breathing. She was asleep. *At least I don't have to deal with her right now.* Lexie made up the couch and flopped down, numb. She was sure sleep would come quickly. She was wrong. She was haunted by nightmare flashes of fighting with her mother pushing out the vision of Emma's ravaged body. *If I can just get through the next couple of days Cassie'll go back to Atlanta.*

Lexie rolled over into a ball willing sleep to come. Instead her thoughts turned to the enigmatic Étienne de Benoit. There was something about him she didn't trust. *Wonder what his story is.* That was her last thought as exhaustion took over and she drifted into sleep.

Chapter 4
Étienne's Story

What is that noise? Lexie's eyes flew open as she tried to identify the annoying sounds coming from her kitchen. She sat up and the reality of Emma's death and the vision of her mutilated body doubled her over with pain. *Shit, shit, shit.* She waited for it to ease.

"Momma, what are you doing?"

Cassie poked her head around the corner. "Sorry, didn't mean to wake you," I just find these French coffee machines impossible."

"Hang on, I'm comin'." Lexie pulled on her robe and made her way into the kitchen. "Stop! You'll just make a mess."

"I've been thinking about Étienne," Lexie said, punching the ON button.

"What about him?"

"You said he and Granddaddy came to Atlanta shortly after you and Daddy announced you were pregnant. How old was he then?"

Cassie was quiet for a moment. "Why do you ask?"

"Don't answer my question with a question," Lexie said. "How old was he?"

"I don't know exactly. Probably in his mid-to-late twenties."

"Then he must be in his fifties now, right?"

"I guess so."

"He's certainly well preserved. You've known him all these years. How does he do it?"

"That's something you'll have to ask him."

Frustrated, Lexie poured a cup of coffee and thrust it at Cassie. She took her own cup to the living room where her phone was ringing. Étienne Benoit showed up on the call display. *That's creepy.*

"*Bonjour,*" she answered.

"I must see you," his silky voice raised goose bumps on her arms. "There is much for us to talk about."

"Ya think?" her tone spiteful and harsh. "Sorry, that was uncalled for. When and where?"

"You could come to my place, or I could come to you. I would prefer we meet privately."

"My place is hardly private with Cassie here."

Cassie had overheard the last sentence. "Honey, I can make myself scarce," she whispered.

"I'll come to your place," Lexie said ignoring Cassie's offer. "What's the address?" She was excited to see him. "Got it, shall we say in an hour?"

"I'll be waiting," Étienne said and hung up.

"Are you sure it's wise to meet with him alone?" Cassie asked.

"It'll be fine. Besides it'll give me a chance to get to know him. He's quite the mystery."

"I'll be here by the phone. Call if you need me."

Not wanting to fuss with parking, Lexie took the Metro to the George Pompideau stop and walked the remaining four blocks to Étienne's apartment in the *Marais*. She had always loved this section of the city, often referred to as 'Old Paris'. Its quaint cobblestone streets were lined with restaurants and bars, and although somewhat modernized, it still was reminiscent of the aristocracy and grandeur of a golden era. Arriving, she buzzed the doorbell and was surprised when the door clicked open without him answering. *He's a trusting soul.* There was no elevator, and as she climbed the three flights of stairs she took time to appreciate the Italian marble walls and floors and the ornate design of the iron railing on the staircase.

"*Bienvenue,*" he said from a doorway as she climbed the last flight. "I am delighted that we are able to meet alone."

She glanced up and had to grab the handrail, tripping on a step when she saw his black jeans, deep purple silk shirt and black leather vest. *Grace.* He was scrumptious.

"It was easy. Em and I loved this area and we spent hours exploring – at least we did." Sadness gripped her cooling the heat in her body that had soared at the sight of him. *Fifty my ass, he looks thirty.*

He stood aside to allow her to enter. "Please come in." As she passed him his musk enveloped her.

"Your place is beautiful," she exclaimed her eyes alighting on beautiful antiques and artwork. "Is that an original Toulouse Lautrec?"

"You have an eye for beauty," he said. "Yes, that is a Lautrec. He painted it for me."

"What do you mean you mean he painted it for you?"

He ignored her question. "I wanted to meet with you because it's time to finish the story Tom began yesterday."

"You mean there's more? I'm still tryin' to wrap my brain around the possibility of vampires and some secret society that fights'em. Cassie gave me a letter from my Dad that says I'm this special being called a *vampire executioner.* What do you know about that?"

"All in good time. May I offer you something to drink before we begin?" Étienne motioned her to take a seat.

"Water would be great," she replied, sitting gingerly on the edge of a velvet covered settee.

Étienne returned from the kitchen with two glasses of water. Handing her the drink, his hand brushed hers. She flushed as her nipples hardened. *Man he's hot.*

"Let's get to it," she said her voice sharp in her attempt to sound unimpressed.

He smiled, settled back into the chair opposite and picked up the book from a table.

"What's that? I thought we were going to talk."

"*Histoire de la famille.* I had hoped we could eventually reveal everything over time. Emma's death has accelerated our plan. I think it's the best way for me to relate my story."

Lexie stifled a yawn and leaned back against the cushions of the settee.

Étienne opened the book with gentle hands and the yellowed pages crackled as he turned them.

Despite herself, Lexie was immediately drawn in by his deep voice. It's silky tone a lover's caress.

"Five hundred years ago the Marquis Benoit, his wife Lisbeth, and their two teenage children, François and Céleste lived on a large estate near the town of Grignon in Southern France. Except for occasional trips to Paris, the family led a quiet life in the country. Life was good."

"Things changed for the worse when François turned eighteen. Tall, like his father, François was widely known as a 'good catch' amongst the other noble families. Céleste, at sixteen, had inherited her mother's delicate beauty, and the Marquis and Lisbeth knew it would not be long until she had her fair share of suitors."

"Their custom was to hold a ball on Christmas Eve. Invitations to the ball were highly sought after, and were sent to all the surrounding nobility as well as the elite of Paris. Included in this assemblage were their closest friends, Pierre and Justine de Bergerac."

"Pierre and Justine had no children, and always spent several weeks with the Benoit family at Christmas enjoying the festivities and warmth. To the Marquis' and Lisbeth's surprise, they arrived with a young woman whom they had never seen before."

"She was breathtakingly beautiful, with eyes so blue they appeared like huge pools of water, silvery blond hair, high cheekbones, a delicate, slightly upturned nose, and her skin appeared almost translucent in the pale winter light. Pierre quickly introduced the stranger as Mademoiselle Marielle Garcia de Catalan, a cousin from northern Spain, who had, on the spur of the moment, arrived at their château two days before to spend a few weeks with them."

"'I know that this is unexpected,' Pierre said. 'Her family mysteriously disappeared in June and have not been seen or heard from since. The police are completely baffled.'"

"'It's not a problem,' the Marquis assured him. 'There is always room for one more in our home.'"

"The Marquis could tell François was completely taken with the young woman. He couldn't take his eyes off her, and she appeared to be equally smitten, gazing into his eyes with disturbing intensity. The Marquis sensed folly and something indefinable from the young woman. He wondered if Lisbeth felt the same."

"On the day of the ball, Lisbeth drew the Marquis into the library."

"'I've observed how smitten François is and I've mixed feelings about it. We know almost nothing about her. When Marielle first arrived, I experienced a strange sense of foreboding and fear. On the other hand, I'm pleased that François is finally showing an interest in a young woman. But let's slow it down until we find out more.'"

"Nodding his agreement, the Marquis kissed her on the cheek. 'I will talk to François.'"

"Later that afternoon, encountering his son alone, the Marquis took him by the shoulder. 'Your mother and I've noticed you seem to be spending a great deal of time with Marielle. We know almost nothing of her background and her family. Has she shared anything with you?'"

"'No Papa she hasn't,' François replied. 'She has only mentioned how much she misses her family.' François rushed on, his face flushing with emotion. 'I am in love with Marielle, and she loves me. I want your approval to ask Pierre and Justine for her hand in marriage at the ball.'"

"'This is too fast. You only met her a few days ago. You must wait and court her for a few months at least.'"

"'No Papa, I've never met anyone like Marielle, and I want to spend the rest of my life with her.'"

"The Marquis put his arm around François' shoulders and gave him a quick squeeze and searched for the right words. He took the easy way out."

"'If you are sure about this, you must talk to your mother and win her approval.'"

"They parted with an embrace. 'Don't worry Papa, I will convince Mama.'"

"Still uneasy, the Marquis found Justine and Pierre and drew them into his sitting room."

"'François and Marielle say they are in love. He plans to ask you and Pierre for her hand in marriage. Lisbeth and I are pleased but a little apprehensive. Is there anything more you can tell me about Marielle's background and the mysterious disappearance of her family?'"

"'You know as much as we do,' Pierre replied. 'She is the daughter of my first cousin by marriage. We rarely saw them given they live in the Pyrenees. Her arrival was a complete surprise and when she told us her tragic story we hadn't the heart to turn her away.'"

"As Pierre spoke, the Marquis noticed that Justine glanced repeatedly at the door, looking afraid."

51

"'Justine, are you alright? You seem jumpy,' he remarked."

"'I'm afraid of Marielle,' she whispered. 'Since she arrived at our home I've had a premonition that something awful is about to happen. I know it seems silly, she is so beautiful and sweet, but I can't seem to shake the feeling.'"

"'Lisbeth had the same feeling,' the Marquis said."

"The Marquis hastened to find his wife. 'I spoke with François. He's in love and wants to ask Marielle to marry him.'"

"'It's too soon.' Lisbeth said."

"'That's what I told him, but his mind is made up.'"

"Lisbeth's face wrinkled with concern. 'Have you spoken with Pierre and Justine?'"

"'They don't know much about Marielle either. Justine said she's afraid of her and has a premonition that something bad is about to happen.'"

"'Then I forbid the marriage.'"

"'Mama don't say that.' François said as he entered Lisbeth's sitting room. 'You have no right to deny me happiness.'"

"Lisbeth looked to the Marquis for support and he nodded. 'It is too soon. We know almost nothing about her and the circumstances around her family's disappearance are very strange.'"

"'Please Mama…'"

"'You heard your mother,' the Marquis said. 'We can discuss this further after the ball.'"

"François stormed from the room, his face red with anger."

"'He'll come to his senses,' the Marquis assured Lisbeth. 'Don't let this spoil the magic of this evening.'"

"That night the ballroom was filled with elegant, dancing couples, and the mood was festive. At eight o'clock, the guests were ushered into the dining hall aglow in all its finery. Crystal goblets, silver and gold place settings and their best Wedgwood dishware were complimented by bouquets of blue Hydrangeas sprinkled with Baby's Breath."

"After dinner, the Marquis invited the gentlemen into the smoking parlor for cigars and port. The women followed Lisbeth into the large sitting room to discuss their children and share the latest gossip. Everyone returned to the ballroom at around 11:30 to continue dancing, and the Marquis and Lisbeth resumed their duties as hosts and spoke to their guests."

"The Marquis leaned down to whisper in his wife's ear, 'François and Marielle seem to have disappeared. No doubt they're somewhere plotting how to win us over.'"

"Lisbeth turned her head quickly to scan the room, nothing. 'I think you should look for them. There's something about that girl. She makes me very uneasy.'"

Étienne paused. His eyes no longer brilliant but haunted. He reached for his glass of water.

"Are you okay? You look paler than usual," Lexie asked. Questions swirled in her head but she was sensitive to Étienne's mood.

"I always find this next passage difficult." He set the water down and lifted the book.

He hasn't turned a page. "We could take a break."

"I don't need one." He took a deep breath and continued.

"The Marquis left the ballroom and finding the butler in the hallway asked him to search the upstairs rooms. Moments later the butler returned shaking his head. He offered to continue looking but the Marquis felt a sense of foreboding and insisted on searching himself. Taking a lantern from a table to the terrace door, he walked out into the snowy night. He made his way around the slippery portico and hesitated at the top of the staircase. He could hear strange sounds coming from the bushes at the bottom of the stairs. Lifting the lantern higher, he saw dark splotches in the snow, and Marielle bent over François holding his body to her."

"'Marielle what has happened? Are you hurt?'"

"Getting no response, the Marquis made his way down the slippery stairs, and rounded the corner, moving toward them. Hunched in the snow, barely illuminated by the Marquis's lantern, was Marielle with François in her arms, both covered in blood. She bent over François' body crying, but as the Marquis approached, she lifted her head and snarled at him. Her petite mouth dripped warm blood that steamed in the crisp night air. Her face was barely recognizable."

"He recoiled in repulsion. 'Monster, what are you doing?'"

"Terrified for his son's life, he rushed to them. Quicker than the human eye could capture, Marielle dropped François' lifeless body, and launched herself at the Marquis, throwing him to the ground, straddling him before he could defend himself. He thrashed violently, but he was no match for her."

"'I had hoped to save you and the rest of your little family for later,' she purred. 'Now that you have discovered my secret, I cannot let you live. But do not fret, I will bring your François back to life and together we will create our own family of indestructible beings. Humanity will sustain us.'"

"The Marquis fought for his life. Pinned to the ground, unable to move a muscle, he looked into Marielle's eyes. They were no longer a beautiful sapphire blue, but blood red."

"She grasped both his arms in her delicate hands and shoved them into the snow."

"'Relax, this will only hurt for a moment, and then you will experience great pleasure before you slip into nothingness.'"

"She leaned close, sank her fangs into his neck and began to feed. The Marquis continued to fight, but she was too strong. He weakened and surrendered to the promised pleasure. He experienced pain and incredible lust - a blinding desire for her. He tightened his arms around her and pulled her closer, his penis strained against the front of his trousers, begging for release. She stopped. But not wanting to lose the euphoria that had settled over him, the Marquis attempted to pull her head back down to his neck. Marielle laughed at his vain attempts, Marielle pulled away from him."

"'I must leave you for a moment and tend to François. It is time for him to share my blood so he becomes immortal. We will spend eternity together.'"

"Marielle lifted François' head to rest in her lap and bit her wrist. She held the wound over his mouth. There was no response from François."

"'Ah, foolish boy, have I waited too long to give you my blood?' he then heard her ask. 'Ah no, there you are. Suck my blood and embrace immortality.'"

"The Marquis watched in horror as his son sucked hungrily at Marielle's wrist."

"She pulled her wrist away from François' eager mouth. 'That's enough!'"

"'Hungry, I am ravenous.' The Marquis could hear his son growling."

"'Hush everything is fine. Be patient.'"

"The Marquis watched helplessly as Marielle moved back to him. As if from a long distance away, he could hear Lisbeth's voice."

"'My love, where are you? Have you found François and Marielle?' Too far gone to respond, the Marquis screamed in his mind, *Run and hide. You are in grave danger.* As blackness descended, he was aware Marielle had stopped drinking from his throat, and had pressed her still bleeding wrist to his mouth."

"'Drink, Marquis. Receive the gift of immortality.'"

"The warm blood seeped into his mouth. At first, repulsed by the taste, he struggled feebly to get away. But as the warm liquid trickled down of this throat, he craved more. He sucked voraciously at her delicate wrist. Then, blackness overtook him, and he knew nothing more."

Étienne turned the page and continued to read.

"Sometime later, the Marquis regained consciousness in his bedroom, with the taste of blood in his mouth. Hunger burned at his insides. The horror flooded back. His only thought was *Lisbeth.*"

"He leaped from the bed, and almost fell down the grand staircase. A coppery odor slammed into him. There were pools of blood everywhere. *Where are the bodies?* As he gazed in shock, an uncontrollable hunger rose – and that hunger was for blood. He forced himself to walk through the puddles. He could hear crying coming from the ballroom."

"At the doorway, his senses were overwhelmed by the smell, and his incisor teeth sprang painfully from his gums. His guest's bodies lay strewn about, blood seeping from great holes in their necks. Unable to control the craving any longer, he knelt down and began sucking the first ravaged throat. Oblivious to anything other than satisfying his insatiable appetite, he flew from body to body, sucking out any blood that was left, and licking the blood that had spilled to the floor. Through his bloodlust haze he became aware of soft whimpering coming from behind him. He whirled, fangs bared and saw Lisbeth standing there, her eyes red from weeping. Behind her, his daughter, Céleste, gazed at him wide-eyed."

"'What are you doing?' Lisbeth whispered."

"Mindful of the blood dripping down his chin, he quickly wiped his mouth with the back of his sleeve. Not knowing how else to respond, he held out his arms. Lisbeth and Céleste rushed into them and he gathered them close."

"'It was Marielle. I knew something was wrong about her,' Lisbeth wailed."

"As he held his wife and child, stroking their hair in an attempt to quiet them, he became aware of the seductive smell of Lisbeth's blood pulsing through the artery in her neck, and the pounding of her heart against his chest. His hunger returned, and unable to control the overwhelming need for blood, he sank his fangs into her neck and began to drink of the warm, satisfying blood."

"The Marquis heard his daughter's sweet voice screaming as if from a great distance. Her small hands pulled at his arms. 'Papa, let Maman go. You are hurting her!'"

"Céleste's small hands pummeling his back and arms were annoying. With his free hand he swiped at her, sending her flying against the wall where she sank to the floor."

"No longer distracted by his daughter, lust surged and his cock hardened. At first Lisbeth struggled in his arms beating at his chest, but as the pheromones from his saliva took effect, she sighed and pulled him closer. He thrust himself against her body seeking relief from the pulsing in his groin."

"He continued sucking at his wife's neck, thrusting against her again and again, desperate to assuage his arousal. Finally, the excruciating blood lust satisfied, and the hardness in his groin dissipating, he opened his eyes for the first time since he had begun to drink from Lisbeth's throat. He gazed into his wife's beautiful eyes which were now lifeless, and realized what he had done to her. Horrified, he clutched her unresponsive body to his chest, raised his head and screamed."

"'*Mon Dieu*, what's happened to me?'"

"'Papa, you have killed Maman,' Céleste cried. But she crawled toward him. The gash in her head seeped blood down the side of her face. His daughter's expression, so trusting, sent a pain so deep inside him he thought he would die. Silently, he gathered Céleste close, and sat cradling his dead wife and his beloved daughter. He noticed he was no longer out of control. The all-consuming hunger for blood had dissipated. Harming Céleste was impossible."

"As the cold dawn broke, he was still sitting in the ballroom holding his wife's lifeless form. Céleste lay with her head on her Mother's lap weeping. The Marquis wiped the dried blood from his mouth and face with the sleeve of his coat, and fearing that others might soon be about, he stood, gathered Lisbeth's body in his arms, and nodded for Céleste to follow him. As they climbed the stairs they encountered no one. In Lisbeth's sleeping quarters the Marquis placed her body on the bed. He stroked her alabaster cheek and willed her to smile at him. Her lifeless eyes stared at him and he swore they held reproach. He was consumed by the magnitude of what he had done. At that moment, he wanted nothing more than to end his own life."

Étienne paused to take a sip of water and continued.

"Justine and Pierre and a few of the Paris aristocrats had managed to survive the massacre by fleeing to the stables and hiding in the bales of hay. Other Royals were missing and the Marquis feared that François and Marielle had 'turned' them into vampires. If this were so, then vampires were now part of France's ruling class."

"When Justine and Pierre learned Lisbeth had perished they were devastated (the Marquis failed to admit he was her killer)."

"The Constabulary was called in. Fearful that they would be considered insane and to avoid too much questioning, they lied. They related they were attacked by a large pack of wolves. Not knowing how to process the carnage, the constabulary investigated no further. Justine and Pierre chose to remain at the château for as long as they were needed. François and Marielle had disappeared without a trace."

"The Marquis discovered that although not as satisfying as human blood he could assuage his hunger by drinking the blood of animals. He was stronger and faster than any human. Exposure to the sun burned him and at dawn the need to sleep was so powerful he had to retire to the cellar until after sunset. Although curious at the Marquis's unusual behavior, Pierre and Justine had no idea what he'd become, and in the aftermath of the attack, chalked it up to shock and grief."

"On the fourth night the Marquis sought out Justine and Pierre."

"'There is no easy way for me to tell you what I am about to reveal,' he said. 'And, I am counting on your love and friendship to help me through this.'"

"'My dear friend,' Pierre began. 'We are here for you and Céleste. We brought a monster into your home. We will do anything to make this easier for you.'"

"The Marquis gathered his courage and sat in the chair opposite Justine and Pierre."

"'Marielle is indeed a monster. She is a *Vampyre*,' he said, using the old French word for vampire."

"'But my friend, *Vampyre* are only legends,' Pierre protested. 'There must be some other explanation.'"

"'I thought so too until that night. But I was witness to her turning François into one.' The Marquis paused for a moment to let his news sink in."

"'You must be joking,' Pierre said."

"'I only wish I were, and he's not the only one.'"

"'What do you mean?' Justine and Pierre said in unison."

"'I too was turned into a *Vampyre*.'"

"Pierre and Justine cringed back holding each other for protection."

"'Please don't be afraid of me,' the Marquis said. 'I am learning to control my hunger by drinking animal blood. As long as I feed frequently, there is no urge for human blood. I would never hurt you. Other than Céleste, you are the only family I have left.'"

"He paused for a moment reluctant to reveal the rest. 'I need to know that you are on my side.'"

"'We will do our best my friend,' Pierre replied. 'But this all seems too preposterous for words.'"

"'I know,' the Marquis replied. 'And you may not trust me after I tell you the worst. I killed Lisbeth. When I woke the morning after, the urge to feed was stronger than anything I have ever known. I found her and Céleste in the ballroom, and couldn't control myself. I murdered my wife.'"

"'Oh, *Mon Dieu*,' Justine whispered. 'Pierre, we must leave immediately. Our lives are in danger.'"

"'Hush, Justine,' Pierre said. 'We're responsible. If he were going to kill us he could have done so by now.'"

"'I swear to you both that I'm so repulsed at what I've done I could never hurt you or any other human.'"

"'To say that we're not afraid would be lying. But you and Lisbeth are our dearest friends and we are prepared to stay with you for as long as you need us.'"

"'*Merde*,' Justine said. 'Why do you always have to be so noble?' She paused. 'I have no life without you. I will stay, but I am not happy about it.'"

"Burying Lisbeth was the most painful thing the Marquis had ever done. He stood by her graveside and swore he would never touch another drop of human blood as long as he survived, however long that might be."

"As for Céleste, she was never the same after that night. The Marquis would often find her wandering the gardens at odd times of the night calling for her Mother and weeping. He would coax her back to her room. One night, several weeks after the attack, the Marquis was hunting small game, when he heard screams in the distance. He dropped the rabbit he'd killed and sucked dry, and ran in the direction of the cries. As he broke through a stand of thick bushes near the house, he found François bending over Céleste. There was blood everywhere. He snatched his son's hair, yanked him away from his daughter and flung him to the ground. He was about to pounce for revenge but he was grabbed around the waist and thrown against a tree by Marielle. Although he was stunned only briefly, by the time he got to his feet, François and Marielle had disappeared into the night."

"Torn between chasing after them and saving his daughter, he knelt by her side. His sweet Céleste lay lifeless and pale in the moonlight. Revenge became his reason to exist."

"As the weeks passed, reports of other gruesome attacks on nearby estates reached the château. With every story, the Marquis rode off in an attempt to apprehend the killers always hoping it might be François and Marielle. With every journey, he was a day too late, his hunger for revenge thwarted. As his determination and frustration grew, he realized working alone was insufficient. One evening while talking with Pierre, he expressed his frustration and sense of helplessness."

"Pierre listened and had an idea."

"'Why don't you form an alliance to support your commitment? Given the stories we've been hearing, surely there must be others who feel as you do and would be more than willing to hunt these creatures.'"

Étienne stopped, and the ticking of the clock was like gunshots. Lexie realized that she was hugging herself and unfolded her arms. She took a deep breath and picked up her glass of water. Her hands were shaking so badly that water splashed on the antique coffee table.

"Shit, I'm sorry…your table…"

Étienne came to her and set the glass back on the table.

"And that, *ma chérie*, is how the Society was formed. With Pierre's help, the Marquis recruited others to join him. Soon, humans and other sympathetic vampires began arriving at the château. Like the Marquis, the vampires were humans who had suffered great loss or were horrified by what they had become. All swore an oath to protect mankind, and like the Marquis, learned to survive on animal blood."

"Has the whole world gone berserk? Just yesterday vampires were a myth."

He pulled her into his arms. At first, she struggled against his powerful embrace pushing against his chest with her fists. But as he continued to hold her, murmuring erotic French words in her ear, she succumbed. He smelled wonderful, like vanilla, and he was cool to the touch. He stroked her back and she pressed against him shocked she wanted more. Her body responded to him and she felt his erection pressing against her. A small moan escaped her lips and his arms tightened in response. Without warning he lowered her to the sofa and retreated to the other side of the room. Lexie saw Étienne breathing deeply and when he faced her, he was calm.

"I assure you, vampires are very real. As for my age...." He regarded her for a moment and took a deep breath. "I am the Marquis."

"I figured that out already," Lexie said.

"And you're a vampire executioner."

"If I'm a vampire executioner doesn't that make me your enemy?"

"In theory it would. However, I walk on the side of the light. I've sworn to protect humans and have seldom touched human blood in five-hundred years. I've worked with many executioners through the centuries. Charlie and Jeremy were two of my dearest friends."

Isn't this a pisser? Lexie looked at him her mind seesawing between belief and doubt. She wondered what the seldom meant and decided she didn't want to know.

"Show me your fangs," she demanded, thinking to trip him up.

She heard a soft click and his incisor teeth protruded from his mouth, long and sharp.

She leapt to her feet putting distance between them. "Thunder crap!" but she was curious "Are those real?" She reached out to touch them. Étienne remained motionless as she probed each one. Fascinated, she tugged, half-expecting them to come out.

"Satisfied?" He asked. She heard a soft click and the fangs disappeared.

"Satisfied is not the word for what I'm feeling right now. Dumbfounded is more like it."

She sank down on the settee keeping a good two feet between them.

Étienne gazed at her with a perplexed expression. "What does thunder crap mean?"

Surprised by his question, Lexie smiled. "It's an old habit I picked up. Cassie used to smack me whenever I'd use a curse word. I started usin' other southernisms instead. It doesn't mean anythin' special."

Étienne was silent.

Her brain seemed unable to process the math. "How old are you?"

"Five-hundred-years-old – give or take."

"Tom isn't......is he?"

"Tom is human."

"How did he get involved?"

"Fifteen years ago Tom was a special agent with MI6. While he and his family were vacationing in Southern France his wife and eight month old baby were killed by vampires."

"How awful. Was it François and Marielle?"

"Most likely, but we could never prove it. When he and I met, I did my best to recruit him into the Society. He didn't believe me and told me to get lost. I kept an eye on him knowing he was taking crazy risks and one night as he returned to his hotel, he was attacked by vampires. I managed to fight them off. Finally convinced, he begged me to turn him. I refused and he became a Guardian. He's one of the best."

"Thank the Lord for small favors."

As if on cue her cell rang. It was Tom.

Really...? Spooky.

"Hey," she answered.

"Where are you?"

"At Étienne's, he's been sharin' his life story with me."

"Splendid, I'll be there shortly."

"Why?"

"Just wait for me." He disconnected.

"Tom's on his way over."

"I heard," Étienne said, his brow wrinkled in displeasure.

"You don't look too happy about it."

"I was hoping for more time alone with you." His silky words stroked her. She felt hot. Before she could respond the front door buzzer sounded.

"He must have been right around the corner," she said. "Odd"

"He's a real *vexé de façon exagérée* when it comes to beautiful women."

Lexie smiled at the eager beaver description. *Friendly competition?*

"Are you okay?" Tom asked as he strode through the doorway and past Étienne without acknowledging his presence.

"Your timing *sucer*," Étienne said to Tom's retreating back.

"I'm fine. My molecules have been rearranged and put back together funny, but I'll live. What're you doin' here?"

Tom smiled. "I called your apartment and Cassie said you'd come here alone. I had planned to take you to the Paris branch of the Society today."

"Whatever for?"

"It's important that you become familiar with everything."

"I'd planned to take her once we finished here," Étienne said. "There was no need for you to make a special trip." He moved to stand close to Lexie.

"No worries, old man," Tom replied. "It's my pleasure."

"*Merde*, sometimes you are *tres iritant*." Étienne's tone left no doubt he was displeased.

"Wanker," Tom retorted.

"Stop it you two!" Lexie said. "Right now you are both as irritatin' as a dawg that don't hunt. If it's that important we can ALL go."

Chapter 5
The Society

The short walk to the Society's branch located in the Place de Voges passed in silence. Lexie was aware of the tension between the two men and found their hostility amusing. *Male rivalry is a good thing.* Tom paused in front of a wrought iron gate and pressed a button. He spoke a couple of words in French and the gate creaked open. The curved driveway was lined with trees, and as they approached the building Lexie marveled at the beautiful 16th century architecture. It was difficult to believe a business operated behind the ornate mahogany doors.

Étienne bent low to allow a scanner to move over his eyes. The doors clicked open and Étienne motioned her forward. Lexie entered eyes wide in awe of the opulence. Dark wood, polished to a brilliant sheen, had been matched to stone giving the entry a warm peaceful dignity. Precious antiques were placed strategically for optimum effect and the pattern of the marble floor was reminiscent of a Monet painting.

"This is amazing," she said. "How long has this branch been here?"

"Since the 17th century," Étienne replied. "*Le Organisation de Fraternite et Solidarite* or the Society is headquartered at the family estate in Southern France. This is one of eight branches around the world."

"We have offices in London, Edinburgh, Bucharest, New York, Los Angeles, Hong Kong and Rio de Janeiro." Tom offered.

"Please follow me," Étienne continued touching Lexie's elbow. Her heartbeat accelerated. "I want to show you our offices."

"What's on the other floors?" Lexie asked him as they ascended the spiral staircase.

"The third floor has more administrative offices, and the top two are living quarters for visiting members."

Étienne ushered them into an outer office where several men and women were busy talking on phones and Lexie heard a cacophony of different languages.

"This is where we gather reports of vampire activity around the world. François and Marielle are pushing hard to strengthen their forces and engage us in war."

"How strong are they?" Lexie asked.

"Thousands," Tom interjected.

"And how many like me are there?"

"A few. That's why it's imperative we bring you up to speed as soon as possible."

We're screwed.

Étienne unlocked a closed door and motioned them inside. The room was huge. Bookcases lined the walls filled with what appeared to be rare books. There were four large glass cases containing old artifacts. An ornate desk drew her attention. Standing behind it was a tall ancient man who smiled at her.

"*Bonjour Mademoiselle* Lexie, *ça va?*" His voice was breathy and rough as if unused for a long time.

"*Bonjour Monsieur, bien merci.*" Lexie said.

Knows my name?

"This is Monsieur Lavallée. He is the curator of our small archives," Étienne said.

"It's a pleasure Monsieur." Lexie said. *He looks like a strong wind would blow him away.*

He seemed to float as he moved toward her. "The pleasure is all mine." He towered over her and as he shook her hand, an unexpected impression of peace fell over her. "Please call me Anastase," he said.

"Archives?"

"Through the centuries, we have collected artifacts and treasured items of memorabilia from the Originals." Étienne said.

"What are you talking about? What originals?"

"The Strygoi and the Divinati," Anastase replied, still clutching her hand as he led her to one of the cases. Daggers of all shapes and sizes lay displayed on blue velvet.

"These are beautiful," Lexie exclaimed. "But who or what are the Strygoi and Divinati?"

Anastase released Lexie's hand.

"Three thousand years ago there were two warring factions of vampires. The Strygoi were evil and dark. Blood thirsty demons who believed they were the ones who deserved to rule the earth and subjugate mankind to use as a food source. The Divinati were light, sworn to wage war against the Strygoi to protect humankind. Both have good and evil in their blood."

"Where did they come from? They sound like angels and devils."

"We don't know. We just exist."

We? She waited for Anastase to explain further but he didn't. "And these weapons?"

Anastase moved his hand over the lock on the case and it sprung open. "These are the daggers that have been used by vampire executioners throughout the ages. They are forged from the first Claidheamh Solius (Swords of Light) wielded by the Divinati. One of them is yours."

"Which one?"

"Move your hand over the blades. It will come to you."

Not likely. Lexie glanced at Étienne and he nodded his encouragement. She reached out and began moving her hand over the ornate daggers. They trembled as she progressed over them.

68

"Holy crap," she exclaimed as one flew toward her and slapped her palm. It had a fifteen-inch blade sharpened on both sides. The handle was simple with a fairly small grip and a large guard between it and the blade. As she closed her hand around the hilt, it warmed.

Not knowing what to do with it, she set it back in the case where it continued to vibrate. "That was creepy."

Anastase gave the barest semblance of a smile and handed her the dagger. "This one is called Requiem and recognizes your bloodline. It will be your best friend and life saver in the months to come. When used by the owner it can slice through a vampire's neck like butter and burns its body to ash. Keep it with you and guard it well."

"Let's show her how it's done." Tom said to Étienne. He picked up a dagger and brandished it at his friend.

"Are you sure you want to take me on?" Étienne replied. His smile was wicked.

"Come on old man, don't be such a wimp."

Étienne grabbed another and the two circled each other as if looking for an opening. Tom saw one and slashed at Étienne drawing first blood from the vampire's shoulder.

They could kill each other.

"Don't worry, I won't let them do too much harm." Anastase remarked.

Did he just read my mind?

As Tom stepped back, Étienne pressed in and opened a long shallow wound on Tom's arm. Tom spun away and circled, looking for another opportunity. They lunged at each other over and over, Étienne clearly the faster and stronger. He took a vicious swipe at Tom and slashed open his shirt marking his chest with a scrape.

"Enough." Anastase thundered. "Your male competition is boring. These daggers are not toys. Now I have to clean them. Idiots."

69

Looking sheepish, they placed the daggers on a table.

Lexie reached out to examine Tom's arm and chest. "Are you okay?"

"I'm fine. They're just a scratch."

"He's tough," Étienne said. His own wound was already healing.

"As I was saying," Anastase continued. "The Divinati's mission is to wage war against the dominance of the Strygoi. Today, the Strygoi are known as vampires or 'the dark ones'. The Divinati are now known as Vampire Executioners. I am one of the original Divinati. You have my blood in your veins."

"Divinati, shmivinati, you're pullin' my leg, right?"

Étienne jumped in. "As much as it would give me pleasure to pull your leg, what Anastase is telling you is no joke. And, there's more. Marielle was turned by one of the original Strygoi."

Lexie interrupted. "Does that mean you're one of them?"

"Please stop interrupting," Étienne said. "We're getting to that."

Aren't you just an overbearing ass? She felt a little tickle in her brain. *That's odd.*

"Vampires like Étienne who have chosen to work with the Divinati are called 'the light ones'." Anastase said.

Lexie noticed a smile playing about his lips. "Because he is second generation, his Strygoi blood is diluted. He had a choice of whether or not to become a blood-sucking vampire. He chose the 'light side'."

"And that makes everything okay?" Lexie said shaking her head in disgust.

Étienne glared at her. "Still not convinced? Just listen." Lexie held her tongue.

Étienne went on. "When we formed the Society the Divinati joined us in fighting the Strygoi. We have been working together for over four hundred years."

"The Divinati can have children?" she said.

"The original Divinati were human in appearance and breathtakingly beautiful," Anastase said. "At one point they mated with humans to preserve their bloodline. Not all Divinati were fertile. Your bloodline is one of the ten originals."

"Are you tellin' me that I'm descended from vampires? What a load of malarkey," Lexie sputtered, heading for the door. "I'm outta here."

Étienne blocked her way, moving as a blur.

She spat at him. "Get out of my way, you arrogant butt head."

"Please hear us out," he said, touching her cheek. "The Strygoi become more powerful every day and you are essential to our cause."

Lexie's shoulders slumped and she faced Tom. "I don't want to be. Help me out here. Can't you provide some sanity in all this?" She knew she sounded pathetic. She didn't care.

"Sorry Lex, I'm with Anastase and Étienne on this one." Tom said.

Lexie turned back to Anastase.

"Do I really have your blood in me?"

"You do."

"And you think my destiny is to defeat the Strygoi?"

Anastase touched her cheek. "It's your choice. No one can do that for you. I know you will do the right thing."

Although his touch was feather soft, Lexie felt her blood rush to meet their gentle connection. It made her dizzy. He broke the link and her world righted.

Pressure much?

The ancient Divinati floated back toward the huge desk. Lexie was sure it was a trick of light but he seemed to be fading in and out.

"Let's leave Anastase in peace. We can continue this discussion in my office," Étienne said.

71

They walked a few paces down the hallway. Étienne paused in front of another door and another scanner read his eyes and clicked open.

The room was minimally furnished with none of the opulence of his apartment. "This is your office?"

"I am rarely here so I keep it simple."

He took a seat at the conference table and motioned Tom and Lexie to join him.

"Tell me more about this cause," Lexie said.

"Our mission is simple. To ensure the continuation and safety of the human race, and create a brotherhood between our species." Étienne replied.

"How many vampires and humans are there in the Society?"

"Our number grows every day, but approximately ten thousand worldwide."

"How do y'all tell the good vampires from the bad ones? Y'all look the same to me."

"Because we refrain from drinking human blood we have a distinct natural odor from taking antiserum every day. Vampires who consume human blood have a distinctly pungent smell and their eyes turn red when they are about to feed. We can also walk in the daylight, which I will explain in a minute. As for the humans, due to the antiserum they take daily, their odor resembles cinnamon."

Lexie interrupted. "What's this antiserum you mentioned?"

"For years, the Society scientists have been working to perfect an antiserum for humans. Our hope was that when taken regularly, it could prevent them from being turned into vampires and increasing François and Marielle's army. Until Emma came to us, it was a disaster. When administered to human volunteers it killed them instantly."

"You used people to test the antiserum? That's barbaric."

"They were volunteers," Tom interjected. "They gave their lives for the cause."

"It's still barbaric. What did Em have to do with all this?"

"She was a brilliant bio-chemical engineer and discovered the chemical compound that allowed humans to ingest the antiserum safely."

"Em was my closest friend. How did she keep something like this from me? Thunder crap, she was going to work in your lab when she told me she was going home for a 'surprise visit'. How did she keep this from her Dad?"

"She didn't." Tom said. "She comes from a long line of scientists who have been working with the Society for generations. Heinrick is one of them."

"What we now have are two forms of the antiserum." Étienne continued. "*Redemption* or 40C prevents humans from being turned into vampire. *Destruction* or 41P, as we originally called it, was useless until Emma perfected it. She devised a compound when mixed with the *Destruction* antiserum makes us stronger and faster. We call this particular formula 88P. It allows us to withstand the burning rays of the sun. As long as we aren't exposed for long periods of time, we can walk during the daylight hours and function as if we were human. It also eases the craving for human blood."

However, there is a dangerous side effect. In an unfortunate incident at the château a few years ago, Emma discovered that if a vampire who has been taking the 88P antiserum ingests human blood he or she becomes virtually unstoppable. We had to decapitate and burn the vampire who tried it. Nothing else worked."

"Is that why Em was killed? Are François and Marielle after the 88P?"

"Two of our informants, Jacques and Emile have alerted us that François and Marielle found out about the antiserum and formula. Both are missing. For security purposes, only Emma knew the entire formula."

"Isn't THIS just a pig in a poke?" Lexie struggled to wrap her brain around what she was hearing.

Tom reached over and took her hand. "There's something else you need to hear. Emma was most likely the leak. We think that François and Marielle found out about her work with us. One or both of them 'compelled' her, and forced her to get them the formula."

Lexie jerked her hand back. "No way," she said. "Em would never….."

"Bloody hell, let me finish. We believe she was killed because somehow she managed to recover sufficiently from their influence to hide the antiserum and formula. They found out she'd betrayed them and killed her. Étienne smelled them when we went to the site. Fortunately, prior to dying she had given each vampire who works with the Society a month's supply of the antiserum. She was not a traitor, but a true hero."

"Sounds like Em. What the heck is compelled?"

"It is a form of hypnosis. Older vampires like myself, François and Marielle are more adept than the young ones," Étienne replied. "It's also very probable that François hit on her. He is very handsome and it would have been easy for him to gain her confidence. It must have been very flattering to Emma to have such a man be interested in her."

"He raped her and killed her." Lexie snapped.

Étienne ran his hand through his hair, his expression inscrutable. "I miss her too. We have no idea where she might have hidden the 88P and formula. Our month's supply is running low. The outcome would be disastrous."

"Knowing Emma, she must have some clues where she hid them," Tom said. "We just need to find it."

"Man, talk about a pig in a poke," Lexie said. "What about the château, do you think she hid them there?"

"Too obvious," Tom replied. "We're really stumped."

Lexie's phone pinged. "It's Cassie," she said. "I need to take this."

Lexie walked to the other side of the room. "Hey I'm fine. I'm with Tom and Étienne. I didn't realize it was so late. I'll be home soon. Bye."

"Is she okay?" Tom asked.

"Getting concerned 'cause I was gone for so long. She'll get over it. Is there anything else we need to cover right now?"

"I think we're done." Tom said glancing at Étienne who nodded. "Emma's funeral is tomorrow at 11am at St. Chappelle. I spoke with Heinrick earlier. Everything's arranged."

"Wait, there's one last thing. You need to start taking 40C," Étienne said, pulling a small vial from his pocket. "One drop under your tongue daily will protect you from being turned."

He handed her the vial and their hands brushed. She flushed, her heart pounding in her ears. *What WAS that?*

Her voice when she spoke was breathy with desire. "Can one of you drive me home?"

"I'll take you," Tom replied before Étienne could offer.

"And, I'll join you." Étienne said.

Tom took Lexie's hand. "That won't be necessary."

"I want to," Étienne said. "Just let me check my e-mail and messages before we leave."

"Bullocks, fine. I'll go get my car. Meet you out front."

Lexie wandered around marveling at Étienne's book collection when she was startled.

"Merde, there's an e-mail here from Emma."

"What? How? When?"

"The night she was murdered."

Lexie peered over Étienne's shoulder. "What does it say?"

"Tom will want to hear this too. I'll print a copy to read and then delete it. "

Her cell phone pinged.

"I'm waiting," Tom texted.

"Hurry up, Tom's out front."

"What took you so long?" Tom grumped.

"We found an e-mail from Em."

"Bloody hell, what does it say?"

Étienne read.

> *Dearest Étienne and Tom,*
>
> *I am sending this to you from an outside computer as I fear my computer has been hacked.*
>
> *If you are reading this e-mail and do not know what I am about to tell you, then I did not survive the night. Someone from the Society is a traitor and has leaked the existence of the 88P to François and Marielle. For the past several weeks I have been meeting with François. His attempts to compel me don't last very long because of the 40C antiserum I have been taking. But I remember enough to know that I haven't given them the 88P or its formula. I've hidden them in a safe place. I have created a riddle to give you the location. The first clue is concealed on the Society property in Grignon and should be fairly easy for you to find.*
>
> *I am in love with François and I pray that he is in love with me. I have made every effort to convince him to make peace with you and join the 'light side.' Tonight will tell the tale. I'm so sorry I couldn't tell you. Marielle threatened to kill my father. When you and Tom take Lexie into your confidence, ask her to forgive me for not sharing my 'other' life with her. It was for her*

protection. I love her like a sister, and I know she will be a great Vampire Executioner.

Trust no one.

Love, Emma

Lexie broke the silence. "That's just more than I can say grace over. It breaks my heart to know that she was so alone and died so bravely. I'll never stop missing her."

"She was *une femme forte et superbe*," Étienne said acknowledging Emma's strength and character. He reached through the front seats to take Lexie's hand. She squeezed back surprised at his show of affection.

They pulled up to Lexie's building. Étienne got out of the car and opened the door for her.

"Why don't you guys come over in the morning and we can all ride to the funeral together."

"Sounds good," Tom said. "Lock your doors and windows and don't let anyone in and I mean ANYONE."

"A little paranoid are we?" Lexie teased.

"Maybe, but we can't be too careful right now."

She got out of the car, and Étienne escorted her to the door, steering her with one hand. Suddenly she couldn't breath and a slow heat radiating from her solar plexus spread to her groin. *Crap, is this going to happen every time he touches me?*

"*Bonne nuit, ma petite*," Étienne murmured, kissing her on each cheek. Before she could respond he was gone.

Cassie greeted her eagerly. "Thank goodness, I'm hungry and tired of bein' cooped up all day."

"There was nothin' stoppin' you from going out. I left you a key."

"I know, hon. I just don't feel comfortable alone with all these foreigners."

"You're the foreigner here." Lexie said.

"Please don't fuss sweetie. Let's just go out for some dinner and have a good chat. You can tell me all about your day."

Lexie remembered she had a dagger in her purse and needed to find a safe place to stash it. "Give me a minute to freshen up." She locked the bathroom door behind her and scanned the room trying to decide. Anastase's words drifted through her mind. "Keep it with you and guard it well." *I guess I'm stuck with it.*

"What's takin' you so long," Cassie called through the door.

Lexie snapped her purse shut. "I'm ready. Let's go eat."

Chapter 6
Lexie

The next morning the alarm on Lexie's phone jarred her awake. Groggy, she wondered what she was doing on the couch in her living room. *Oh right, Cassie's here.* Rain pattered against the French doors to the balcony. Today was her birthday, and Em's funeral. *So much for happy birthdays.* Emma was gone and she would never talk to her again. *I miss you Em.*

She paused to check the weather on her way to the kitchen. It was that gloomy gray that disappointed the tourists. A presence behind her unnerved her. She heard the soft pad of feet on the floor, the rustle of clothes, the smell of perfume, Hermes' Santal Massoia, and breathing. She could even detect a heartbeat.

"Happy birthday, honey pie." Cassie held out her arms for a hug.

"What's happy about it?" she snapped back. "I wish it would all go away." She ignored her Mom's outstretched arms and continued to the kitchen.

"Honey, I've been thinkin'," Cassie said following her. "Why don't you come home with me after Emma's funeral?"

"You've gotta be kiddin' me. Why on earth would I want to do that? I've been mad at you my whole life. Findin' out that you've been lyin' to me has only added fuel to the fire."

"You just said you wish it would all go away. Comin' home would be a way to put some distance between this tragedy and healing. Besides your grandmother Bessie misses you and you know she's not going to live much longer. Don't you want to spend some time with her?"

"Don't pull that guilt trip on me. Bessie's stronger than a mule. My life is here not back in Atlanta. The answer is no."

"But hon, I don't want you to be a vampire executioner. I can't stand the thought of losing you too."

"It's not your decision to make. I feel like I'm bein' torn apart with Tom and Étienne on one side and you on the other. No more talk. I'm done."

Lexie fixed coffee and headed for the bathroom to be alone with her grief and anger. Her phone pinged a message. It was painful knowing it wasn't Emma. It was a text from Tom.

We'll be at your place between 9:30 & 10:00.

Lexie finished her make-up just as the intercom buzzed.

"Cassie can you buzz'em up?" she called out.

Cassie's voice drifted into the bathroom. "Who is it?"

"It's Tom and Étienne."

"You brought that – that THING with you?"

"Not now Cassie, just let us in." Tom said.

"Against my better judgment," she said.

Lexie applied lip gloss, and fluffed her hair one last time. Despite her foul mood, she tingled with excitement at the prospect of seeing Étienne. She hurried back to the kitchen to lay out breakfast. Cassie was already there, slicing melon and the croissants had been piled on a platter.

It provoked her. "I could have done that."

"I know sweetie, but I wanted to help," Cassie said.

"Don't think for a minute this makes up for anything," Lexie said.

"Oh hon, I've always done what I thought was best for you."

"Let's not start that again," Lexie said as the doorbell rang.

"Good mornin'," she said opening the door.

"Happy birthday Lex," Tom said, He gave her a peck on each cheek, and handed her a huge bouquet of red roses. "You shouldn't have," she said taking the flowers.

"Today is a tough day but it's also your birthday. I wanted you to know that someone remembered."

"Thank you, they're beautiful."

Étienne was still in the hall. "What are *you* waiting for?" she asked. He looked delicious dressed in an all-black leather suit with a white shirt. His cologne smelled like winter fir trees and mixed with his natural vanilla musk made her want to jump his bones. *Jesus he's hot.* Tom was grinning.

"You'll have to invite him in or he can't cross the threshold," Tom said. "You'll have to rescind it if you ever want to get rid of him. My advice is you keep him out."

"Bâtard, better watch your back. You'll pay for that remark." Étienne fired back.

"Come on in." Lexie said.

He stepped through the entryway and kissed her cheeks. "*Joyeux anniversaire.*"

Her cheeks tingled. Heat surged through her and she backed up willing the lust to subside. "What, you didn't bring me roses too?" she said to cover up her embarrassment.

"Honey pie are you okay?" Cassie asked. "You look flushed."

"I'm fine."

Cassie played the gracious Southern hostess making sure everyone was served. The rain drummed harder and only gray light filled the apartment. Lightening flashed with occasional claps of thunder. *The beginning of a storm.*

"I think it's time to talk about the hippo in the room." Lexie said plunking her coffee mug down on the table. "Y'all have been peein' down my back and tellin' me it's rainin'!"

Cassie waggled a finger. "Language, young lady," she said.

"Thunder crap, this is no time for manners," Lexie said. "I'm pissed. In the last twenty four hours the life I thought I was livin' has turned out to be nothin' but a pack of lies. You claim to be so virtuous and pure - a good Christian by any standards. I thought 'good Christians' didn't lie. You made my life a livin' hell. It was church every Sunday and two nights a week. I had to sit through the preachin' hatin' every minute of it. Why do you think I moved across an ocean? It was to get away from you. I don't know how Daddy stood it. I saw him leavin' the house just to get away from you."

"Steady Lex that's a tad harsh," Tom said interrupting her tirade.

She glared at Tom and Étienne. "And, you two, pretendin' to be soooo supportive and actin' as if you were sensitive to my feelings. You're just as two-faced. Maybe I don't want to be a vampire executioner. Like I said, what if I just disappear? It would serve all of you right."

In the silence the rain sounded like hailstones hitting the windows.

It was Étienne who broke it. "You have no idea what it's taken and is taking to protect you from François and Marielle, not to mention the Strygoi. It's not all about you. This legacy of yours is for everyone. The sooner you come to terms with that the quicker we can move on. You are acting like a spoiled brat."

Lexie's mouth hung open at his outburst. "Well, aren't YOU just nastiness waitin' to happen," she fired back. "It doesn't excuse the lies and deceit. Y'all should've trusted me. And Em, how could she have kept this from me, even if it was for my protection? She was like a sister to me and now I find out it was all a bunch of hogwash. You guys are a piece of work. And speakin' of protection….Em died because you weren't there for her."

Tom slammed his fist down on the table. "Bollocks! We didn't know she was seeing François and Marielle. The fact of the matter is you *are* a vampire executioner. At this point the lies and deceit are moot. We have a crisis on our hands. Whether you like it or not you're an integral part of managing that crisis."

Étienne reached across the table and took her hand. "You can trust us. I swear to you." His piercing green eyes held hers.

"Don't do that!" Lexie said, jerking her hand away. "I'm not some silly school girl you can seduce with your good looks and charisma." She could feel herself moistening at his touch and she hated herself for it.

Cassie put her two cents in. "That's right honey, he's from the devil. He may be on our side now, but you can't trust any of'em."

Lexie was aggravated by her Mom's words and found she wanted to defend Étienne. *Are you crazy?*

"I need time," Lexie said. "This is a lot to swallow."

"Then swallow faster," Tom said. "Time is one thing we don't have."

Étienne took a small black velvet box from his pocket and handed it to her.

"What's this?" She asked.

"I have brought you a locket with verveine in it to prevent you from being compelled."

Lexie opened the box. Inside was a beautiful eighteen carat gold locket mounted with a huge sapphire. *This is too personal.*

She snapped the lid closed and shoved it back across the table. "I hardly know you. I can't accept this."

Étienne sighed and shook his head. "Must you resist everything? Consider it a birthday gift."

Tom glared at Étienne. "Ruddy hell, are you daft? Can't you see she doesn't want it?"

"Yeah, what he said," Lexie piped up, crossing her arms in defiance. *It is beautiful.*

83

Étienne slammed his hand down on the table causing everyone to jump. "I insist. You can return it after we've confirmed you're safe from being compelled."

He removed the locket, and fastened it around her neck. Lexie shivered as his hands brushed her neck and she ducked away to cover her reaction.

"Tosser, you're a stubborn ass," Tom said.

"Tosser or not, I don't want to take any chances Do you?"

"Of course not," Tom grumbled.

"We should leave for the Society this afternoon," Étienne said.

"So soon?" Cassie asked. "I just got here and want to spend more time with Lexie."

"You're welcome to join us."

"And enter that den of iniquity? Not in a coon's age. Besides Lexie hasn't chosen. She might choose to go back to Atlanta with me."

"I'm not goin' back to Atlanta and that's final." Lexie said. "Nor am I ready to choose. We're on our way to Em's funeral and I don't want to discuss this right now. You guys go pick up Heinrick. Mom and I will grab a cab."

"I have a better idea," Tom said. "Let's you and I go pick him up."

"Or Étienne and I could take your car and fetch Heinrick and you and Mom could take a cab." She glanced at Étienne and despite her hesitancy at being alone with him, she liked how he seemed pleased at her suggestion.

Tom's eyebrows knitted together in annoyance. "Bloody hell Lex, we haven't had time to talk in the last couple of days. Besides, I prefer to drive my own car,"

"Okay, don't get your knickers in a wad," Lexie said. "It really doesn't matter."

"You expect me to ride alone in a car with a vampire?" Cassie said, her eyes big as saucers.

84

Give it a rest," Lexie said. "You'll be fine."

"What in the world was that all about?" Lexie asked as she and Tom pulled away from her apartment. His sleek Mercedes blended into the heavy traffic. "You were downright rude."

"I wasn't rude," Tom protested. "I just wanted a few minutes alone with you. A lot has happened in the last two days and I'm concerned." He reached over and squeezed her hand. "How are you really?"

"Hmmph," she said surprised at his show of affection. She peered at him in an attempt to read his expression. She couldn't. "I'm angry, frustrated, and sad. I miss Em so much it hurts. How's that?"

"Straight enough," Tom said. He was quiet for a moment, avoiding a motorcycle. "Why are you so bloody beastly to your Mom? Some of the things you said today were extremely harsh."

"She's been meddlin' in my life ever since I can remember. When all the lies came out it was just the last straw. I love her, but she can be so manipulative and sneaky at times. This mornin' she asked me to go home with her. Said it was about seeing Grandmother Bessie before she dies. The truth is she thinks if she gets me away from you and Étienne I'll choose not to be a vampire executioner."

"Can't say I blame her. She loves you a lot and she's afraid for you."

"Maybe, but enough is enough. It's time for her to let go and let me live my life. What's it to you anyway?"

To her surprise, Tom abruptly pulled into an empty parking spot.

"What are you doin'? We're gonna be late."

"You know Lex, I care for you deeply, but sometimes you can be dead from the neck up," Tom said. "She's the only Mum you have and you're lucky she's still alive. She's lived with danger all her life and she's protected you from the worst possible threat a human being can face. She's handled a lot of tragedy and kept it together."

"Are you takin' her side?"

"I'm just pointing out some facts," he replied. "Someone needs to remind you who she is and what she's endured. Now she's about to hand over her only daughter to a vampire and a life of extreme risk. And you are clear how she feels about vampires." He took one of her hands and held it gently in his warm one. "Give her some slack, she deserves it."

"When you put it that way… I just feel like I'm up to my butt in alligators."

Tom chuckled and pulled back out into traffic. They spent the remainder of the ride to the hotel in silence.

Chapter 7
Goodbye to Emma

The Saint Chappelle had always been one of Lexie's favorite churches. A royal, medieval, gothic cathedral, situated on the Île de la Cité in the heart of Paris, it retained one of the most extensive collections of thirteenth-century stained glass anywhere in the world.

There were about fifty people already there with more pouring in. Lexie and Tom took their place in the family's row. She stood for a moment and scanned the crowd. She recognized a few colleagues but most were strangers. *Are they from the Society?* She was moved by the number of people in attendance.

She saw Étienne and her Mom arrive and she raised her hand and waved. Cassie waved back and hurried down the aisle leaving Étienne to fend for himself.

In spite of her earlier outburst, Lexie felt safe. "I'm glad you're here Mom. It's good to have your support."

"Thanks darlin' that means a lot to me." She squeezed Lexie's hand and held on as the service began.

The priest opened the service with the Lord's Prayer in French. Lexie was thankful when Cassie discreetly handed her a Kleenex. She dabbed at her wet cheeks, as tears of anger and sadness slid down her chin. After the priest finished speaking, Emma's father walked to the podium. As he delivered the eulogy a break in the weather allowed a ray of sunlight to shine through the rose window. Multicolored, it danced like a kaleidoscope, changing even as Lexie watched it. *How can the world be beautiful?*

"Thank you all for coming," Heinrick began, his excellent French tinged with a German accent. Tall and distinguished looking, his looks failed to broadcast 'brilliant scientist.' He looked more like a mature male model. The thick lenses of his eyeglasses gave him away. "It is a fitting testament to Emma that there are so many here to pay their respects." He paused, clearing his throat before continuing. Lexie could tell that he was struggling to maintain his composure and her heart ached for him. "Emma was a gift. Her quick mind and gentle spirit made it easy to love her."

Heinrick's voice became a drone in the background as vivid memories of Emma flooded her mind. *Hell's bells Em, why didn't you confide in me?* Cassie's hand moved in hers, and Lexie realized she had been squeezing hard. She eased up, and Cassie pulled her hand away to slip her arm around Lexie's shoulders, and kept it there through the rest of the service.

As they rose to view the open casket, Lexie stopped so abruptly that Tom ran into her, and she lost her balance.

"What's wrong?" he whispered his lips close to her ear as he righted her.

"I don't know," she muttered. "It felt like someone touched me and my scalp started itchin' like crazy." She was drawn to the balcony, and thought she saw a woman's face. It was gone as quickly as it had appeared, and she moved on to take her place in line to view Emma's body.

Emma's throat was wrapped in one of her favorite scarves, and Lexie shivered knowing what it hid. Unable to stop her hand, she reached out. Although no longer bloody, Emma's neck looked like something from a Frankenstein movie. She rearranged the scarf. *Thunder crap, you didn't deserve this.*

"What are you doing?" Tom murmured at her side.

"I had to see it again. Now I wish I hadn't. How could anyone be so brutal?"

"They're not just anyone. They're monsters."

"Beheaded monsters if I have anything to say about it."

Lexie squared her shoulders and walked to the receiving line at the church door. Her heart went out to Heinrick. She shook people's hands and accepted their sympathies, but Lexie felt an internal anger growing.

"Is this service ever going to end?" she whispered to Cassie. "This is torture."

"Easy darlin', this is all part of it."

After the last of the mourners had left, Emma's casket was loaded into the hearse for the ride to Charles de Gaulle airport. Heinrick was taking Emma's body back to Frankfort to be buried in the family plot with her mother.

"I'm still havin' trouble believin' she's gone," Lexie said turning to Heinrick. "It's so unfair. I can't wait to get my hands on….."

"Now is not the time to discuss this," Étienne interrupted, touching her elbow.

"Aren't you angry?" Lexie said. "She was our friend and they…."

"It's okay darlin,'" Cassie said. "She's in heaven with the angels now."

"What an inane thing to say. And it doesn't make things any easier."

"I understand *liebes*," Heinrick said, his eyes glistening with tears. "The loneliness without her will be difficult but acts of revenge are not the answer. Fighting the good fight is what she would have wanted."

Lexie didn't understand. "Fighting the good fight?"

"Accept your legacy and fight the forces of evil," Heinrick responded, taking her hand. "Don't let Emma's death be for nothing."

Before Lexie could respond, a young man touched her elbow and startled her.

"Mademoiselle, I think you have dropped a necklace in the church," he said. "Please follow me."

89

Lexie's hand flew to her throat. The necklace that Étienne had given her was gone.

She hurried after the man before Étienne or Tom could stop her. "Y'all, I'll be right back,"

"Tom, why don't you and Cassie wait for Lexie, and Étienne can come with me to the airport," Heinrick said. "You can follow in your car."

The last thing Étienne wanted was to be separated from Lexie right now but he acquiesced to Heinrick in honor of Emma's passing. "I'll meet you in front of the Air France terminal," he called as he joined Heinrick in the limo.

"I'll get the car. Cassie I won't be a sec," Tom said. He hurried off.

Lexie followed the young man anxious to retrieve Étienne's necklace. They entered the cathedral, now dark and deserted.

"Where is it?" she asked him.

"It's just over here," he said, motioning her to follow.

Intent on getting the necklace back she was stunned when a blow to the back of her legs sent her crashing to the stone floor.

Ignoring the sharp pain in her knees, Lexie sprang to her feet, assuming the defensive stance from Gaétan's training. Three men closed in on her. She prayed that her new abilities were sufficient. There was no one else.

She delivered a devastating kick to the head of one of her attackers as he lunged forward and heard the snap of his neck breaking. A blow to her temple sent her reeling. Dizzy and disoriented, she was unable to fend off the strong arms that encircled her from behind and the simultaneous crushing right hook to her jaw. She lost consciousness, and when she came to, she had a huge boot pressing against her windpipe.

I can't die now.

Chapter 8
Étienne

The limo Étienne had hired to follow the hearse was as luxurious on the inside as the outside. Beige leather seats and extra padding to filter out any external noise provided maximum comfort as they crawled through the heavy Paris traffic.

"I'm so sorry about Emma," he said. "I only wish…"

"It was not your fault," Heinrick replied. "She knew the risks." He turned away to stare out the window and Étienne could think of nothing else to say. *I know his pain.* Memories of his own daughter, Céleste, reminded him. He thought of Lexie. He must stop her resisting and join them. Yet, her stubborn nature and anger was both frustrating and alluring to him. *There is something about her.* His blood rushed to his groin remembering her delicious lilac perfume and he struggled to remain detached. But an unfamiliar panic gripped his insides.

"Something's wrong," he said, touching Heinrick on the shoulder.

"What is it?"

"It's Lexie. I must go to her, now!"

"But we're almost at the airport."

"I'm sorry, but I have to go."

He opened the limo door, and with the car still in motion Étienne disappeared before Heinrick could stop him.

Étienne heard Tom and Cassie talking as he neared their car.

"Lex is taking a long time," said Tom.

"Should we be worried?" Cassie said.

Étienne appeared at Cassie's window. "Tom, come with me. Lexie's in danger. Cassie, stay in the car. Lock the doors."

Étienne didn't wait; confident Tom would be right behind him. He entered the cathedral and saw two men standing over Lexie, a third one lay on the floor blood seeping from a large gash in his head and his head twisted at a funny angle. *Merde, they mean to kill her.* His bloodlust rose as he caught the scent of Lexie's fresh wound. *Blood.* Ignoring the urge to respond to his vampire nature Étienne was amongst them. He grabbed the man who had his boot planted on Lexie's throat and tossed him in the air as if he were made of feathers. The man landed with a crunch and didn't move. The other attacker drew a stake. Étienne lunged for it, shouting over his shoulder to Tom.

"Make sure Lexie's alive. I've got this." He kicked the man in the gut, and as he doubled over in pain Étienne twisted his neck, breaking it. His insides knotted, fearing the worst for Lexie.

Tom was kneeling over her. As he reached for her neck to find a pulse, her eyes flew open. She coughed once then threw a hard right toward his jaw.

"Relax, it's me," Tom said, ducking. "Are you okay?"

"Yeah," she replied as he pulled her to her feet. "But I'm angry enough to fry bacon from a distance." She winced as Étienne gripped her shoulder.

"Ma petite, Êtes-vous bien?"

"A little bruised, but fine," she replied rubbing her throat. Her jaw was bleeding where she'd been punched. "Who were those guys and why did they attack me?"

"I suspect they're three of François and Marielle's human servants," Étienne replied as he turned each man over with his shoe. "Unfortunately they are all dead so we cannot ask them."

He stared at the line of blood dribbling down Lexie's neck from the cut on her jaw. *The smell...intoxicating.* His nostrils flared in hunger and he felt his penis stiffen. He pushed away his bloodlust and desire.

"Maybe they were sent to test Lexie's strength," Tom said.

"Did I actually kill one of them?" Lexie asked.

"You did," Étienne replied, going through the dead men's pockets.

"What're you looking for?" Tom asked.

"The necklace. I'm sure one of them had it."

"Let me help." Lexie bent down to search the pockets of the man she'd killed and promptly threw up just missing the body.

"Christ Lex, are you okay?" Tom said, touching her back.

"I guess killin' someone for the first time affected me more than I realized. Sorry about the mess."

Étienne gave a grunt of satisfaction as he pulled the necklace from an inside pocket.

"I have it! The clasp isn't broken. They removed it from her somehow."

"When you stalled at the pews earlier, Lex, you felt something." Tom prompted.

"That's right, I thought someone touched me and my scalp itched like crazy. When I looked up I saw a woman's face, up there in the balcony."

Could it be Marielle? Étienne sniffed the air but could detect nothing.

"Let's get out of here before anyone or the police show up," Tom urged. "We don't want to explain what happened. Besides, Cassie must be frantic. I'm calling the clean-up crew now."

Lexie walked with Étienne. "I thought you left with Heinrick. How did you get back here so fast?"

He responded handing her the locket. "I have my ways, ma petite. Right now we need to get out of here."

As Étienne followed Lexie down the aisle, one thought screamed through his mind. *Merde, she almost died.* Nothing was more important than getting her trained. François and Marielle were a threat and he would have his opportunity for a battle, but if they lost Lexie nothing could replace her and her lineage would be broken. *We must leave for Grignon at once.*

Chapter 9
Choice

As Lexie exited the church she was almost knocked over as Cassie ran to her and hugged her tight. "Sweet Jesus honey. Are you okay?" She was grateful for the familiar hug of her mother, but also felt for the first time, truly separate from her in a way that all their miles apart had never accomplished. She had just killed a man, and in the moment, she had done so without remorse. It was a side of herself she hadn't known existed and it made her feel powerful. At the same time she was a little freaked out. *Maybe I am cut out for this.*

"I'm fine, just a few cuts and bruises. Some vampire executioner I am. I'm pretty useless in a real fight. I'd be better off takin' up knittin'."

"You did great," Tom said squeezing her shoulder. "You killed one of them."

Cassie squeaked her arm tightening around Lexie's shoulders as they walked toward Tom's car. "I'm so sorry you had to go through that. Now more than ever I wish you'd come home with me."

"Stop it Momma, I'm not goin' home with you. Tom, don't remind me. My stomach still feels queasy."

"The next one will be easier," Étienne assured her as she and Cassie climbed into the back seat. *When Hell freezes over.* He locked the car door and joined Tom in the front.

"Maybe, if it's François or Marielle," Lexie said. "I think I could kill them without getting upset," but her stomach lurched at the thought.

Étienne nodded. "It would give me great pleasure to detach Marielle's head from her body. But my son is a different matter."

"What about François? I for one couldn't give a bleeding hell that he's your son. If I get half a chance he's dead meat," Tom said.

Étienne's tone turned icy. "That would be *très désastreux* my friend. For then I should have to kill you. My intention has always been to bring François over to the light side."

"In your dreams mate," Tom retorted.

"I don't dream," Étienne shot back.

"All this talk of killin' is givin' me hives and palpitations not to mention it's un-Christian," Cassie interrupted. "Can we please talk about something else?"

"I do apologize, Madame," Étienne said. Lexie heard a tinge of sarcasm in his tone. "I do not want your last hours with us to have any more unpleasantness."

That seemed to end the heated conversation. Exhausted, Lexie leaned back against the soft leather upholstery. As she tried to relax, the words she had uttered the day before came to mind. *'Lexie, you need to get a life, girl.'* It had become a reality beyond anything she'd imagined. *Be careful what you wish for.*

"Where are we headed now?" she asked, noticing they were on the outskirts of Paris.

"To the airport," Tom replied.

"But Cassie's flight doesn't leave until five."

"Our immediate departure for Southern France is imperative. I've arranged for the Society's private helicopter to take us," Étienne said.

"Hold your horses. I haven't agreed to go anywhere. I've just said goodbye to my best friend. I was in my first fight where three men were killed. Granted I killed one of 'em, but I would've died if you guys hadn't showed up. Maybe I'm no good at this vampire executioner thing." Lexie stopped to catch her breath.

"This is your destiny, Lex, whether you like it or not," Tom said.

"It doesn't have to be," Cassie said. "She can still choose somethin' different."

"I can fight my own battles Momma." Lexie knew her tone was harsh and felt a pang of guilt. *Too bad.* Her anger spurred her on. "Why does it have to be me? Maybe I want a life of glamour and travel. Or a husband and children and the house with a white picket fence. I know I need to choose but it's all jumbled in my head."

Étienne pierced her with a look that took her breath away. "Tap into that anger. It will give you power and strength."

She sat for a moment. "Stop the car!"

"What?" Tom said.

She opened the car door a fraction. "Stop the car, I have to get out."

Tom swerved to the side of the road and before he could stop, Lexie was out of the car and pacing.

"Bloody hell Lex, get back in the car. You'll get yourself killed," he said.

"Can't," she yelled back.

Étienne jumped out and reached for her.

She batted at his outstretched hand. "Don't touch me. I hate François and Marielle for killin' Em. Especially François. He raped her for God's sake. He's your son and all I can think about is how much I would enjoy rippin' his heart from his chest." Her hands balled into fists. "I hate that my life is out of control. I hate that you and Tom are pushin' me in one direction and Cassie is manipulatin' me in another." She stopped to breathe. "I even hate myself for bein' so indecisive and conflicted."

"You must choose, and it needs to be now," Étienne said.

Lexie walked away from him. "Talk to the butt, the head is tired."

"And a lovely butt it is, but where are you going?"

"Back to Paris even if I have to walk there." Her head bent down in determination, she didn't notice Étienne was suddenly in front of her, and she plowed into him. She shoved him, but he grasped her shoulders forcing her to look at him.

"Stop *ma petite*. I'm sorry. I forgot that in spite of your being special, you are still human. I've been insensitive and cruel."

"No kiddin'," she fired back. "Now get the hell outta my way." She reeled away from his grasp and continued to walk in the direction of Paris.

Étienne's voice taunted her. "What about your vow to avenge Em's death?"

She stopped her heart pounding. "That's not fair. How dare you throw that in my face?"

"I'm sick of your theatrics and whining. I've asked you to trust me as your father and grandfather did, and countless others before, and you refuse. Go back to Paris and live your safe little life. We're better off without you."

The words hurt and before Lexie knew what she was doing she grabbed his arm and swept his legs from under him, sending him crashing to the pavement. She stood over him yelling, "Better off without me? You arrogant butthead. I don't want to be a vampire executioner."

Étienne rose and dusted himself off. "Are you so afraid of failure? Or are you just a coward and don't want to admit it." He turned and walked toward the car.

Lexie watched him go her body trembling in anger and frustration. "I'm NOT a coward!" He kept walking.

Out of the blue images of life after denying her legacy flashed across her mind. More years as a translator, maybe finding a man and having the white picket fence. Boring. Returning to Atlanta with her Mom, no way. It wasn't pretty. In fact it was downright depressing and scary. *Shit, shit, shit.* Every molecule in her body urged her to keep walking toward Paris, away from the dangerous life that had been offered. She couldn't do it. She had to follow her destiny. If not for her own sake, then for Emma. And, as much as she hated to admit it, Étienne was right. She was afraid she wasn't good enough. That she would fail.

"Étienne wait," she called.

"Too late," he said. "I'm done trying to convince you."

Lexie ran after him. She caught his arm and whirled him around. His green eyes were black. She hated the way he was looking at her, cold and contemptuous.

"I'm sorry," she blurted. "I'm sorry I've been such a pain in the butt. And, you're right. I'm afraid of failin'. But I am not a coward." Unwanted tears trickled down her face and she brushed at them in annoyance. "Damn it! I never cry."

Without hesitation Étienne gathered her into his arms. She pushed him away not wanting to appear weak. But as his musk enticed her she relaxed into his embrace.

"*Ma petite*, I will always be there for you. I promise."

"Do you mean that?"

"With all my heart and soul, but you must choose and you must choose now."

Here goes nothin'. She stepped back and studied his face for any deception. There was none. "I'm gonna hold you to everything you just said. I'm done resistin'. Thunder crap, let's go to Grignon."

"No more doubts?"

"Of course I have doubts. I have no idea what's in store. But in my heart I know this is the right choice."

Étienne smiled as they walked back to the car, hand in hand.

Tom was anxious "Well?"

"I'm in," Lexie replied. It's still a bad idea.

"Dadgummit, kiss my ass and call me a hooker!" Cassie said. "Darlin' are you sure? Étienne and Tom are pressurin' you. Come back to Atlanta and think things through." Cassie reached over to take Lexie's hand.

Lexie ignored her. "For the umpteenth time Momma, no. Everything I thought was real in my life was false. And, everything I thought was unreal is true. Can we please just get a move on before I change my mind?"

Tom gunned the Mercedes.

Lexie leaned forward to urge Tom to stop. "Wait, I don't have any clothes or things. I need to go to my apartment."

"I took the liberty of having my assistant purchase a few things for you." Étienne said.

"Pretty sure of yourself aren't you?"

"I am used to getting my way."

Chapter 10
L'Organisme de Fraternité et Solidarité, AKA – The Society

Wake up sleepy head we're about to land," Tom said, shaking Lexie's shoulder. "You snore like a stevedore." He grinned at her and she smiled with embarrassment.

The private helicopter from Charles De Gaulle airport was luxurious with leather upholstered seats that reclined to a prone position. Lexie had tried to stay awake for the short trip to Grignan, but exhaustion had gotten the better of her and so in under two hours they were circling the heliport.

Lexie gazed out the window, captivated by the view of the French countryside. Mile after mile of grape vines, interspersed with olive groves and orchards of apricot and coin trees spread beneath them. She smiled with delight. There on a rocky promontory was the Château des Adhémar de Monteil, looming over the medieval village of Grignan.

She had read during one of her classes at Emory that the eleventh-century castle had stood proud and formidable until it was severely damaged during the French Revolution. Evidence of its restoration showed from the air, and in spite of vestiges of the beating it had taken, the beautiful three story building took her breath away. Its commanding presence dominated the skyline.

"What a beautiful old castle. Is the Society nearby?"

"It's ten minutes by car once we land." Étienne said.

The helicopter began its descent and she could see a landing pad on the outskirts of the town. Stepping into the warm Provence sunlight was a welcome relief from the cold rain in Paris. She noticed a man approaching, whose face broke into a broad smile, transforming his handsome looks into drop dead gorgeous. He wore a tan, suede jacket that flattered his broad well-formed shoulders, and a forest green shirt was tucked into trim sage leather breeches. His dark brown eyes exuded warmth and intelligence from an ebony complexion. Well-kept dread locks of black hair hung to just below his ears giving him a youthful appearance.

Étienne greeted him. *"Bonjour,* André,*"*

"Bonjour Comte."

"I would like to introduce you to the newest member of our Society, Lexie Miles. Lexie, this is André Le Clair, head of our security and a dear friend."

Lexie took his outstretched hand. *"Bonjour, Monsieur Le Clair."* Her scalp itched and her heart rate accelerated. It was getting annoying. *What is that?*

"Please Mademoiselle, call me André," he replied taking her suitcase.

"No problem and call me Lexie," she said.

"And Monsieur Tom, you are well?" André asked.

"I am excellent," Tom replied as he shook André's outstretched hand.

André escorted them to the two Range Rovers where three other men stood ready to escort them to the château. Étienne greeted them warmly and completed the introductions.

"Lexie, this is Antoine Moreau, one of our scientists and these two are Hamish McClellan and Ken Turner. They're bodyguards who accompany us whenever we leave the compound."

Lexie greeted each man with a handshake, noticing that Antoine's touch did not elicit any reaction. Hamish and Ken's touch made her scalp itch. *Hell's bells, three vampires – really?*

It's good to meet y'all," she said. Hamish's tall, blonde good looks and Scottish brogue and Ken's shorter, stockier physique with his

102

strong Texas drawl amused her in their striking difference. In turn, each man greeted Tom, shaking his hand and welcoming him back. Lexie was impressed by the easy camaraderie that existed between them. Hamish accompanied Lexie, Tom and Étienne while the other car with Antoine and Ken led the way.

The men were engaged in Society talk and Lexie listened keenly as they spoke of increased killing around the world. The Rovers stopped at a large iron gate and the driver of the lead car spoke into a black box attached to a guard house.

"Tom, there are men with guns standin' on either side of the car. Who are they?" she asked, uncomfortable at the sight of the firearms.

"Given the recent rise in vampire sightings and attacks, the security here is extremely high at the moment," he replied. "Those men are two of a hundred soldiers who maintain permanent residences on the property. The gates are guarded around the clock and are electrified, as is the entire perimeter wall surrounding the château's grounds."

"It's a state of the art security system, deadly not only to any human who tries to invade us, but also stops any vampire attack," Étienne added. "It doesn't kill but it renders them helpless which allows us to capture them."

"What do you do with them?" Lexie said.

"We do our best to turn them to our side." Étienne said.

"And if you can't?"

"We burn them."

Wicked gross. She shivered. The brutality of this new world slammed into her consciousness.

At that moment, the car came out of the trees which lined the long drive to the house, diverting her attention from the grizzly picture in her head. To her delight she finally saw the large and charming home that Étienne had described so clearly when he had told her his history. It's peaceful surroundings, made it hard to imagine François and Marielle here causing such carnage and violence so many centuries before. The grounds were

103

meticulously kept. Manicured bushes, flower beds, and off to the side, were fenced pastures and large stables.

"Do you have horses?" she asked. "I love to ride, but I haven't done much since arrivin' in France."

"We have thirty horses which we use at different times to patrol the grounds, and train our new members in the art of horsemanship," Étienne said. "I'd love to go riding with you and show you the rest of our property."

Lexie flushed as desire spread through her. "I'd like that very much." *Too hot to handle.* She was relieved when the Rover pulled up in front of the château. A row of smiling faces greeted her eyes and Lexie wondered who they all were. She hoped they weren't all vampires.

Étienne introduced her and indicated she was to shake each person's hand. As she moved down the line, her scalp itched intermittently and her heart raced. She chalked it up to excitement.

Étienne touched her arm and they entered the château together. She froze on the threshold from the grandeur. The Italian marbled entryway sparkled and reflected the elegant spiral staircase that seemed to go on forever. Louis 14th cabinets graced each wall and ornate floral arrangements had been placed in fancy vases, giving the illusion of a wild English garden. French Doors led to a stone balcony with stairs leading down to the back gardens.

"This place is gorgeous. It's hard to believe a grim Society for huntin' down and killin' vampires is housed here. Where are the labs and the trainin' facilities?"

"Underneath the stables," Étienne replied. Lexie sensed he was pleased at her praise of his home. "During the French Revolution, the stables were burned to the ground, and when we rebuilt them, we built an entire compound underneath. Let's get you settled. Our chef has prepared a light lunch for us and we can tour the facility before dinner. You can meet more of the staff."

He escorted them up the elaborate curving, staircase to the third floor, and showed Lexie and Tom to their rooms. She learned the second floor was devoted to administrative offices.

The smell of pine logs burning in the fireplace greeted her, reminding her of childhood, sitting with her father as he read to her. She took off her shoes and her toes squished in the plush Persian rug. Enchanted by the huge four-poster-bed she bounced on it a few times. Its soft mattress was delightful. Perched on the bed, she scanned the rest of the room. Next to the balcony doors was a gorgeous, mahogany armoire she was sure dated back to the fourteenth century. *The antiques in this place must be worth a fortune.*

A glimpse of herself in the large framed mirror above the fireplace flattered her and she stopped to admire her reflection. *Damn, I look good here.* From the balcony the gardens resembled Versailles. The beautiful vista of cypress trees, horse trails and rolling hills seemed to stretch forever.

Inside the armoire was a selection of couture designer fashions already hanging on one side with a note from Étienne.

> *Lexie,*
>
> *I took the liberty of ordering some clothes to wear while you are here. I hope they fit. I guessed at the sizes.*
>
> *Étienne*

She smiled at his thoughtfulness, and couldn't resist opening each of the five drawers filling up the other half. They were filled with silk bras, camisoles, and heavenly cashmere sweaters. *A little personal.* Captivated by the soft aroma of lavender emanating from the drawers, she wondered if he'd arranged that as well. Now, thoroughly intrigued, she surveyed the en-suite. Although completely modernized with a huge soaker tub, separate shower, and a huge vanity with a large well-lit mirror, she could tell that the mirror and marble flooring were old and had been artfully restored. She took a few moments to brush her teeth and run the silver brush through her curls.

Tom called through the bedroom door. "Are you ready to go down?"

"Be there in a minute".

She applied a sheen of lip gloss, gave her hair a last minute plumping, and nodded in satisfaction. Tom and Étienne were waiting in the hall. At the sight of the handsome vampire, moisture seeped from between her labia and perspiration dotted her upper lip. She flushed with embarrassment and hurried ahead hoping Étienne hadn't noticed her reaction. She could smell her arousal and wondered if his super sensitive vampire nose could do the same. *Get a grip girl.*

The breakfast room was awash with sunlight. Lunch had been laid out on a long sideboard that covered one wall. Platters of smoked salmon, sliced beef, green beans, eggplant prepared with homemade mozzarella cheese, sliced potatoes roasted in local herbs covered one end of the table. A huge bowl of green salad, with tomato and avocado slices tossed in light vinaigrette stood in the center. Olives, slices of homemade baguette, and finally several different types of desserts, including homemade cheesecake covered in cherries, a chocolate concoction that looked sinful and an apple crisp with a side of whipped cream took up the remaining space. As the delicious smells reached her nose, she realized she was starving (another change since her transformation).

"I'd hate to see what y'all call dinin'," Lexie said. "Are we feedin' an army?"

Étienne laughed. "Hardly. The administrative staff and scientists will eat once we are complete. Please help yourself to everything you see, and if there's something you want that you don't see, please feel free to ask for it. I am at your service."

He moved closer touching her elbow. His smell made her stomach get all squishy and her nipples protruded through her shirt. *Damn it, what is going on?*

She reached for a plate and was surprised to see her hand shaking. *Hell's bells girl, get over yourself.* Befuddled by her reaction to Étienne she barely noticed the food she dropped on her plate, but mortified at the quantity she considered putting some of it back. *Too late.* Instead, she sat at the table and pretended to be engrossed in the view through the French doors.

The back gardens and the lake spread before her. The trees still held leaves of bright yellow, red and orange. The lake glistened in the afternoon sun.

"This place is a fairyland," Lexie said. "And the food is amazin'. If you keep feedin' me like this, I'll be as fat as a hog in slop."

"I don't think you need to worry about that," Étienne replied. "Once we start your training you'll work off anything you eat."

"Awesome. When does my trainin' begin? I can't wait to get started."

Étienne smiled at her. "All in good time. Once we have finished lunch, I will show you the rest of the château."

"Great, let's go now. I've eaten enough to last me a week." She rose from the table waiting for him to lead the way.

"I'll let you do the honors without me. I have some calls to make and work I need to finish," Tom said.

"Are you sure you won't come with us?" Lexie asked, not sure she wanted to be alone with Étienne.

"You'll be fine without me." Tom replied. "Étienne is an excellent host."

Nervous, Lexie followed Étienne chatting inanely as he gave her the grand tour of the château. The openness and friendliness of the employees made her feel more at home. But it was still jarring whenever she would shake someone's hand and her scalp would itch and her heart raced. *Oh man, this is creepy.* They returned to the entrance hall, and Étienne led her toward the stables.

They moved from stall to stall. "Good heavens! You told me you had horses, but these are all pure-blood Arabians. The most magnificent animals I've ever seen."

"Yes, we are quite proud or our collection," he said. One of his rare breathtaking smiles lit up his features. "They're truly amazing and each one has a particular personality. Tomorrow, we'll come back and you can choose which horse you'd like to adopt while you are here."

He gestured toward a stunning black stallion. "The only one unavailable is this black beauty I named Brute. He's mine and will not suffer anyone else riding him."

Brute was at least eighteen hands, coal black, with a white star on his forehead, and four white stockings. He whinnied as his master approached. Obviously there was a deep bond between the two.

"He's gorgeous. I can tell that he's yours by the way he nuzzles you. Do you have any treats for him?"

"Always", he chuckled, slipping Brute two pieces of apple.

They moved away, laughing as Brute snuffled after them and reached the last stall. Lexie wondered where the entrance to the lab and training facility was located. She was about to ask when Étienne guided her into the tack room. Expensive handcrafted saddles and bridles hung along both walls. He strode to the back wall and pressed a panel. It swung open to reveal another door with an entry pad to the right. Leaning down, he pressed a button and a scanner moved across his eye. A green light flashed, the door opened and he stood to one side. He motioned for her to enter.

"Welcome to the hub of our Society; this is where we conduct all of our research and train our new recruits."

Automatic lights flooded a deep stairwell, and Lexie found herself at the top of a long flight of stairs that seemed to go on forever. To her right were a set of doors, and when Étienne pushed a button, they opened to reveal a large elevator. She could feel Étienne's eyes on her as they entered. Lexie glanced up, drawn in to their green depths. Breathless, her heart pounding so loud she was afraid he could hear it she reached out to touch him. He took her hand and drew her against him. His arms encircled her and she surrendered. She twisted her arms around his neck and delighted in the feel of his silky hair. Lexie lifted her head for his kiss. It was feather light and soft, and she leaned in closer for more. His arms tightened around her as his kiss became urgent. His cock hardened as it pressed against her.

Lost in the passion and the feel of his body responding to hers, she almost fainted, but without warning, he thrust her away. He held on to her shoulders until she was steady, then whirled away from her. She caught a glimpse of eyes which had turned black and thick veins protruded around his eyes and mouth.

She reached out and touched his shoulder. "Shit what happened to your eyes?" she asked.

He spun, knocking her hand away. His eyes were black pools flecked with green, his face distorted and evil looking, and as he spoke, she could see a hint of his fangs.

"Don't look at me. I never want you to see me this way," he snapped. "You arouse feelings in me that... I almost lost it and bit you. I wanted nothing more than to taste you. I can never taste you. The consequences would be disastrous. It would send me back to the dark side."

He struggled as his face and eyes returned to normal. Dismayed at his violent outburst, Lexie reached out to touch him again.

He jerked away. "It's still too soon. I have never forgiven myself for what I did to Lisbeth. I can't risk doing the same to you."

"I only want to assure you that I'm not frightened. I know you'd never harm me." She heard the tremor in her voice. She didn't sound brave.

"You should be terrified," he said. "A vampire out of control is dangerous, and I'm no exception. You have no idea how powerful the bloodlust is."

"You're right, I don't. But I know you'd never hurt me."

The elevator stopped, ending their conversation, and as they exited, she was overwhelmed by the high tech world that lay before her.

Chapter 11
The Society Continued

Eerily quiet, the lab smelled of herbs and chemicals. Everywhere Lexie looked there were computer stations, centrifuges with test tubes processing different colored fluids, and microscopes on cement counter tops. Dozens of men and women dressed in white lab coats performed various tasks, and chalk boards filled with equations took up one wall. So engrossed in their work no one even glanced their way, Lexie admired their concentration. She heard an occasional whisper as two or more of the scientists conferred. Étienne paused in front of the elevator and his voice boomed through the silence like a bass drum as he asked for their attention.

"*Bonne aprèsmidi, tout le monde*, I want to introduce you to Lexie Miles, Vampire Executioner, and the newest member of our team. Please come and meet her."

Heads turned in their direction, and blushing at the sudden attention, she stood self-consciously as each one greeted her, shaking her hand and murmuring their name as they did so. Many of the hands she touched made her scalp itch and her heart race. She experienced a strong sense of trepidation assuming they were probably vampires. *Thunder crap, I'm surrounded.*

Introductions complete, Étienne guided her through the lab. "This is where we do all of our research and production of the antiserums. Everyone is working on trying to reproduce Emma's formula for the 88P antiserum. Our supply is running dangerously low, and without the formula, we have no way to produce more. The consequences are beyond comprehension. The 'dark ones' could easily overtake us."

110

"What do you mean? A vampire is a vampire."

"Because their kind drink human blood and we don't, they are twice as fast and strong. It is the antiserum that keeps us equal. The risk to humanity and to us would be doubled. I cannot allow that to happen and must do everything to prevent it."

Lexie felt ill.

"You mean anything?" she said.

"Anything," he replied.

Lexie heard the determination in his voice.

"But let's not dwell on that right now. Étienne said. He gestured to a door. "This is my private office. Only my assistant Claudette, André, and I have access. Claudette will return this evening in time for dinner, and you will meet her. Come, it's time to show you the training facilities. I want you at your fighting fit within the next six weeks."

Whatever Lexie had expected in no way prepared her for the state-of-the-art work-out equipment that filled the gym. A running track encompassed the circumference and at one end an Olympic size swimming pool shimmered under the fluorescent lighting.

"Wow, this is amazin'!" she said, moving ahead of him to examine the equipment. "I can't wait to get started. When do we begin?"

"Patience *ma petite*, patience," he said smiling down at her.

Term of endearment?

"Tomorrow morning at seven you are scheduled for tests to determine the extent of your powers. We'll create a schedule best suited to your abilities. Training will begin the following day."

"Sounds like a plan." She left his side and wandered through the maze of equipment, work-out mats, and punching bags hanging from the ceiling. The pool invited a quick plunge but they continued on.

"Men and women's locker rooms are there," Étienne said. We have saunas, a coed steam room, and three whirlpools." His breath in her hair unnerved her. She hadn't heard him approach.

"I would love to take a dip in the pool before dinner."

"There are extra swimming suits in the women's locker room. Wine and cocktails are served in the library at 7pm and dinner is at 8pm. I have shown you everything I wanted you to see today, so feel free to enjoy yourself."

"Will you join me?"

"Not this time. There are things I must do before cocktails. By the way, dinner is formal tonight. There's something appropriate hanging in your closet."

"I'll be there." She was disappointed at his excuse.

The locker room was larger than her apartment. Muted lighting reflected the decor of *Eau de Nil* or pale green, and peach. Private change rooms lined one wall. Luxurious lounge chairs surrounded a faux fire pit. Beside each was a cherry wood table with burning tea lights which gave it a spa-like atmosphere.

A large closet revealed a selection of designer bathing suits, terry-cloth robes and towels. Lexie chose a sexy black number and was well-satisfied with her image in the floor to ceiling mirror. *He doesn't know what he's missing...*

She dove into the deep end and the water felt heavenly. She swam laps, and could feel the tension of the last two days begin to dissolve away. At the end of her fifteenth lap she rolled over and floated on her back. Sad images of Emma drifted through her mind. She let the feelings go and surrendered to the soothing caress of the water. *Heaven.*

She remembered the saunas, and the thought of the warm, dry air penetrating her tense and tired muscles brought her out of the pool.

The sauna was all cedar, and cushions covered the bench seating. She set the controls for fifteen minutes and sat down to enjoy the heat. Her thoughts drifted to past events and Étienne. *New life, new me.* Despite the coziness of the sauna, she shivered recalling the effect he had on her in the elevator and her nipples hardened reliving their kiss. It hurt that he had broken off their embrace. The attraction was mutual but dangerous. He'd said he didn't want to kill her, but damn it sure felt like rejection. Memories of Justin's betrayal in college bombarded her. *Thunder crap, complicated anyone?*

The timer dinged, startling her out of her musings, and she padded back to the change room. She glanced at her watch and was astonished to find an hour had passed. She needed to hurry to be ready in time for cocktails. She entered the lab, nonplussed when people stopped their work to wave and smile at her. *Vampires for friends, really?*

Back at the château, Lexie rifled through her closet. She spotted a vibrant teal cocktail dress, checked the size, and satisfied that it would fit her, hung it on the closet door. She felt like a princess as she showered and washed her hair in the elegant bathroom. She took extra care with her make-up and hair, and then felt foolish as she remembered Étienne's harsh rebuff. *I can still hope.* The dress and three-inch-high black pumps fit perfectly. She checked herself in the mirror and was stunned. She was a beautiful, vibrant stranger. Her hair seemed thicker, her cheeks rosier, her eyes brighter and larger, and her body seemed more toned and strong. She surmised that it was a side-effect resulting from the vampire executioner changes she'd been experiencing. The sapphire necklace that Étienne had given her sparkled against her skin, and delicious languorous sensations rose as she relived Étienne's kiss in the elevator, over and over.

A soft knock on her door brought her back to reality.

"Come in."

Étienne entered, and she stifled a gasp. The turtle neck he wore matched the blue/black of his hair, and the black silk Armani suit accentuated his powerful physique. He looked good enough to eat, and it took all of her willpower not to throw herself into his arms. *Down girl.*

"You look incredible," he said. "I'm glad you're wearing the necklace."

"Thank you, you look pretty great yourself," she replied and then blushed at her boldness. Her heart was banging against her rib cage at his nearness. "All my new dresses are beautiful. I had a difficult time decidin' on which one to wear. Even the lingerie fits like a glove. Please thank your staff for me and tell them how much I appreciate the care with which they chose the clothes."

"I would be happy to do that," Étienne said, smiling down at her. "However, I believe it would mean a great deal to Claudette if you were to thank her personally. Tonight during cocktails will be the perfect opportunity for you to acknowledge her."

"Perfect." She replied, smiling and hoping he couldn't hear her pounding heart.

Arm in arm they descended the long staircase. Lexie had never felt so elegant. *I could get used to this.* The sound of music and laughter coming from the library drew her forward eager to socialize with her new acquaintances. A festive spirit permeated the château. About twenty people were gathered in the library, and as she and Étienne entered they turned their attention to her. Someone started to clap and the others joined in. Étienne let go of her arm and stepped back, leaving Lexie alone. She blushed and fought the impulse to run. But Tom came to her rescue, stepping forward he took her hand and led her to a chair.

His eyes were wide with approval. "Wow, Lex, you look smashing. How was your tour?"

"Enlightenin'. I enjoyed meetin' everyone in the lab and your facilities are the best."

"She even had a swim," Étienne said from behind them. He touched her back but it made her uncomfortable.

"It was so relaxin'. The water was perfect, and the sauna just topped it off. I hadn't realized how tense I was."

"Good for you," Tom said. "What would you like to drink?"

"Red wine please."

She scanned the room, waiting for her drink, and realized all of the guests were people she had met during the day. Out of the corner of her eye, she noticed a tall, drop-dead-gorgeous redhead moving their way. Étienne motioned her over.

"Lexie, I'd like to introduce you to Claudette Roberge, my personal assistant, and the person responsible for your wardrobe. Claudette, meet Lexie Miles, vampire executioner."

"*Enchantée Mademoiselle* Miles," Claudette said. Her smile was dazzling and her golden-brown eyes twinkled with welcome. "I am pleased to meet the beautiful American that everyone has been talking about. I knew your Grandfather and father. They were extraordinary men." Claudette extended her hand and before Lexie touched it, her scalp itched and her heart raced. *This is getting old.*

"The pleasure is all mine, Claudette. Call me Lexie. Mademoiselle Miles is so formal. Thank you for such a stunnin' wardrobe. Your taste in clothes is impeccable."

"It was my pleasure. If there is anything else you need, please feel free to ask. I am at your service."

The butler entered the library, announcing dinner was served, and without further conversation, Étienne took her arm and escorted her into the dining room. Lighted candles, crystal, fine bone china, and Birds of Paradise flower arrangements dazzled the eye. At each place there was an embossed place card, and Lexie was relieved to find herself seated between Tom and Étienne.

Everyone applauded as each course was served, each new bottle of wine poured. There was duck foie gras served on homemade baguette, a goat cheese and pear salad, roast lamb garnished with tiny potatoes and carrots, and for dessert a platter of assorted French cheese accompanied by more freshly baked baguette. With each course, an appropriate bottle of wine was served. Beaujolais with the foie gras, a 2008 Macon Village with the salad, a 2010 Gigondas Côtes du Rhône with the lamb, and with the cheese a wonderful Sauterne, Semillon topped off the meal.

Despite the jovial atmosphere, Lexie had little to say, and sat picking at her food. Tom and Étienne were caught up in conversation with the person next to them. She was too sad and tired to care. *Em would have loved this.*

After the desert, Calvados was poured as the digestif. She sipped the wonderful liqueur allowing it to soothe her. She yawned, trying to conceal it with her hand.

Étienne noticed, looking concerned. "Are you alright?" he said, placing his arm along the back of her chair. "You are oddly silent this evening, and you barely touched your food. Has something happened?"

She forced herself to smile. "I'm just a little overwhelmed and tired. It's all so sudden and fast. I think Em's death and this place has worn me out."

"You look so beautiful tonight. I am mortified that I have not been more attentive." He bent his head toward her, and she felt his lips brush her hair with a soft kiss. *Mixed messages much?*

"Don't take it personally. I've enjoyed every minute of this evening." She glanced around the table to see if anyone had noticed the kiss.

Claudette had, and Lexie felt the violent reaction again as she met the beautiful vampire's stare, her eyebrows were raised in surprise. But in a flash, Claudette caught herself and smiled. *That was a little odd.* A sip of wine steadied her. Étienne leaned in close once more.

"What's wrong? You're shivering."

"It's nothin'," she lied. "As I said, I think all the excitement and grief of the past few days is finally catchin' up with me."

"How thoughtless of me," he said, rising from his chair. "You've had three full and difficult days. This evening must have seemed endless to you. And, even though there are things I need to discuss with you and Tom, they can wait until tomorrow. We'll postpone your testing for a day so you can rest. Breakfast is served at eight. We can speak then. Come, I will escort you to your room."

"Lex are you okay?" Tom said.

"I'm fine, just exhausted. I'm goin' to bed," she replied, smiling to reassure him. He smiled back but she could tell he wasn't convinced. She bid everyone goodnight and allowed Étienne to escort her to her room. At the door, he kissed the back of her hand. *"Bonne nuit, ma petite,"* he whispered.

Once her dress was back in the closet and her heels tossed in a corner, she set the alarm for seven thirty, slipped on a silk nightshirt and crawled into the huge bed. She turned out the light and pulled the covers up around her shoulders. *This is all more than I can say grace over.* And with that thought, she slept.

Chapter 12
Étienne

The taste of Lexie's skin lingered on Étienne's lips as he walked away from her. He ran his tongue around his mouth and felt his fangs lengthening. His penis stiffened straining against his zipper. *Merde, this could get complicated.* He paused at the head of the stairs to rearrange himself before rejoining the others. It didn't help. The strong beat of *Cold Play* floated up and he knew that people were now dancing. He paused at the door to the salon to observe the scene before him.

Claudette and André were among those dancing. Tom stood off to the side engaged in conversation with several of the scientists. Happy that his friends were enjoying themselves despite the chaos that surrounded them, he was too obsessed with what was happening between him and Lexie to join the revelry. Unnoticed, he backed away from the entrance. *I need air.* And left the château. With no particular destination he wandered the wooded property, his emotions jumbled and in turmoil. He remembered his reaction when earlier in the day Lexie had kissed him in the elevator. The passion she'd ignited in him had left him breathless. He'd wanted her so desperately he'd almost lost control. His cock swelled as he recalled her scent and the softness of her lips. His knees buckled as passion fired through his body and forced him to lean against a tall oak to steady himself. He wanted her underneath him, open, juicy, ready. In all his five-hundred-years he'd never experienced such longing and desire. *Old man you've got it bad.*

The smell of hay and oats hit Étienne's nostrils as he entered the stables to check on Brute. He stood at the stallion's stall stroking his neck when Claudette's silky voice interrupted his thoughts.

"We were wondering where you were? You're missing all the fun."

He turned to face her; the smell of her desire slammed into his already heightened senses.

"I needed some air and time alone to think."

"No need to ask who or what you were thinking about." She stood in front of him, her eyes locked on the bulge in his trousers.

"What are you talking about?"

"Lexie. It's obvious to everyone that you are attracted to her."

"It's none of your business, or anyone else's."

"Why her and not me?" Before Étienne could respond, Claudette's hand snaked out and stroked him. His cock throbbed at her touch and lust coursed through him.

"Don't do that," he gasped. His mind urged him to run. His body had other ideas and pushed into her hand.

Claudette didn't hesitate. She ground her hips against him. Her arms encircled his neck and as she lifted her face to his he was overcome by the smell of her lust. He pulled her closer, all reason gone in the wake of his need to release. He captured her mouth and forced his tongue inside, thrusting in and out as if he were inside her. *This is so wrong.* The thought left as quickly as it came as her hands removed his belt.

"Fuck me," she demanded, her voice low and husky. She grasped his penis and began to stroke it, running her thumb over the tip where a drop of liquid silk had escaped.

He lost control, ripping the dress from her shoulders, baring her full breasts and kneaded them hard, not caring if he hurt her. She groaned and pulled his turtle neck over his head. Her mouth found his nipples, nipping at them drawing blood, and he grew harder in her hand.

119

He threw her down on a pile of hay needing to be inside her. He shoved her head back and wrenched her thighs apart. He grabbed her hips raised them slightly and plunged the full length of his shaft into her.

He grunted in satisfaction, his thrusts hard and explosive. His need for release eclipsed any sense of wrong doing.

"Take my vein *cher*," Claudette whispered, her body lunging towards him, matching him stroke for stroke.

His blood-lust slammed through him and he sank his fangs into her jugular, drawing hard on her warm blood.

She screamed in ecstasy. "That's it. Let me erase that *pathétique* human from your heart."

Lexie's beautiful face hovered in Étienne's mind. He froze. His lust dissipated. He flung himself away from Claudette, landing on his hands and knees.

"This can't happen," he panted. "I don't love you and I won't use you this way."

"Fuck, your nobility is disgusting." Claudette sprang to her feet, pulling the remnants of her dress around her. "Go to your beloved vampire executioner. But beware, one day she may have to kill you."

Claudette disappeared before he could respond. Étienne lay back in the hay, with Claudette's warning ringing in his ears. He felt dirty. *Tom, talk to Tom.* He needed someone to talk to. He hated what he'd done.

The château was quiet with only a few lights burning as he entered the foyer. The butler took his jacket.

"Is Tom in his room?"

"*Oui Monsieur*. The dancing ended some time ago and Monsieur Grant has gone upstairs."

"*Merci*, that's all for tonight."

Étienne tapped on Tom's door. No response. Étienne knocked harder.

"Bugger off," Tom's sleepy voice drifted out.

"Open the door, I need to talk," Étienne said.

"Get stuffed. I'm knackered."

"*Ne fais pas l'andouille*, this is important."

Tom threw open the door, his body highlighted by the soft glow of the hall lights. "I am not a fool." He stomped back to the bed and put on his robe. "What's so important that you have to wake me at one in the morning? Breakfast is in a few hours."

Étienne loitered inside the doorway curiously uncomfortable in his friend's presence. His eyes wandered over the sparse furnishings.

"C'mon man, I'm awake now," Tom said. "What new crisis are we facing?"

Étienne paced, attempting to clear his thoughts. Tom's eyes followed him.

Étienne took a deep breath. "I think I'm in love with Lexie and I don't know what to do about it. I have all these questions running through my head. Is it even possible? Can we make it work? What if something happens to her? What if she has to kill me? How can a vampire and a vampire executioner have a lasting relationship?"

He collapsed into an armchair and dropped his head into his hands.

"Say something, I'm dying over here."

Tom's voice boomed through the room. "Bloody hell, are you crazy?" "Crazy doesn't even TOUCH what you've said. How could you let this happen?"

"Letting has nothing to do with it," Étienne growled. "It just happened. Every time I think of her my blood heats up. I have to constantly control my urges. I've never felt like this before and I don't know how to handle it. I can't be near her or hear her voice without feeling out of control"

"FUCK!" Tom shouted as he sagged into the other chair. "Does she have any idea?"

"I don't think she realizes the depth of my feelings, but yesterday when I was showing her the layout we kissed when we were in the elevator. It didn't go well,"

"What happened?"

"I almost lost control and she saw my fangs. It wasn't pretty."

"What'd she do?"

"She told me it didn't bother her which made it even harder. It would have been easier if she'd freaked out."

Tom launched himself at Étienne slamming both of them to the floor. "You can't have her," he growled, slamming his fist repeatedly into Étienne's jaw.

At first, too stunned to react, Étienne didn't defend himself. *I deserve this.* Self-preservation kicked in and he flung Tom away sending him crashing against the wall. Tom sprang to his feet and Étienne side-stepped as he charged him again.

"She's too good for you," Tom said. "You'll only hurt her."

"You don't know that," Étienne said, dodging Tom's fists. He swirled around behind Tom and wrapped his arms around him.

Tom struggled furiously and Étienne waited, holding his friend tightly. "I promise you I won't hurt her. I love her more than words can express. Please trust me, my friend."

Tom slumped in his arms, panting, and Étienne released him. "If you hurt her, I'll..." Tom said.

122

"I promise I won't. But there's more."

Not what I want to hear," Tom replied.

"Tonight, after I took Lexie to her room, I was so turned on I couldn't face going back to the party. I went to the stables. Claudette followed me and one thing led to another. We were goin' at it, but I couldn't finish. All I could see was Lexie's face."

"You bloody asshole! How could you do that to Claudette? You know how she feels about you."

"You don't have to remind me. I feel guilty enough. What do I do? I can't think straight."

Étienne stared at Tom wanting an answer. The temptation to read Tom's mind was strong and Étienne had to look away to stop himself.

When Tom stopped pacing, Étienne could tell he had suppressed his emotions. The only giveaway was the gruffness in Tom's tone. "You have to tell Lexie how you feel. I don't have to tell you that this situation could be dangerous. In a fight, priorities will be different. It could cost one of us our life."

"*Merde*, this is one complication we so don't need right now."

"By the way, how does it work?" Tom said.

"How does what work?"

"A relationship between a vampire who's descended from the Strygoi and a vampire executioner descended from the Divinati."

"It doesn't. It shouldn't. I'm not even sure that it can."

Tom resumed his pacing, anger emanating from him in hot waves.

Étienne broke the silence.

"You're right. I'll talk to Lexie in the morning at breakfast. It's unfair, not to mention, dangerous to keep her in the dark."

"That's the first sensible thing you've said since we started this conversation. What about Claudette, is she okay?"

"I think so. I can't worry about her feelings right now. She'll just have to get over it."

"Wanker."

Étienne smiled at his friend and rose to take his leave. "We can all be jerks at times."

"Some of us more than others," Tom said. "Are we finished?"

"For now, go back to sleep and I'll see you at breakfast."

Étienne walked down the dimly lit corridor toward his suite. As he passed Lexie's door he halted in his tracks. Her unique scent drifted into his nostrils. His cock stiffened and his bloodlust surged as his body reacted. *Fuck, I want her now.* He reached for the doorknob the urge to go to her was overwhelming. It took willpower to walk away.

He crossed the threshold to his room, slamming the door behind him. He undressed and as he removed his shorts, his cock was swollen and throbbing. He fondled the silky hardness, lightly squeezing the tip as a drop of wetness seeped out. His scrotum tightened in anticipation.

Unable to ignore his need any longer he stepped into the shower and turning on the spray full force stroked until he was panting with need. He imagined Lexie underneath him, her cunt wet and dripping for him. He could feel her juices, slippery as he entered her. His semen exploded, but he wasn't done. Four more times he ejaculated and on the fourth screamed. He sagged against the wall to regain his equilibrium. He wrapped his lower body in a towel. He sprawled across his bed, still wet knowing he wouldn't sleep but reveling in the sense of contentment that washed over him.

Tomorrow, I will tell her tomorrow.

Chapter 13
Message from Emma –
Claudette and André's Stories

It was just getting light when Lexie's alarm sounded. Opening one eye, she peered at the room disoriented by the strange surroundings. Then she remembered. *New life, new me.*

The cool, morning air gave her goosebumps as she washed her face, ran a brush through her hair, and threw on jeans and heavy sweater. She squared her shoulders ready to face the day and descended the stairs following her nose to the wonderful aromas of coffee drifting through the house. Her stomach growled outside the breakfast room. A fire burned brightly in the fireplace, and sunlight poured in through the windows.

Étienne greeted her as she entered. "Good morning, how did you sleep?"

What do you care? "Mornin'," she replied. Her heart fluttered. He looked great in his riding outfit. His eyes tracked her as she walked over to the sideboard and filled her plate. "I slept well, thanks. How about you?" She spoke coolly as she could.

"I don't sleep." He joined her and poured another coffee.

"Never?"

"Never." He placed his coffee on the table next to her and removed his tweed riding jacket, hanging it over the back of his chair. The black turtle neck he wore clung to his body and accentuated his broad shoulders and narrow waist.

125

"Do you mean that in five-hundred-years you've never slept?" Lexie said between mouthfuls.

He smiled in the wonderful way he had that made her toes curl. *Crap he's hot.*

"*À peu près.* In the very beginning, I slept during the day but as I grew older, it was less and less important. At one point I realized I no longer needed it at all."

"Wow," she said her eyes wide with amazement. "What's that like?"

"It's boring. Five-hundred-years is a long time. I've seen everything there is to see, and been everywhere. The only thing that keeps me going is my commitment to destroy the Strygoi and Marielle, prevent the destruction of the human race and living in harmony with humans."

He paused and took a deep breath. Lexie sensed he was struggling.

"There's something I must to say to you —"

"Hey you two, how's it going?" Tom breezed into the room.

"*Merde*, your timing sucks," Étienne mumbled to himself. He ran his hand through his hair, glanced at Lexie, and shrugged. "Grab some breakfast and come join us. Now that you're here, we have much to talk about."

Tom sat at the head of the table and Lexie saw him raise an eyebrow at Étienne and Étienne shook his head. *Wonder what that's about?*

"You said last night at dinner that you had things to discuss with us. I got the impression they were urgent." Tom said. His phone rang and he mouthed 'sorry' and answered it.

"Hang on, let me just move to a better location," he said, getting up and walking onto the terrace. Lexie could hear him through the door which he'd left ajar. She couldn't tell who he was talking to.

"What were you about to say before Tom came in?" Lexie asked.

"It can wait," Étienne said. He seemed uncomfortable and kept glancing at the terrace. Lexie felt like he was putting her off with continued rebuffs.

"Gotta go," Lexie heard Tom just before he hurried back into the room.

"Is everything okay?" she asked.

"I told work you needed some time and you've gone back to the United States to visit your Mom for a bit. I explained my absence by telling them I'd been called to Berlin for a meeting."

"I wondered how you were gonna handle that." Lexie said. *Nice lyin'.*

Tom prodded Étienne. "You were saying,"

Étienne reached behind himself and pulled a folded paper from his coat pocket.

"It's time for us to revisit this. Let me just make sure we are not overheard." He closed the breakfast room doors.

"From Emma's email we know that she thought François was in love with her and that she hoped to turn him to the light side."

"That didn't go well," Lexie interrupted, her voice angry.

Étienne ignored her and continued on. "We also know that François and Marielle have discovered the existence of the 88p and formula. This means there's a traitor in our midst. Emma hid the antiserum and formula and created a riddle with clues to help us find it. She died protecting us."

The three of them sat in silence. Tears trickled down Lexie's cheeks, and she grabbed her napkin to blot them away.

"Are you going to be okay?" Tom asked.

"I'll be okay," she said, blowing her nose. "It's more than missin' my best friend. It's such a waste of an extraordinary human being. Those last few hours must have been awful for her. If only she had confided in me. I might've been able to save her."

"Don't go there Lex," Tom said. "There's no guilt here. She didn't confide in any of us."

127

The doors to the breakfast room flew open. "Why the somber faces?" Claudette asked from the doorway. She and André headed for the buffet.

"Good morning," Étienne replied. He quickly folded Emma's message with the riddle and stuck it back in his coat pocket. "We were just remembering Emma and the brutality of her murder."

"Ah, now I understand. She was your best friend, *n'est-ce pas?*" André said to Lexie.

"Em and I were very close," she said, wondering how much Claudette and André had overheard. She rose and poured herself more coffee. The simple act calmed her. *Too close for comfort.* As she neared Claudette and André her scalp itched and her heart rate increased.

"Please, both of you, come and join us," Étienne said. "We were just finishing up, but we will sit with you while you eat." Lexie could tell he was as anxious to get going as she was and was trying to avoid raising suspicion.

Claudette poured herself coffee and ignoring the food, came and sat beside Étienne. André took a bit of the rare roast beef from the buffet and seated himself on Étienne's other side.

"Mademoiselle, Lexie, when will you start your training?" André said.

"That's up to Étienne and Tom," she replied. "Right now, it's planned for tomorrow mornin' with... some testin'."

"It will be interesting to see how fast you progress," he said. "You sound very much like your father."

"It's the southern accent," Lexie said. "His was actually stronger than mine. I've worked hard to curb it."

"Why would you do that?" Claudette said.

"So the French can understand me. I'm just hopin' I don't make a complete fool of myself, but I guess every now and then even a blind pig finds an acorn," Lexie said.

"*Qu'est ce que c'est que ça?* What does that mean, I do not know this expression," Claudette said.

"Sorry, it's just a Southernism. Never mind."

"Now I understand," André said, he grinned.

The next few minutes were spent in small talk, and Lexie was aware of being scrutinized by both André and Claudette. She was relieved when Étienne interrupted.

"I have a few items to discuss with Tom and Lexie. If either of you need me, I'm on my cell." He picked up his jacket and headed for the door.

Lexie glanced back over her shoulder as she followed Tom and Étienne, and saw Claudette and André speaking quietly, heads together. She had the feeling they were talking about her, and it made her uneasy. She promised herself that she was going to talk to Tom and Étienne about them at the first opportunity. She was curious to know their backgrounds and how they came to the Society.

Tom, Lexie and Étienne entered the stables. Étienne immediately went to Brute and gave him a morning treat, before leading them to the elevator. Standing next to Étienne, visions of yesterday's disastrous kiss made Lexie uncomfortable. She stared down at his riding boots.

"Where are we going?" she asked.

"To my office," Étienne replied. "We can talk there in privacy. André sweeps it for bugs every night."

As they entered his private office, Lexie was impressed with its size and opulence. It was very much like him – sophisticated and graceful. His work space contained a large, intricately carved mahogany desk, and his chair was the latest ergonomic creation. There were two chairs, also covered in dark leather placed in front of the desk. His art collection was impressive and one wall boasted a floor to ceiling bookcase containing volumes of what appeared to be original manuscripts. Étienne motioned them to sit as he shut and locked the door.

129

"So who do you think the traitor is?" Lexie asked as she settled into a chair.

"It has to be someone close to me." Étienne replied.

"Bloody hell, I hate to think of any of our people as traitors." Tom interjected. "But we have to suspect everyone. Right now I think the most important thing for us to focus on is the location of the riddle, and then solve it. Do you have any ideas where she might have hidden it?"

Lexie was anxious to get started.

"I have several ideas, but we must be careful in our search," Étienne replied. "Since we don't know who the infiltrator is, we don't want to arouse any suspicion or give any indication that we are on to something."

"That reminds me," Lexie interrupted. "Before we start workin' on the riddle, tell me more about Claudette and André."

"Why do you ask?"

"Just curious," she replied. She noticed that Étienne seemed a bit uncomfortable.

"Claudette was made a vampire almost two hundred years ago by François and Marielle during an attack on her village in northern France near Dijon. She stayed with François and Marielle until we met a hundred years later at a ball in Paris. Claudette and I were drawn to each other. We had a brief affair and she developed feelings for me that I didn't return."

Étienne stared at Lexie and she felt a little twitch in her brain. *Must be a habit with him.*

"In spite of that, she begged me to become a part of the Society. I accepted her and she accompanied me to the château. We weaned her from human blood to animal. She kept insisting that she wanted support our mission. I suspected that it was mainly to be near me, so I tested her and she passed. I made her my personal assistant. She has been with us now for more than a century, and I have learned to depend on her. I trust her."

"That's good to know, and André?" Lexie said. *Wonder what test.*

"André has been with me since the French Revolution. I knew him as the son of one of our estate's Moroccan peasant farmers. He joined the National Assembly and was mortally wounded during one of the battles. I found him near death and he begged me to take his life. I could not bear to. I offered him immortality and he accepted." Étienne paused for a moment, frowning. "I drained him of blood and then gave him mine. He is like a brother to me and has stood by my side through many battles."

"My side as well," Tom interjected. "Why the curiosity?"

"I'm just tryin' to sort out who I can trust." Lexie said.

"My life as well as Tom's has depended on each of them on many occasions."

"Good, it'll be nice to have another female friend, even if she is a vampire. *And beautiful to boot.* Not that Claudette could ever replace Em." She wasn't entirely sure she believed what she said, but she'd started to doubt her suspicions as paranoia. "Em said in her e-mail that she'd hidden the first clue to the riddle somewhere on the property that only you would know about."

"I've searched my room as well as my administrative office to no avail," Étienne said. "I need some time to think about it further. Unfortunately, time is the one thing we don't have. Our supply of 88P is running very low. I have been in contact with other branches of the Society, and the vampire attacks around the world are escalating. Their numbers are increasing rapidly. We must find some way to contain this escalation, or figure out how to get the Redemption antiserum to humans."

"Rather than you thinkin' about it on your own, why don't we brainstorm right now," Lexie urged. "We've postponed my testin'. Let's use the time to list the places where Em might have hidden the first clue."

"What about this office?" Tom said, leaning forward in his chair.

Étienne shook his head. "Doubtful since she had no way to enter without me."

"We have to think from Em's point of view," Lexie said. "She was scared and riskin' everything."

Lexie was interrupted by a knock on the door, and Tom opened it to Claudette with a serving cart.

She pushed through the door. "I have brought refreshments, water and fruit for Lexie and Tom and animal blood for you. Is there anything else I can provide?"

"What do you think you're doing? I didn't want to be disturbed." Étienne said, his eyebrows knit together in anger. "You're intruding on a private meeting."

Claudette visibly recoiled at his words. "I was just trying to be helpful and thought..."

"That's the problem, you didn't think. Now leave the cart and go."

She whirled, the door slamming behind her. "Bastard!"

How odd.

"What was that all about?" Lexie said, keeping her first thought to herself.

Étienne grabbed a bottle of animal blood, popped the top and drank. It was the first time Lexie had seen him drinking blood, if it *was* animal blood. She swallowed the bile that rose in her throat. *Eww, too nasty for words.*

Lexie realized she was staring and her mouth hung open. She grabbed a bottle of water, and returned to her chair.

"I know that this is the first time you have seen me drinking blood. If it bothers you, I can wait until later."

"It's somethin' I'll have to get used to," she stammered. "It took me by surprise. Please don't stop on my account."

She managed to smile at him, hoping she had covered her disgust. He nodded, and took another long swill.

"Let's begin by making a list of all the places in and surrounding the château where Emma could have hidden clues," Étienne said, opening a lined pad of paper. "It would have had to have been the last time she was here which was about two weeks prior to her murder."

"I don't know the château very well, and since you have already searched your room, I have no clue." Lexie said.

"What about the admin offices?" Tom offered.

"It's possible," Étienne said. "But seems too public."

"Maybe she hid it in Brute's stall," Lexie said. "Would he tolerate her knocking around in there?"

"Possibly, he's pretty gentle unless someone else tries to ride him."

They continued to brainstorm, listing every place imaginable where Emma might have hidden the first clue. At the end of two hours they had several pages full of locations.

"Bloody hell, searching in all these spots could take forever, and time is of the essence," Tom groused. "There has to be some way to narrow this down, any ideas?"

"Not right now," Étienne replied, leaning back in his chair, stretching. He glanced at his watch. "It's noon. Cook will have set out the buffet for lunch. Let's take a break and reconvene here at one-thirty this afternoon. We'll start the process of eliminating any locations that are too obvious. Lexie, I'd like to have a private word with you. When we get back to the château, please come to my study. Tom, we'll meet you in the dining room."

The barn was in chaos when they exited the elevator. Horses were being led from their stalls to be saddled. Men and women shouted instructions to each other. Lexie saw Claudette talking on her phone with a serious expression on her beautiful face.

"I was just coming to get you," she said hurrying over. "The de Villeneuve-Flayosc estate was attacked last night by François and Marielle. I'm just on the phone with Jacques. Apparently there was no time to warn us."

Étienne grabbed the phone from her. "Talk to me Jacques. How bad is it?"

The look on Étienne's face told Lexie the news was bad.

"Shit! This is too close to home," Étienne said, flinging the phone to the ground.

"Brute has been saddled for you and the team is ready to ride," Claudette said.

Étienne faced Lexie. "Our private conversation will have to wait. This news takes precedence."

Lexie wondered what he kept wanting to talk to her about. *More rejection?*

"Saddle horses for Lexie and Tom as well," Étienne said. "Saddle Bella for Lexie, she is perfect for her."

"Do you really think she's ready?" Tom said.

"She has to confront what she's up against. Now's as good a time as any." Étienne said.

"Why horses rather than cars?" Lexie said.

"It's faster over ground. Villeneuve is an influential member of the French government. If he's been turned...not to mention how close to home this is. Is there anything you two need before we ride out?"

"I need riding boots", Lexie said looking down at her black pumps. "Other than that I'm ready to go."

"Claudette, we need riding boots for Lexie," Étienne shouted. "Please check the tack room for an extra pair. I believe a size seven is correct?"

Lexie changed her pumps for a pair of soft, leather riding boots, and ran back to the stable yard. She was delighted to see that the horse chosen for her was a beautiful Arabian chestnut mare with four white stockings and gentle brown eyes.

"This is Bella," Étienne said as he stroked her gleaming coat. "Trust her. She will take good care of you."

"Thanks, she's gorgeous. I'm sure she and I will do just fine together." Lexie swung into the saddle and settled in for the ride.

"Is everyone ready?" Étienne shouted as he mounted Brute. He turned the big stallion toward the pastures and spurred him into a gallop.

Thrilled to be riding again, Lexie forgot for a few moments the grizzly mission they were on. The knot in her stomach reminded her. She was anxious at the prospect of seeing the attack scene. *Can't think about that right now.* She had her hands full staying in the saddle as they jumped fences and splashed through streams. It was a mad chase through pastures and forest and she had to concentrate to keep from being swept off Bella's back by low hanging branches.

The Villeneuve estate teemed with local Gendarmerie.

"*Putain,*" Étienne exclaimed dismounting as Brute was coming to a halt. "I hope they haven't compromised the scene. *Qui est le responsable?*" A fat sergeant raised his hand.

"I'm in charge."

Étienne captured the man's gaze with his own. The sergeant's eyes dilated and he nodded yes before Étienne even spoke.

"Gather your men. I want to be briefed on your findings."

"What just happened?" Lexie asked Tom as the sergeant began calling for his men. "That cop is acting like Étienne is his boss."

"Étienne compelled him."

As the police milled round the sergeant and Étienne the sergeant spoke. "This is everyone including the medical examiner."

Étienne addressed them holding their attention. "This was a false alarm. When you arrived here the place was empty except for a servant who told you the family was away on vacation. Any other thoughts you have about what you've witnessed here will be gone. You will not remember seeing us."

"Oui Comte Benoit," the men and women responded with obedience. They climbed into their cars and drove away without a backward glance.

Étienne spoke to his team. "I want ten of you to remain outside guarding the house. The rest of you help us search."

Étienne motioned for Tom and Lexie to follow him. *Spooky.*

As they entered the house Lexie's curiosity piqued. "How did you do that?"

"I compelled them," Étienne responded.

"I knew you could compel one-on-one, but control a crowd?"

"After five-hundred-years I have perfected the art."

Her curiosity vanished as she viewed the carnage that lay before her. The walls dripped with blood and bits of flesh. Bodies lay in pools of blood, their faces contorted in horror, hands frozen in time, grasping at throats that no longer existed. Their dead eyes staring. She swallowed hard as the scent of fresh blood assaulted her nostrils. She spun back toward the front door wanting to escape into the fresh air and ran into Tom.

"Are you okay?" he said, grabbing her shoulders to steady her. "You look a little pale."

"Sweet Jesus, this is horrible," she said, doing her best to keep down her breakfast.

"These poor people – they must have been so terrified! I can't imagine what it must have been like for them."

"Get used to it," Tom said.

"I don't think that will ever happen."

"Forgive me," Étienne said, placing a hand on her back, "I should have prepared you for this. Perhaps it was a mistake to bring you."

She pulled away and stepped closer to Tom, shivering. Instead of the explosion of warmth in her groin she usually experienced when Étienne touched her, this time it repelled her. His eyes flashed in anger and Lexie could sense he was reacting to her revulsion.

"Nothin' could have prepared me for this, but I guess if I am a vampire executioner, I'd better get used to seein' blood and mutilated bodies."

Étienne's voice turned cold. He spoke harshly. "We need to determine if everyone was killed, or if some are missing."

She took a deep breath and followed the two men through each room of the ground floor. They encountered more death and destruction. They climbed the grand staircase to the second floor. Lexie could see the team taking blood samples and dusting for fingerprints.

Étienne led them to the nursery and school room. Here she stopped, unable to contain herself any longer.

"Thunder crap you guys – even the children? What kind of monsters are these?" She found the scene before her unbearable.

"It's a very powerful message," said Étienne. "Nothing and no one is safe from their brutality. They're not people. As you said, they are monsters and this is a vile attempt to goad us into action. Help me check the bodies. It may be that one of the children is still alive. If they have a heartbeat we can revive them. They may be able to help us."

Steeling her nerves, Lexie checked for a pulse in each of the five children.

"Gotta faint pulse, but he's alive," she said. Her finger was pressed to a little boy's neck. "He needs a doctor fast."

"Got another live one here too," Tom said, his fingers touching a little girl's carotid. Étienne started toward him. Tom motioned him away. "Take care of the little boy. I'll give mouth to mouth until you're ready for her."

Étienne placed his fingers where Lexie's had been and nodded his head. He pulled up the sleeve of his jacket. She heard the pop as his fangs bit into his own wrist. Blood flowed and he placed the dripping wound over the young boy's mouth, forcing the liquid between his lips. Horrified, Lexie scrabbled backward, falling over, not believing what she was seeing. Too shocked to say anything, she pointed, her mouth moving with nothing coming out.

She was aware of Tom as he moved to her side and laid the little girl next to Étienne. "I've done what I can for her. Her pulse is steady."

He focused on Lexie. "Lex, it's okay. He's giving the boy a little of his blood to save his life." He helped her up off the floor, and steadied her as her legs didn't want to cooperate.

"What do you mean he's savin' his life?" She managed to stammer. "He's forcin' the child to drink his blood. Won't it turn the boy into a vampire?"

"His blood has incredible healing powers," Tom reassured her, placing his arm around her shoulders. "As long as the boy's heart is still beating, it will not turn him. Watch, the boy should be better in a few minutes."

To her amazement, as she watched, the boy grabbed Étienne's arm, and was now sucking the blood, a rapturous expression on his face. Étienne continued to let the boy suck for a moment more, and then gently, but firmly pushed the boy away from his arm. He licked his wrist and as he pulled his sleeve over the puncture marks Lexie noticed they had already begun to close. Étienne looked up at her. "There was no time for explanations."

"He won't turn into a vampire, right?" she said, not sure she wanted to hear the answer.

"No he will not turn, but he will have enhanced senses, and I will always be able to feel when he is in danger," Étienne replied, pushing the boy's hair from his face.

The boy stirred, opening his eyes, and with a small cry struggled to get away from Étienne. Tightening his grip, Étienne concentrated on the boy's eyes, and murmured. "*calmez-vous les enfants, vous êtes en sécurité.*" Étienne's soothing words that the boy was safe calmed him immediately. The boy stopped fighting, relaxed against him and sighed.

"Compelling?" Lexie asked.

Tom nodded. "He needs to keep the boy calm until the blood has a chance to work, and we can get him back to the château."

Étienne handed the boy to Tom who cradled him gently in his arms. Étienne repeated the same blood exchange on the little girl. Within a few seconds, she grasped his arm and began sucking. Still appalled, Lexie concentrated on the little boy who rested peacefully in Tom's arms. Holding the small boy with one arm, he put his other arm around her waist and squeezed. She managed a faint smile. The little girl's eyes fluttered open, and as soon as they did, Étienne captured them and murmured the same reassuring words he had spoken to the boy.

"I think we're finished here," he said, picking her up and rising to his feet. "They are incredibly lucky. I have never known François and Marielle to leave anyone alive. It's an indication that they are getting overconfident and careless."

"Maybe it was their recently turned and human servants that did this," Tom said. "Is anyone missing?"

"As far as I can tell, the parents are missing as well as two of the servants," Étienne replied. "The Villeneuve are too important in the French government to risk sending newbies. Given they are first and second generation Strygoi, François and Marielle are the only ones capable of turning them. It's likely that this is an indication they are beginning to infiltrate governments. I fear the worst."

"Does that mean they've been turned and joined forces with François and Marielle?" Lexie said.

"I'm afraid so."

"Bloody hell, this really throws a spanner in the works," Tom said. "This can only mean they have the numbers and are now focusing on influence."

When they reached the ground floor the children were laid on the sofa. Étienne took out his phone and punched in a speed dial number.

"Claudette, we have survivors – a boy and a girl. Please bring a car so we can transport them back to the château. Yes, I've given them my blood. Also, have the clean-up crew come. This place is a mess. I told the gendarmerie the family was on an extended vacation."

A clean-up crew – how convenient.

"Tom, I want you to ride back in the car with Claudette and the children," Étienne said. "Lexie and I will return on horseback with the others. Watch yourself my friend. François and Marielle's human servants may still be lurking around."

"I'll be careful."

The two walked into the foyer to wait for Claudette. Lexie knelt beside the children. As she softly stroked their heads she could actually see their wounds healing, and marveled at the miracle of Étienne's blood. *Miraculous…and repulsive.*

She could hear Tom and Étienne speaking with the other members of the team. She yawned and laid her head on her arms to rest.

"Two children surviving is amazing." Claudette's voice woke Lexie. She couldn't believe she'd fallen asleep and pushed to her feet just as Claudette, Tom and Étienne walked into the room.

"If they're not too traumatized, they will have information we can use." Claudette said.

"We'll have to wait and see," Étienne said. He picked each child up and led the way to the car. "This is very precious cargo. Drive carefully, and I'm sending Tom with you in case anything happens."

"Now what?" Lexie asked as she and Étienne watched the car drive off.

Étienne slammed his hand against the door frame and it cracked. His eyes blackened and his fangs protruded from his lips.

"Mon Dieu! I feel like we're fighting a losing battle."

Lexie touched his arm. "I know it seems that way right now, but we cannot give up. Em's death aside, after what we saw today we must keep fighting."

Étienne took her hand. "Thank you. I needed to hear that from you. To answer your question, we return to the château and find the first clue."

The team had finished gathering evidence and waited by the horses. Étienne motioned to them to mount up and they headed off in the direction of the château. He swung into the saddle and Lexie followed suit mounting Bella in one smooth motion. They cantered side-by-side in silence. Étienne seemed lost in thought, and Lexie hesitated to intrude. She remained silent as her own thoughts were chaotic. Despite her earlier bravado she was scared.

"Are you okay?" he asked breaking the silence.

"I don't know. The reality of what we're facin' just slapped me upside the head."

"Good, it's important that you realize the magnitude of the battle we're fighting."

Lexie decided it was best to let that one go, and turned her attention back to Bella and the ride.

"You ride well."

"It feels good to be back in the saddle. Bella is wonderful, and so responsive. When we get back to the château, I want to unsaddle her and brush her down myself. She deserves a little TLC. And after what we just witnessed I need to do something practical."

"TLC?" he asked.

"Tender loving care." She smiled at his bewilderment.

"Ah, perhaps it would be good for Brute as well. If you don't mind, we can do it together."

"Hells bells, I don't know what to feel right now. I've just been exposed to somethin' so gruesome I can't wrap my brain around it. You're a vampire capable of that kind of brutality. Yet, I'm supposed to trust you with my life. You say you've chosen to 'live' in the light, but how can I be sure of that?" she replied.

Their eyes met and Lexie saw Étienne's pain.

"You've only my word and that will have to suffice." He paused for a moment. "There's something I must talk to you about."

What now?

He didn't get to begin as his phone rang. Lexie heard Tom's voice on the other end.

"We've arrived safely. The team came back several minutes ago. Where are you two?"

"Shit," Étienne hissed under his breath. "We're just coming across the last pasture. We'll be there in five." He hung up and without another word urged Brute into a gallop.

Lexie didn't know whether to be disappointed or relieved that Étienne kept getting interrupted. She wondered if he wanted to apologize for the fiasco in the elevator or if he was going to further enforce his commitment of keeping their relationship strictly professional. Frustrated, she gave Bella a good kick and the mare responded without hesitation.

Chapter 14
The First Clue

Lexie and Étienne dismounted in front of the stables. "Do you think Brute would allow me to unsaddle him?" Lexie asked. "I'd love the opportunity of gettin' to know him better."

"Give it a try," Étienne replied, stepping away from the stallion's head. "The worst he'll do is shy away from you. He would never harm you." He watched Lexie.

"He's so beautiful," she said, stroking his white star. She murmured to him, and moved her hands down his neck toward his shoulders. She was careful not to make any sudden movements. Brute turned to watch her, and as if satisfied she was okay, snorted, dropped his head, snuffling for bits of grass.

Étienne couldn't help but imagine her stroking his penis and he felt it swell in response. *She's incredibly sexy.* "You really have a way with him. He usually takes much longer to warm to strangers." *Control yourself fool.*

"I love him already," she replied.

She seemed oblivious to his plight and he was thankful her attention was focused on Brute.

Lexie ran her hand across Brute's shoulder until she reached the saddle and lifted the stirrup out of the way. Étienne heard her singing softly to the stallion as she unbuckled the belly strap. Brute raised his head and eyed her over his shoulder. Lexie smiled and lifted the light English saddle off his back. She reached for the saddle pad and Étienne saw her stop to examine one of the leather corners.

"This stitchin' doesn't match the rest," she said.

"Let me see." She lifted the pad to show him the odd stitching. "You're right, it is different."

"Here hold the saddle so I can have a better look," she said.

Étienne watched as Lexie picked at the haphazard stitches.

"This is definitely new mending, and it was done sloppily, like someone was in a hurry. I wonder," she paused. She glanced in the direction of the château and then whispered, "Could this be the location of the first clue? Em said that it would be somewhere only you would know about. Do you have a knife?"

Étienne withdrew a small pen knife from his back pocket, and handed it to her. He watched as she cut the new stitching until she had opened a slit about two inches long. She reached inside.

"There's a piece of paper in here."

Étienne stopped her with his hand on her shoulder. "Wait, if this is one of the clues, we're way too exposed to take it out and read it."

"What's taking you two so long?" Claudette's voice came from behind them.

"We're just finishing up with the horses," Étienne replied. *Merde, did she hear us?*

Étienne stepped toward Claudette blocking her view of Lexie and the saddle pad. "How are the children doing?"

"They're resting and waiting for you to visit them."

"I'll visit them after we've finished here."

"See you then. Are you okay Mademoiselle Lexie? That murder scene must have been hard for you."

"I'm okay and thanks for asking. Étienne and I are cooling the horses down and I'm getting acquainted with Brute."

Étienne saw she had removed the saddle pad. It was folded and tucked under her arm. *Clever girl.*

144

Lexie was smiling at Claudette with all the innocence of a newborn baby.

"*Bon*, I will see you two later."

"That was close," Lexie said when they were alone.

"*Oui*, hopefully she didn't hear anything."

Lexie didn't answer, and held up a folded piece of paper. "I couldn't resist."

"Damn woman, are you always so contrary?"

"Not always, only when the spirit moves me," she replied.

"*Vous êtes une femme tenace.*" He loved her stubborn streak but would never let her know that. "Let's finish with the horses and go to my office. We can examine the note and hide the pad. "

They brushed and curried the horses, led them to their respective stalls, and headed for the tack room. Étienne took the note from Lexie and stuck it back in the opening of the saddle pad and they rode the elevator in silence. Étienne heard Lexie's heart rate speed up and he wondered if memories of their kiss affected her as much as it did him. His penis stiffened as he recalled the softness of her lips and the feel of her breasts pressed against him. Embarrassed he held the pad in front of him hoping she wouldn't notice.

There were only two or three people in the lab, and they were hardly noticed as they hurried through to Étienne's office.

"I can't get over how amazin' your office is," Lexie said forgetting for a moment their urgent task. "Your artwork is beautiful." She examined each painting. "I really love this one of the lavender. Is this Van Gogh?"

"Thank you," he said, locking the door behind them. "They're all originals that I have collected over the centuries. I find the light of

Provence particularly captivating in that one. It is an original Van Gogh. He was quite mad but devastatingly talented."

"It must be worth a fortune," she said, peering closer. The intimacy they were sharing with no one else present felt awkward. She glanced at him and was drawn into the depths of his eyes. Her heart pounded *He's so beautiful.* She fiddled with the large world globe that stood on a pedestal in the corner to cover up her reaction.

"Here, you do the honors," Étienne said, breaking the mood. He handed her the saddle pad. "I would never have noticed something as simple as irregular stitching. That was good work on your part."

She stuck her fingers into the opening, and withdrew the piece of paper, holding her breath. She unfolded the note.

"It's in Em's handwritin'. I'd know her chicken scratch anywhere." She read,

"Mes félicitations Étienne, voici votre premier indice:

Ce qui est vert et bleu et aimé partout

Pour trouver le prochain indice, allez à la sortie

Une fois que vous trouvez la sortie, demandez des instructions

Bonne journée."

"It reads slightly differently in the English translation:

Congratulations Étienne, here is your first clue:

What is green and blue and loved all over?

To find the next clue find the egress.

Once you find the egress ask for instructions.

Good luck"

"I have no idea what any of this means, do you? Damn, this is so frustratin'. Why does everything have to be so complicated?"

"I have no idea either." He took the clue from her and read it again. "I cannot imagine what is green and blue and loved all over. And, what is an egress? That's an English word I don't know, and the French word Emma uses means exit. This makes no sense."

"I think an egress is a door or a way out, but I'm not sure." She leaned closer to read over his shoulder. "We definitely need more time with this." His musk filled her nostrils and she swore she could hear his heart pounding in time with hers.

"Time we don't have," he countered and backed away.

Coward.

"We also need Tom in on this. He is masterful at deciphering clues and riddles. I'll just call his cell and find out how he and Claudette are managing with the children."

He punched the speed dial for Tom's phone, and put it on speaker.

"Lexie and I are finished with the horses. How are you and Claudette faring with the children?"

"They're settled in as well as can be expected." Tom replied. "Are you on your way to the château?"

Étienne ignored Tom's question "Have they said anything?"

"Not yet. Doc Gavin gave them a mild sedative. My guess is they'll sleep most of the afternoon."

"You and Lexie must be famished," Étienne said. "Have Claudette order some snacks for the two of you. Tell her I'll meet her in the nursery." He snapped his phone shut before Tom could say anything else.

"I am famished," Lexie said. "But first we must find a safe place to hide the clue. I hesitate to put it back in the saddle pad. It would be disastrous if it fell into the wrong hands."

"I'll hang on to it for now," Étienne said placing the folded paper in his inside coat pocket. "We'll come back here with Tom once you and he have eaten and I've checked on the children."

He gathered up the saddle pad and turned toward the door. His hand had just touched the handle to open it when there was a soft knock and they could hear Claudette's voice on the other side calling their names.

"Lexie? Étienne? Are you in there?"

Merde, where did she come from? Oui, we'll be out in a minute." Étienne said.

Claudette continued, "Tom is with the children, and I wondered where the two of you had gone, so I came looking."

Étienne moved so fast even for Lexie's enhanced vision he was a blur. He shoved the pad into a desk drawer and nodded at Lexie. "Can't be too careful," he whispered." Before Lexie had time to respond, he was back at the door and had it open.

"We were just discussing her training routine which starts tomorrow." He blocked the doorway just enough to prevent Claudette from entering.

He stepped aside to allow Lexie to exit the office, and closed the door behind him.

Chapter 15
The Children

Claudette, come with me," Étienne said as they reached the château. "Lexie I'll join you and Tom in the lunch room."

"What did Dr. Gavin say about the children?" Étienne asked as he and Claudette climbed the stairs to the third floor.

"He said physically they're doing well given what they've been through," Claudette said. "Mentally, he's concerned that they will have emotional scars. We'll know more after the counselors have examined them. For now, they've been given a light sedative so they can sleep."

"What about other family?"

"André is trying to contact them now."

They arrived at the children's room, and Étienne preceded Claudette inside. Twin beds positioned side by side took up one wall and stuffed toys had been placed near each sleeping child. Only their heads peeked out from underneath soft comforters. A fire burned brightly, and soft lighting made the room look homey and warm.

Étienne sat gingerly on the boy's bed and pulled the covers back to examine his throat. The wound had already begun to mend. He touched the boy's shoulder and his eyes flew open. Étienne felt his fear. Their blood connection was strong.

"Hello, little one," he murmured trying not to startle the child.

The boy sat up rubbing his eyes. "Where am I?" he asked.

"You're in my home and safe. What's your name?" Étienne said.

"Pierre."

"How old are you?"

"Seven."

"Do you remember what happened at your home?" Étienne pressed Pierre. He wanted answers. Now was no time to be careful.

Pierre began to cry. "Mama, Papa, Monique where are you?" His eyes flicked around the room.

Étienne captured the boy's gaze. "Pierre, you're safe here. Who's Monique?"

"She's my sister," Pierre said.

Étienne pointed to the girl sleeping in the other bed. "Is that her?""

Pierre nodded and crawled toward her.

Étienne reached over to the other bed and woke Monique. Her eyes flew open and she jerked away from Étienne's touch. Great sobs shook her tiny body. Étienne placed her on his lap. Monique quieted as Étienne compelled her. He placed her next to her brother who put his arm around her. They clung to each other, their eyes watched Étienne.

"What can you tell me about what happened?"

Pierre took a deep breath. "A man and a woman came to our door last night. They said that they had been traveling all day and were looking for a place to rest for the night. My papa invited them in. We were standing at the top of the stairs..."

"Who is we?" Étienne interrupted...

"My mama and my sister and me." Pierre's voice quavered.

"Very good little one, you're doing great. Can you remember anything else?"

"They attacked my papa. He was all bloody. Mama grabbed us and ran to the nursery where our friends were playing. She told us to be very quiet and she would come back and get us."

"Did she come back?"

Pierre shook his head.

"We never saw her again." Monique said, and then snapped her mouth shut as if she had spoken out of turn. She was clearly older than Pierre, and Étienne waited for her to continue.

"There was screaming and yelling. We stayed quiet like mama told us. The man and woman came and broke down the door. They told us that our mama and papa were fine and waiting for us down stairs. They wanted us to go with them. We refused. They got so mad. They started biting our friends and there was blood everywhere. The woman bit me. Where are my mama and papa?"

Étienne captured the children's eyes. "Your mama and papa have gone away for a little while and you and Pierre will be staying with family until they return." The lie was tricky but necessary. Let the therapists tell them the truth.

The children hugged each other. Étienne could tell that Pierre was very protective of his sister although she was the older. He smiled at the boy's bravery and memories of François and Céleste flitted through his mind. They curled on their sides facing each other and fell asleep. Étienne motioned to Claudette and they left the nursery.

"I think we can be pretty certain that their parents have been turned, don't you?" he said.

"It certainly seems that way given what they said."

"That's not good news. We may now have Strygoi descendants in the French government. We are running out of time. We must find the 88P and formula."

151

Chapter 16
Deciphering the Clue

"What took you two so long?" Tom asked.

"We were in Étienne's office in the lab discussing my training routine," Lexie said. She hated that she had just told him a bold-faced lie but she couldn't risk revealing what she and Étienne had discovered when others might overhear her. The identity of the traitor was still unknown and she was clear that it was not safe to mention anything about their discovery.

She helped herself to the snacks cook had prepared for them. She joined Tom at the table and they ate in silence.

"God I was hungry," she said, leaning back satiated. Tom was watching her. "What's up? You look like you're full of gas with nowhere to go," she said.

"You're probably going to say that this is none of my business, but in a way it is. I think you're falling for Étienne."

"What on earth would give you…?"

"Let me finish. When two people whose life will depend on the other become romantically involved the priorities are dangerous for both parties as well as others. It can jeopardize an entire mission when the team is not completely focused on the task at hand. Then there's the obvious. He's a vampire descended from the Strygoi and you are a vampire executioner descended from the Divinati. Technically you're mortal enemies. What if you were forced to kill him or François? You know how Étienne feels about bringing his son to the light."

"Well, aren't you just the nosy one," Lexie snapped, her cheeks burning with anger. She took a couple of deep breaths allowing her embarrassment to dissipate. "I can assure you there is nothin' going on between Étienne and I. And if there were, you're right, it would be no one's business...."

"What's no one's business?" Étienne said, sauntering in with Claudette and André.

"It was nothing," Lexie said. *Thunder crap, I hope they didn't overhear.*

Tom stepped up. "We were just discussing the importance of beginning Lexie's training as soon as possible given the recent events."

"In fact, that's what Lexie and I were doing in my office while you and Claudette were with the children." Étienne said.

"So she said," Tom replied.

"Speaking of the children," Étienne said. "They're resting now and André has notified an aunt who will arrive the day after tomorrow. We'll have some counselors in to work with them tomorrow. If you and Lexie have finished your meal, we should return to my office to complete the schedule."

"Let's get to it," Lexie said, rising from the table to join Étienne.

"Now that the children are settled, I have some time on my hands. Would you like me to join you?" asked Claudette.

"That won't be necessary," Étienne said. "The three of us can work it out. I'll join you later to look in on the children."

"Perfect, I will be in the nursery should you need me," Claudette said as she headed toward the staircase.

"And I will join you," said André.

As soon as the office door locked behind them, Lexie was unable to contain her excitement.

"I lied to you at lunch." She blurted.

"I rather gathered that," Tom replied. "What *were* you two doing?"

His sarcasm didn't go unnoticed, but Lexie ignored it.

"We found the first clue to Em's riddle. When I unsaddled Brute this afternoon I noticed that the saddle pad had been tampered with. The stitchin' was different on one side. We slit it open, and inside was a small folded note with the clue written on it. We read it, but neither one of us has any idea what it means. We are completely stumped."

"Brilliant!" Tom said. "Let me see it."

Étienne withdrew the small folded paper, and handed it to Tom.

Carefully unfolding the note, Tom read out loud.

"What is green and blue and loved all over? To find the next clue find the egress. Once you find the egress ask for instructions."

"What do you think?" Étienne asked. Tom paced the room muttering Lexie stepped around Étienne's desk, and sat in his chair. Glancing down at the drawers, she noticed the middle one was ajar. A cold shiver of fear suddenly ran down her spine.

"Étienne, where did you put the saddle pad?"

"In the middle drawer of my desk, why do you ask?"

Not bothering to answer him, she opened the drawer and found it empty.

"Because it's gone." She threw open the other drawers just to make sure.

"Impossible, no one has access except for me, André and Claudette. How could such a thing have happened?" he moved around the end of the desk, and checked the drawer.

"Thank goodness you had the foresight to remove the riddle," Tom said.

"I thought I'd been careful." Étienne slammed the drawer shut.

Lexie saw comprehension dawning on Étienne's face.

154

His fist struck the desk top so hard it cracked.

Lexie jumped. "Shit!"

Étienne's face turned ugly. "I have trusted André and Claudette with my life and every secret the Society has. If either one of them is the snitch–"

"–Hold on a minute," Tom said. "We don't know anything for sure. We only know that someone broke into your office and has taken the saddle pad. Is there anyone who has raised your suspicions even slightly?"

"No one," Étienne said, shaking his head. "You know our staff as well as I do. They're highly trusted and faithful to our cause. Besides, Claudette and André are the only two who have retina clearance."

"Maybe André blames you for his mom's death and is working with François and Marielle to get revenge," Tom said.

"Wait, what?" Lexie said. "You never said anything about his mom dyin'. What happened?"

"She got very ill one winter," Étienne said. "André came to the château to ask for money for a doctor and was turned away. Our family was in Paris and she died of pneumonia before we got back. André left shortly after to join the revolution."

"Is it possible that he holds a grudge?" Lexie said.

"Revenge is a strong motivator," Tom said. "I should know."

"I can't believe it," Étienne said. "He's my progeny, he would never betray me."

On the other hand, Claudette fell in love with you, and you rejected her," Lexie said. "Rejection is a powerful motivator."

"But I assumed when she said she understood that it was over. Do you really think...?"

"I think anything is possible when it comes to a woman scorned in love," Lexie said.

"But I gave her the test."

"What test?"

"When vampires exchange blood, which I did with Claudette on several occasions..."

Étienne glanced uneasily at Lexie who did her best to fake indifference. *Yech, too much info.*

"...it allows the person drinking the blood permanent access into the others mind. Ordinarily, vampires can block their thoughts at will. But once we've taken the blood that's no longer the case. I searched Claudette's mind before bringing her into the Society and there was no hint of betrayal."

Lexie addressed the question hanging in the air. "Did she take *your* blood?"

"Never, I always avoided her attempts."

"Thank God for small favors. Could she be clever enough to mask her thoughts?"

"Perhaps, but it would be highly unusual."

"Everything about this situation is unusual," Lexie said.

"There must be something else," Tom said.

"*Non, mon ami*, not that I can think of," Étienne replied.

Tom pressed on. "Okay, then, so what about André?"

Étienne's voice was impatient. "You know his history as well as I do."

"I'm well aware of it, but I'm trying to be as objective as possible here. Just look closer."

"I knew very little of him before I turned him on the battlefield, other than he was the son of one of my family's tenant farmers."

"Maybe Lexie is right and he holds a grudge against you for the death of his mother," Tom said. In the ensuing silence, Lexie had a heart stopping thought.

"Étienne, where's the e-mail from Emma?"

"It's here in my coat," he replied, reaching into his pocket. "Fuck, it's not there. One of them must have noticed me slipping the note into my pocket, and removed it while we were having breakfast."

Lexie saw Étienne streak toward the door. Hatred and anger distorted his handsome face. Tom barely noticed.

"Wait," she exclaimed, catching his arm. "Where are you goin'?"

He shoved her away. "I'm going to find Claudette and André. If I don't like their answers, I will kill them both." His eyes had turned black, and a hint of his fangs protruded from his mouth.

For the first time since they had met, she was afraid of him. "I don't think that's such a good idea," she said.

Lexie gathered her courage and talked fast. "At this point, we're still not sure who the traitor is. If either of them *is* in league with François and Marielle, maybe we can use that to our advantage. I think you should contact our spies in their camp, advise them of our discovery, and see what they can uncover. This could be the break we're lookin' for."

Tom placed his hand on Étienne's shoulder. "She's right. Let's keep this under wraps for now old friend, and see how we can trap the culprit."

Étienne's eyes returned to green. Lexie pried his fingers off the door knob, and he took the seat behind his desk.

"We'll play it your way for now," he said. "But if either is the traitor, I will take great pleasure in extinguishing his or her life and I will feel no remorse in doing so." His voice was cold and brittle.

"Let's have a look at the clue again," Tom said. "Maybe I can figure out what it means. Okay, the first line is 'what is blue and green and loved all over.' Let's take a leap of faith and assume that this is something to do with France. What is France famous for?" he asked, picking up the writing tablet on Étienne's desk.

"The Eiffel Tower," Lexie called.

"Soccer," Étienne offered.

157

"Paris," Tom said writing down their answers.

"Versailles," Lexie said.

"Côte d'Azur," Tom said.

"Perfume, I love French perfume, but I don't know any that are green and blue," from Lexie again.

"Good, good, what else," Tom said, not missing a beat at her girly answer and adding it to his list.

"Wine," said Étienne, thinking of grapes in the field. "But grapes aren't blue, they're purple."

"Good, good," Tom said. "What about fashion? Fashion is a huge industry here. Are there any designers who specialize in green and blue fabric? Or maybe the colors of their design house?"

"None that I can think of," Étienne replied. "Lexie, you must be more familiar with that sort of thing than Tom and I. You do have a certain penchant for beautiful clothes. Anything?"

Lexie squirmed under Étienne's intense gaze.

"As far as I know there are no designers who use blue and green material in their fashion lines. And the last time I went shoppin' in the fashion area, I don't remember seein' any of the houses' logos designed in blue and green."

Tom's hand was poised to take notes. "Okay, what else?"

"Olives and olive oil," Lexie said. "But, again, olives aren't blue, and neither is olive oil."

Tom ran his hands through his hair. "Usually I'm a quick study when it comes to clues. This is going to be a long process, and time is something we don't have a lot of."

"Patience my friend," Étienne said, smiling at his friend "The three of us are smart enough to sort this out. What else is France known for?"

Lexie had been scanning Étienne's office as the men spoke, and suddenly it hit her.

"Lavender! France is known for its lavender," she said, pointing at Van Gogh. "It's got to be lavender. It's blue and green and I believe loved all over the world."

"Wonderful!" Étienne and Tom replied together.

"The first line might refer to lavender," Étienne said. "Tom, give us the second line." Étienne said.

"To find the next clue, find the egress. That's as clear as mud."

"Lavender and a way out don't make any sense," Lexie said. "Étienne do you have a thesaurus on your computer? We can look it up."

Étienne addressed his computer by name. "Geneviève."

"Good afternoon chèr," a female body-less voice purred in response. "How can I assist you?"

"Please look up the English word egress in the thesaurus."

"One moment *chèr*,"

Lexie snickered at the computer's use of endearments, and Étienne scowled at her.

"I found it *mon amour*," the computer's voice was so seductive if she hadn't known better Lexie could have sworn it had the hots for Étienne. "It is a door or a way out, but it is also an outlet. Is there anything else *chèr*?"

"That's all Geneviève, *merci*."

"It is always my pleasure *chèr*."

Étienne growled as he turned off the computer. "Claudette programmed it as a joke. Egress still doesn't make any sense. What does lavender have to do with an outlet?"

The three sat there looking at each other for a moment.

"Outlet, outlet," Lexie kept murmuring. "An outlet in the States is also a place to shop. It's where you can buy designer wear at marked down prices. Is there such an outlet near here?"

"Nothing like what you describe," Étienne replied. "The only outlet we have is the Durance store on the other side of Grignon, but they don't specialize in lavender. They have their own fragrances."

Lexie felt a slight tug on her brain as he stared into her eyes. *Is he trying to read my mind?* Suddenly his face lit up with one of his amazing smiles.

"Hold on, there is the *Distillerie de Lavande* in Nyons. The store specializes in all things lavender. They have other fragrances as well, but lavender is their big seller. Do you think that could be it?"

"I remember Em talking about the lavender distillery in Nyons. It's called *La Distillerie Bleu Provence*. I know she was there just before she died." Lexie replied. "I think we're on to somethin'."

"I think it's worth checking out," Tom said, writing down outlet (distillery) next to lavender. "It's all we've got right now."

"Good, now what's the last line?" Étienne asked his eagerness tangible.

"The last line is, once you find the egress, ask for instructions. What instructions and whom do we ask?" Tom said, scratching the light stubble on his chin.

"I think we have to go there right now," Lexie said, rising from her chair and stretching. "How far is Nyons from here?"

"It's about thirty minutes," replied Étienne, glancing at his watch. "It's three thirty now, if we leave immediately, we can get there before it closes."

"That's great you guys," Tom said. "But how are we going to leave the château without arousing suspicion? We need some kind of excuse."

"Keep it simple," Étienne replied. "We'll tell them that Lexie wants to buy some local tablecloths to send to her mother, and we're taking her to Nyons to buy some. The weekly market is today. A *little* outing in the countryside for our vampire executioner."

"You lie so easily," Tom said, handing the paper clue back to Étienne. "Keep this safe, traitorous eyes would love to see it."

"I'll do better than that." Étienne said. "I'll burn it and our brainstorming list." Moments later all traces of their work lay in an ashtray.

Étienne flushed the ashes in his bathroom and wiped the ashtray.

"There. That handles that," he said. "Let's get out of here."

Leaving the château was uneventful, and Lexie enjoyed the drive through lush vineyards and olive groves to Nyons. Once there Étienne carefully navigated through the narrow streets until he turned into a parking lot.

"This is a beautiful town," Lexie said. "Where is the distillery?"

"Just over there," Étienne replied pointing to a warehouse looking structure with a smoke stack on top. "The lavender blooms in August and has already been harvested and distilled for the year."

"Where's the store?"

Étienne strode purposefully toward the rear of the structure. "It's in the back."

He paused before the entrance.

"Let me do the talking. If required, I can compel whoever is in the store and get the information we need."

"I hope you won't have to," Lexie said, still uncertain about this particular talent. "And, I didn't just fall off the turnip truck."

She was captivated by the delicious aroma. There were shelves filled with perfumes, oils, and soaps. Several customers milled about browsing. Moving as one, the three approached the small checkout stand.

"*Bonjour m'sieu*," Étienne began, and then hesitated as if listening for something, his eyebrows raised.

161

"*Bonjour*," replied the sales clerk. "*Comment puis-je vous aider?*" He was clearly eager to help them.

"We were wondering if in the past few weeks a young woman had been here and left a package for a pick up?" Étienne inquired. Lexie assumed he'd switched to English to avoid the other patrons from understanding.

"No, *m'sieu*, I have not had such instruction," the clerk replied.

Lexie's heart fell. *Thunder crap.*

"Think again," Étienne persisted. "I'm sure you can recall something."

He caught the clerk's gaze. The man's eyes glazed over as he stared at Étienne, mesmerized.

"Ah yes, now I recall," the clerk said. "One moment and I will retrieve it."

The clerk reached under the counter, and rummaged through a small file box. With a satisfied grunt he handed Étienne a small envelope.

"Very good *monsieur*," Étienne murmured. "Now you will forget this entire incident. You will forget the young woman giving you this envelope. You will forget our visit. Is that clear?"

"*Oui monsieur*," the clerk murmured, and as Étienne broke eye contact, the clerk woke up looking puzzled.

"Come dear," Étienne said. "We must find you some pure lavender to take home."

Taking his cue, Lexie browsed through the shelves, selected several bottles and turned to Étienne.

"These are wonderful, honey. Let's buy these."

"Will that be all?" The clerk asked innocently, ringing in their purchase.

"*Oui, merci*," Étienne replied.

The transaction complete, they hurried from the store and Lexie heard the clerk closing up behind them. The sun was dropping behind the mountains and in late November darkness came quickly.

Lexie was the first to speak. "For a minute there, I was afraid we were completely off track," she said with relief, once back in the car.

"I was not concerned," Étienne said, maneuvering the car through the evening Nyons traffic. "As soon as I greeted him, he wondered if we were the ones Emma had told him about. He was just being cautious, and it only took a bit of compelling for him to relent."

"I hope you never have to use that talent on me," Lexie said.

"It wouldn't matter if I did," he replied, smiling at her in the rearview mirror. "Remember, you are a vampire executioner and therefore immune to my special talents."

"Good," she said. "Now, what about the note; can we read it now?"

"Let's wait until we get back to the château," Tom said. "We can't be sure we're not being watched, and I would have to turn the overhead light on."

Leaning back, Lexie glanced at her watch and was surprised to see that it was 5:15.

"Is tonight's dinner formal or informal?" she asked, stifling a yawn behind her hand.

"It is informal, and will be served at seven," Étienne replied.

With little else to say, Lexie relaxed enjoying the fast steady driving. It was Étienne's voice that interrupted her reverie.

"We'll meet after dinner to read Emma's latest instructions. I will make sure that Claudette and André are otherwise occupied."

"Works for me," Tom said.

"Well, it doesn't work for me." Lexie piped up. "Why can't we read it as soon as we get back to the château? The suspense is killin' me."

"It would look too suspicious." Étienne said. "We've just returned from an outing. To sequester ourselves in my office now could raise questions."

Lexie caved. "I guess you're right." but it felt wrong suppressing her eagerness to read the next clue.

They arrived at the château and Étienne took her arm as they walked up the steps. At his touch Lexie almost tripped her legs weak.

"I need to speak with you privately." he said. His grip tightened as he guided her toward his office. "We're going to my office where we can talk."

Thunder crap, here it comes. "But I thought you said that would look suspicious. Besides, I'm really tired. Can't it wait?" Her desire for him hammered her body, and she didn't think she could handle any more rejection.

"For bloody sakes man, give the girl a break," Tom said. "Can't you see she's exhausted?"

"But this is important—"

"Give it a rest Étienne," Tom insisted.

Lexie shot him a glance of thanks. "Would one of you wake me at six thirty? I'm gonna have a quick nap."

"I'll wake you," Étienne responded. His hand slipped up her arm and he pressed gently on her shoulder. Flames of lust flicked through her and she couldn't wait to get away.

Reaching the second floor, Étienne and Tom split off to go to Étienne's office, and after giving them a quick smile, Lexie dragged her butt up the next flight of stairs. She reached her bedroom. Without bothering to change her clothes, she fell across the bed and slept.

Chapter 17
Tom and Étienne

Tom and Étienne entered the vampire's book-lined office on the second floor of the château. As usual it was the epitome of Étienne's well organized brain. The large mahogany desk was devoid of any paperwork and polished to a brilliant sheen. The items on top were strategically placed so that they appeared like decoration rather than office supplies. Two Louis XV wing back chairs sat in front of the desk with a glass end table between them. Fresh hydrangeas adorned a blue porcelain Chinese vase centered on the table.

"Finding that next clue was a stroke of good luck," Tom said as he settled into one of the wingbacks.

Étienne sat in the other wing back keeping the conversation informal. "That was not luck, it was brilliant deduction," he said.

"Have you spoken with Lexie yet?" Tom said.

"I keep getting interrupted. I wanted to just now. You interfered."

"Sorry old man. But the sooner the better. You know I'm not good at keeping secrets."

Étienne regarded his friend. "I'll do it this evening. By the way, who were you really speaking with this morning?"

"What, when?"

Étienne heard Tom's heartbeat accelerate and resisted the temptation to read his thoughts.

"Don't play dumb with me, my friend. This morning during breakfast. I know you weren't talking to your office."

"Bloody hell man, were you rattling around in my head? You wanker, you promised you wouldn't."

"I didn't need to. When you were explaining to Lexie about the call I knew you were lying. Your heart rate and blood pressure skyrocketed. Who was it?" Étienne struggled with suspicion. The last thing he wanted was to think that Tom could be the traitor.

"It's none of your business."

"Actually it is. Tell me or you leave me no choice but to assume the worst."

"Assume what you will, I'm not saying."

Étienne slammed the desk with his fist. "*Fils de pute*, don't do this. You and I have no secrets. We've always been straight arrow with each other."

"What do you mean? And don't call me a son-of-a-bitch. I'll have to hurt you."

Étienne ignored his friend's challenge. "We still don't know who the traitor is."

"Shite man, you really know where to hit a fellow below the belt."

Don't read his thoughts. Étienne poked at Tom's mind then withdrew honoring his promise. Tom blinked a couple of times before he looked away, and walked to the window.

"Well?" Étienne prodded.

"Bugger it, you can be such a tosser. I was talking to Cassie."

Étienne saw Tom's hands were curled into fists.

"What on earth for?"

"It was about you and Lexie."

"*Sacre bleu*, are you crazy? You know how she feels about me. All we need is for her to show up. What did you tell her?"

"I told her you were in love with her daughter and I thought Lexie felt the same. Then I asked her what she thought I should do. I managed to talk her out of jumping on the next plane, but

166

man she's furious and scared. I wouldn't be surprised if she shows up despite my efforts to stop her."

"Did she tell you what to do?"

"Yeah but castration is not an option."

Étienne stared at him for a moment and then burst into laughter. "Trust Cassie to come up with that solution."

"You're not mad?"

"Relieved. I feared something much worse. However, now that Cassie knows, I must tell Lexie. I'd hate for her to hear this from her mom."

"True. But damn it man it's a really bad idea. Why do you have to be in love with her?" He ran his hand through his hair.

"If I didn't know better I'd think you were jealous."

For a minute Étienne sensed Tom was about to blurt something out. Instead he shook his head, and to Étienne's amusement, he blushed to his roots. *Interesting, could he have feelings for her?* Étienne couldn't tell if it was that or something else.

"Don't be an asshole," Tom said before Étienne could question him further. "What about the next clue. Should we have a look at it?"

"Not here. After dinner we'll go to my office in the lab."

A sharp knock sounded on the office door suppressing any further conversation.

"Come in," Étienne called.

André entered, his powerful presence filling the room. "It's almost time for dinner. Everyone is gathered in the library wondering where you are. Has something happened?"

"We were discussing the attack on the de Villeneuve-Flayosc family." Étienne replied. "We lost track of time. Is Lexie in the library?"

"She hasn't come down yet," André replied.

"I'll go wake her and be down shortly. Don't wait for us."

Tom cocked an eyebrow and Étienne nodded. He was going to talk to Lexie now.

For the first time in several centuries Étienne experienced the jitters. He had no idea how his conversation with Lexie would go. He knew how he wanted it to go but she was unpredictable at best and downright contrary at worst. He smiled as he recalled their conversation on the way to the airport.

There was no answer when he tapped on her door so he pushed it open. She was curled on her side, her beautiful face cushioned in her palm. Her lips raised in a soft smile. *Wonder what she's dreaming about.* He walked to the bed and touched her shoulder.

"*Ma petite*, wake up." He could smell her delicious lilac scent and the urge to bend down and kiss her was almost irresistible. She didn't stir. "Wake up sleepy head." He shook her shoulder.

One eye peered at him. "Go away. It can't be time to get up yet." She rolled over and pulled a pillow over her head.

He sat down on the edge of the bed and pulled the pillow away. "It's almost dinner time and we need to talk."

All he got was a moan. He waited for a moment and then shook her again. "C'mon *ma petite*, this is important."

She sat bolt upright. "What's wrong, has somethin' happened?"

"Nothing bad, just urgent."

"It better be important. I was havin' a wonderful sleep."

He was tongue tied. He couldn't seem to gather a coherent thought. *How do I tell her this?*

"Spit it out man. I'm not gettin' any younger here."

"I'm in love with you." He couldn't believe he'd blurted it so blatantly.

"Never in my loneliest moments did I imagine myself falling in love with a human. Don't get me wrong, I've had relationships. They never lasted and I always found an excuse to end them. Then you walked into my life. When we kissed yesterday in the elevator, I wanted nothing more than to drink your blood and be inside you. It took every bit of strength I had to pull away."

He took her hand as he spoke, afraid she might bolt.

"What the…" Her eyes widened and he felt as if he could get lost in their depths.

The smell of her arousal washed over Étienne in waves. His cock seemed to have a mind of its own. He wished he could read her mind.

"It would be good if you said something now." He couldn't stand silence any longer. "Tell me I'm crazy. Tell me I'm a fool to think you could love me. Tell me something."

"You're not crazy," she said. Her voice came out as a squeak. "I've felt the connection between us since the first day we met. But yesterday in the elevator when I tried to kiss you, it seemed clear you didn't want me."

"*Ma petite* that was not rejection that was self-preservation. I want you more than life itself."

Lexie shook her head her. "I'm stunned. And, what about all the problems? You a vampire and me a vampire executioner. I don't know that I trust you, and sometimes I'm afraid of you. I find myself torn between wantin' to be with you and wantin' to run from you and kill you all at the same time." A wayward tear trickled down her cheek.

Before she could protest he enfolded her in his arms and held her. She struggled, pushing at his chest. He didn't pull away but held her closer and began to kiss her. Softly at first and when she didn't object, his kisses became more demanding. His cock hardened with desire and he could feel his fangs pressing against his gums. *Danger, danger.* He told himself he needed to be the stronger. To have control. His body completely disagreed.

169

Lexie laid her hand on his cheek. "I think we'd better slow down. I get the impression you're losin' control and I'm not ready for that."

He groaned but honored her request and released her. "That was a little too much wasn't it?"

"A little, but I'm glad we had this conversation. I was beginnin' to think that I had read the signs wrong."

"There is something else."

"I don't think I want to know."

"I discussed my feelings with Tom."

"What on earth for? It's so, none of his business."

"Don't be angry. I needed someone to talk to and he is my best friend. The problem is, he called Cassie."

"He did what? That was stupid. He knows how she feels about vampires. It would be just like her to jump on a plane and show up."

"Calm down, he says he talked her out of it. But, knowing Cassie she could come anyway. I wanted you to hear it from me not her."

"Can't cry over spilt milk. If she comes she comes. We'll deal with it when it happens. I'm glad you told me though. It's much better comin' from you than her."

Étienne took her hand and brushed a wayward lock of hair behind her ear. "Do you know you smile in your sleep?"

"I've never stayed awake to find out."

He grinned and leaned over to give her a light kiss on her cheek. "You're cute."

"I hate cute."

"I love it."

"Call me that and I'll skin your hide."

"Ummmm. Sounds delightful." He took her hand and licked the palm.

"Don't try to seduce me. You called me cute."

He kept a tight grip on his emotions, but she was so adorable.

The door opened to reveal Claudette. "Am I interrupting something? We're waiting on you two to start eating."

Étienne let go of Lexie's hand and stood up. "*Merde*, I forgot about dinner. Are you ready?"

"More than ready, I'm famished. You two should get out of my way so I can make myself presentable for dinner. I'll be downstairs in a few minutes."

Étienne ushered Claudette out the door and closed it behind them. He could feel the waves of anger emanating from her as they descended to the first floor. He decided he couldn't do anything. She would just have to deal with his and Lexie's relationship.

Chapter 18
The Second Clue

What on earth could be so important that you and Tom and Lexie are meeting after dinner?" Lexie heard Claudette's voice as she rounded the corner to the dining room.

"We must finish planning Lexie's training," Étienne replied. "We're training her in the French discipline of Savate combined with the use of weapons, the Senban Shuriken. I've decided to forego her testing. We're starting first thing in the morning."

Their eyes met as she entered the room and she loved the way they lit up as he gazed at her. Eight other pairs of eyes pinned her with a look. The attention made her uncomfortable.

"Hi everyone," she said, her cheeks flushed. "I'm starvin'. What's for dinner?"

"Dig in," Tom said. "The food's excellent as usual. I'm going back for seconds."

"Wait until I get my firsts. I don't want to have to eat your leftovers."

Chuckling at her feistiness, Étienne took a sip of synthetic blood. "Is there anything else?" he said to André and Claudette

Claudette shook her head. "Let me know if there is anything you need with regard to Lexie's training," she said as she and André left the room. "I am available."

"Me too," André said.

"I think we're fine for now," Étienne said

"I appreciate your willingness to support me." Lexie said.

172

Claudette paused and smiled back. The smile never reached her eyes. Lexie felt uneasy.

"As soon as you two are finished with dinner we can go to my office in the lab and get to work," Étienne said, finishing the last of his synthetic blood.

"I'm almost finished," Lexie piped up, not missing a beat in her chewing. She scooped up the last bite of the delicious chicken from her plate, took a swig of wine, and sighed in contentment. "What is this Savate y'all are talkin' about?" Certain vampires might be listening and she kept up the charade to avoid any suspicion.

"It's an ancient form of martial arts that employs kick boxing as well as hand-to-hand combat. It's very efficient and deadly when combined with karate," Tom said. "It's also fairly easy to learn, and given your present strength and speed it will give you an advantage in short order."

"And a Senban Shiriken?" She stumbled over the unfamiliar name. "I've never been trained in weaponry."

"It's commonly referred to as the Chinese Star which is usually made from steel, but can also be made of wood or iron. It is not particularly deadly, but is a great way to distract your opponent and deliver a killing blow with another weapon such as a knife or sword," Étienne said.

"Great, let's get started on the schedule," Lexie said.

Once inside Étienne's office he withdrew the small envelope from his pocket and tore it open.

"Hurry and read it, the suspense is killing me," Lexie said.

"I'll let you do the honors." He handed her the note.

"Where the Celts once roamed

In this home away from home

Where red flowers grow in

Summer fields of grass

And love abounds in food and fun"

This one is even more complicated than the last one." Lexie said. "Where did Em come up with this stuff?"

"She was a brilliant woman," Étienne replied. "Her mind worked in strange ways."

"My brain is tired from all this thinking." Tom said rubbing his hands over his face...

"I suspect this clue isn't about France," Lexie said.

"What makes you say that?"

"Em wouldn't make it that simple. As Étienne said, her mind worked in mysterious ways. Let's dissect it line by line the way we did the last clue. The first line reads 'The Celts once roamed' which is broad and could be anywhere in Europe or Great Britain. But if we include the second line 'In this home away from home' it begins to narrow the field a bit."

"I don't think we can narrow the field just yet," Étienne said.

"Hear me out. We know the Celts are most commonly known for their influence in Ireland and Scotland, but if I recall my history, they were also prominent in middle Europe."

Étienne raised the top of his computer. "Let's look on the internet and compile a list of all the countries they influenced. Geneviève, it's time to work."

"What do you need chèr?"

Lexie couldn't help but smile again at the sultry voice.

"Stop calling me that or I'll unplug you," Étienne hissed.

"Sorry *mon amour*. Is that better?"

"Not really, but I don't have time to argue. Please look up where the Celts were prominent in middle Europe."

"One moment chèr, I will display everything I can find."

"There's a lot of information here," Étienne commented, scrolling through the listings. "Ah, here we go. Tom, can you write this down?"

"Sure," Tom grabbed a pad from Étienne's desk.

"This says that the Celts were primarily in Germany and Southern Austria, as well as countries now known as Slovakia, Serbia, Croatia, Poland and the Czech Republic. It also mentions that they had some influence in France, Portugal, northern Spain, and of all places Transylvania," Étienne read. "Maybe Emma's imagination took her to Transylvania, but where in Transylvania."

"Hold on y'all," Lexie said. "The second line of the clue reads, in this home away from home. I think this has to mean Germany. Her folks have a place outside Frankfurt in the Taunus Mountains in a town called Kronberg. Étienne, look up Celts in Kronberg."

Étienne punched a few keys. "It says that the Celts settled on the Altkoenig Mountain twenty-four hundred years ago, and today you can still see the Celtic rings on this mountain. Kronberg sits at the foot of this mountain. Do you think that's it?"

"I think we're on the right track," Tom said. "What's the next line?"

"Where red flowers grow in summer fields of grass," Lexie continued. "That could be anywhere in Germany and it could be any red flower."

"But, if we assume, and I do mean assume, that the beginning is about Emma's folk's summer place in Kronberg, then let's look at what flowers grow near there." Étienne said.

"Of course, the clue here is summer." Lexie said. "Poppies bloom abundantly in the summer everywhere in the Taunus Mountains and around Frankfurt. Heinrick's place is ablaze with them durin' May and June. They're like a red carpet."

"Next line." Tom said.

"And love abounds in food and fun," she read, scrunching her eyebrows together in thought. "Hmm, please read what we've come up with so far, maybe that will help me think."

Tom looked at his notes. "So far we've determined that the next clue is probably in Germany in the town of Kronberg where Emma's Dad has a summer home. We've determined that part of the clue has to do with poppy fields or flowers, and now we are at 'and love abounds in food and fun'. You've been to Em's summer home a couple of times. What do you remember?"

"I remember how airy and bright the house is," Lexie said a faraway look in her eyes. "I remember Em and I used to share a huge bed in the loft of the house. But most of all, I remember the grassy meadow on fire with poppy blooms. And in the middle... oh my God! That has to be it. When Em was little Heinrick constructed a beautiful gazebo in the middle of the field. Em once showed me a secret hidin' place in the floor underneath one of the stones. In the recess was a small box where she had hidden memories of other summers spent there. "

"Brilliant!" Étienne said. "I think it's worth checking out. What do you think Tom?"

"I think it's the best shot we've got right now. If she's right, there's a good chance either the 88P is hidden there or we'll discover another clue."

"I'll leave for Kronberg tonight. Do you remember where on the floor the loose stone was?"

Lexie thought for a moment. "The best I can do is tell you it wasn't far from the entrance gate – maybe three or four paces in and to the right a little."

"That's a bit vague, but I guess it'll have to do." Étienne said.

"How can you leave for Kronberg tonight?" Lexie said. "It's almost nine, and I'm sure there are no trains running at this hour, let alone flights to Frankfurt from Charles de Gaulle."

"I will be traveling by, shall we say, an unconventional method," Étienne said. "Another advantage of being a five-hundred-year old vampire. I can teleport wherever I want much faster than any other form of transportation. Depending on the distance, I can reach some places in a matter of minutes and other places within two to five hours. It's very useful when I'm in a hurry."

"I can imagine," she said, shaking her head. Lexie wondered if she would ever get used to his special qualities. "Are there any other attributes you have that I should know about?"

"He can read minds," Tom said. "So be careful what you think."

"Oh great," Lexie said. "That could be awkward. Is there any way to avoid it?"

"Relax ma petite." Étienne said. "I can read every human and vampire's mind. The exception is a vampire executioner's mind and an older vampire if they've blocked me out."

Relieved, Lexie asked. "Can you read Tom's mind?"

"Yes."

"That must come in handy."

"It could, and I've promised him not to. I always try to honor another's privacy. It's a very intrusive talent."

"No kiddin'," Lexie said.

"But never mind that. You and Tom need to be very careful while I am gone. Someone here is a traitor, and your lives could be in real danger if he or she suspects what we have discovered. What little evidence we have points to either André or Claudette, and both have been blocking their thoughts from me."

"Do you think the traitor might try something while you're away?" Tom asked.

The look on Étienne's face was grim. "I don't know, but it would be a perfect opportunity. This place is a fortress, and we have the best people in the world guarding it, but…just, please, be careful."

A cold shiver ran up Lexie's spine as visions of the carnage she'd seen at the neighboring château flashed across her mind. "I promise we'll be careful. I don't take any of this lightly, and am very clear how dangerous François and Marielle are."

"What else?" Tom said.

"I want you to begin Lexie's training tomorrow morning," Étienne said. "We can't delay another day. I recommend you start with yoga moves in the morning to improve her flexibility and then after lunch begin with the basics of Savate. Let's see how quickly she learns and how fast her abilities develop."

"Works for me" Lexie said. "Now you need to get out of here. Even with your ability to teleport, it will take you a couple of hours to get there and then you have to find the right house."

"Do you even know where Kronberg is?" Tom said

"I know that it's not far from Frankfurt, and if you'll give me a minute," Étienne paused, fingers flying over the keyboard of his computer. "Here it is. No worries my friend, I know exactly where I'm going. But finding the right stone in the gazebo could be a whole other issue."

"Maybe I should go with you," Lexie said, wondering how that would work.

"No way," Tom and Étienne said in unison.

"It's far too dangerous," Étienne continued. "Don't take this the wrong way, but you would only slow me down. If I do run into trouble, I don't want to have to worry about protecting you."

"Fine," she retorted unhappy with his response. Her face brightened with a new idea. "I'll put my cell phone by my bed tonight. You can call me if you're havin' a problem. I might be able to walk you through it."

Étienne smiled at her in a way that made her insides turn to Jell-O. "Smart. Plus I'll be able to check on you."

"Are you leavin' now?" she asked, reluctant to think about being without him for even one day.

"I need to speak with Claudette before I go."

Tom stretched and stifled a yawn. "Are we done here? I'm knackered."

"There's just one last item to attend to," replied Étienne taking the note from Lexie. He set it on fire with as he'd done earlier. "We can't take any chances that this could fall into the wrong hands."

Back at the château, the three entered the foyer and Étienne drew Lexie to him. He hugged her and kissed her on the cheek."

She pulled back a little embarrassed that Tom had witnessed this display of affection. "Be careful," she said.

"Promise," Étienne responded. He nodded to Tom, and using vampire speed disappeared up the stairs.

"Are you okay?" Tom said.

"I'm exhausted from the last few days and all the grief and excitement. And, I'm worried for Étienne. What he's doing is incredibly dangerous, even deadly, and I don't want to lose him. He's become important to me."

"I noticed," Tom said. "Be careful Lex. I've cautioned Étienne about how dangerous it could be for the two of you to be in a romantic relationship. It clouds the mind and causes you to lose focus in a fight, and that could prove to be deadly."

"I think it's a little late for that. By the way, if you ever pull a stupid stunt like that again, I'll tan your hide."

"What stunt?"

"Don't play dumb with me. You called Cassie and told her about Étienne and me."

Tom blushed. "Oh that. I'm sorry Lex. I didn't know what else to do. It seemed like a good idea at the time. It wasn't. She flipped. She wanted to jump on the first plane."

"I know, Étienne told me. He said you managed to talk her out of it. No harm done and you're forgiven."

"Thanks, I won't do it again. But what about you and Étienne?"

"All we can do now is be responsible for our feelins', and not let them get in the way of our judgment."

"I hope you're right. Go get some sleep. Five-thirty will come soon enough. Do you want me to wake you?"

"Yes, please. I don't seem to have an alarm clock in my room," she replied.

She gave Tom a quick hug outside her room and entered welcomed by a blazing fire and a turned down bed. She sank back into the soft pillows, and even though sleep called to her she shivered as the experience of feeling small and alone intruded on her thoughts. She wasn't sure why but as she drifted off to sleep, she knew something bad was going to happen, and that it would be soon.

Chapter 19
Amant de Sang

Lexie didn't know how long she'd been asleep. Her eyes flew open, heart thumping. There was someone in her room. She steeled herself for an attack and wished she wasn't wearing only a T-shirt and panties.

A cool hand touched her shoulder. "Relax ma petite," Étienne said. "I couldn't leave without saying good-bye one more time."

She could just make out his features in the light from the fireplace. Relief flooded through her. She sat up and touched his face.

"I'm glad. I already missed you."

Étienne shrugged off his overcoat, and gathered her in his arms, kissing her face. She could feel her body responding to his touch as her nipples hardened and moisture rushed to her vagina. She wrapped her arms passionately around his neck. The soft silk of his shirt was sensuous against her bare arms. She tilted her head, and captured his lips with hers.

Parting her lips with his tongue, Étienne explored her mouth. Shivers of delight raced through her. She thrust her tongue into his mouth, and he groaned as his breathing came in gasps. She could feel the sharp tips of his descending fangs. *Oh man, that's hot.*

He pressed her back against the pillows, and his strong body covered hers. The feel of his cock against her thigh made her squirm as she demanded more. She hated that his leather pants were between them. He slipped his leg between hers and the

181

pressure against her clit brought on the first orgasm. She shuddered as it washed over her leaving her breathless and wanting more. He sighed as his tongue continued to explore her face and neck.

"Your scent is intoxicating," he murmured as he paid particular attention to her pulsing artery.

Without warning, he drew back, his breathing harsh and fast. His eyes had turned black; his face veined. "Wait, *mon amour*, I need a minute. The scent of your blood and arousal is too much."

"Honey, I don't give a hoot about control." She tightened her arms around his neck capturing his lips with hers and forcing her tongue in between his fangs. Her pent-up desire focused in her lips.

He pulled away again. "I don't want to hurt you."

"You won't," she panted her body on fire.

His tongue stroked her neck. "And, I don't know if I can stop before tasting your blood. You know what that could do to me," he said. He gazed at her with dark passion. But worry filled his eyes.

Her desire for him so strong and urgent she was willing to ignore his words of caution. "I trust you."

Lexie reached down and gripped his throbbing penis. He groaned and thrust his tongue into her mouth. She responded matching him thrust for thrust. His lips moved from her mouth down to her neck. She continued to stroke him and he grew bigger in her hand. Her cunt dripped with her juices. Étienne pressed his hand over her mound and slipped his finger inside. She moaned and squeezed his finger and he stroked her to the brink. She protested when he withdrew his hand.

He continued to explore her body with his mouth, nipping at her nipples until they were hard nubs. She pushed against his leg needing release from the sweet tension that was building in her cunt.

"I want you inside me," she groaned. Her fingers fumbled frantically trying to undo his belt to free him.

"Wait," he said, pulling back from her again. "I want to see you – all of you."

He straddled her and ripped off her T-shirt in one move.

"You're beautiful," he said. He ran his hands over her breasts, pausing to tease her nipples then down her belly until he reached the top of her panties. He growled low in his throat, and grabbed the elastic at her waist. With one swift tug, he tore them from her.

"No fair," she said. Her fingers trembled as she unbuttoned his shirt. "I want to see all of you as well."

"No problem," he said. He was naked before she could blink.

She sucked in a breath at the size of him. *He's too big.* She ran her hands over his chest reveling in the feel of his skin and muscles that rippled as he held himself over her. She followed the thin line of hair down his belly and he moaned as she curled her fingers around his cock. She touched the tip and a drop of wetness clung to her finger. She licked it away and his penis jerked as he watched her. Lexie slipped her arms around his neck and pulled him down on top of her.

"I want you inside," she said, kissing him.

"First things first." He sucked at her neck, his fangs scraping the skin, but not breaking it. His tongue explored her body and when he reached her already hardened nipples he nipped at them gently. Each lick and stroke brought her closer to ecstasy. He spread her legs and his tongue found her labia. He tantalized her clit until she bucked wanting more. He slid his fingers into her while his tongue continued to tease. Her body contracted hard around his fingers as she climaxed in a long, shuddering spasm that left her weak and panting.

"*Mon Dieu, ma petite* this is torture. I cannot wait any longer," he moaned. He slipped his fingers from her wetness, and licking his way up her body he knelt over her.

She could feel the smooth head of his penis as it pressed against her, stroking and teasing the folds of her cunt. The sweet pressure began building inside her. She wanted more. She wanted to taste him. "Not yet," she murmured. She flipped him over and straddled him. She licked his chest and his hands gripped her shoulders as she flicked his nipples with her tongue. Étienne was panting and his cock stroked her crack as he moved under her.

Lexie slithered down his body until her mouth found his penis. She wrapped her mouth around him and he gasped, his grip on her shoulders tightening. Lexie sucked and ran her tongue around the tip. She kneaded his scrotum gently and it swelled in response. Her lips slid up his cock and she tasted the beginning of his climax.

"Enough," he rumbled and effortlessly laid her on her back. "I'll be as gentle as I can," he said. His cock probed her cunt sending her closer to the edge.

"I want you now," she cried out.

He gave a powerful thrust that plunged deep inside her body. The pain as she stretched was quickly replaced by waves of ecstasy. Lexie heard a soft click. She opened her eyes. Coal black eyes glittering with passion stared at her, and Étienne's fangs were fully extended. *Oh shit, can I handle this?*

He turned his head away from her in an attempt to hide what he had become. "Don't look at me," he said. "I'm capable of killing you with one bite."

"Look at me, damn you. I want you more than I'm afraid of you, and yes I'm afraid." She clutched his face in her hands and kissed him hard. The coppery taste of blood spread in her mouth as his fang nicked her tongue.

Étienne pulled back coal black eyes bearing into her. "It's as sweet as I knew it would be. I want more." He continued to thrust into her.

"Then take it," she said, forgetting in the throes of passion what might happen if he drank her blood. "I want to experience everything."

"I cannot, my love," he said. He nuzzled her exposed neck, and licked greedily at the delicate skin. "I am afraid that I would lose control if I were to bite you."

His fangs graze her neck. The sensation brought her to the brink of climaxing.

"I want it all."

"*Merde, ma petite,*" he said leaning back to stare into her eyes.

"Thunder crap, do it!"

He sank his teeth into her neck, and he began to suck. Every nerve ending in her body sang with pleasure. He began moving faster inside her, each thrust penetrating deeper and more powerful than the last. The sensations were exquisitely unbearable. She writhed beneath him. Her hips matched his rhythm thrust for thrust. There was no holding back. Her body shuddered and her cunt exploded. Lexie screamed thrusting faster and faster against him, every feeling narrowed to her cunt.

"I can't stop..." he gasped. He lifted his head from her neck and he cried out. His body convulsed against hers, and she could feel his cock spasm as he released inside her.

She held him in her arms, too spent to do anything else, feeling him relax as he continued moving inside her. She heard a soft click, as his fangs retracted. He licked her neck where they had punctured the skin and when she opened her eyes, found emerald green ones gazing back at her.

Étienne shifted his weight to the side. "Did I hurt you?"

"Oh sugar, do I look like I'm hurt?"

He chuckled. "You look like a woman who has been thoroughly satisfied."

"I'm happier than a frog on a lily pad catchin' flies." She reached up to touch her neck which had begun itching a little. "Will the marks take long to heal?" She wasn't sure she cared.

"As a vampire executioner, your healing powers are much greater than a normal human, so I suspect.....ah yes, it is already happening. I licked your neck to help them close."

"Good, I'd hate to have to explain bite marks on my neck to Claudette and Tom." She was quiet for a moment and then said, "Are you okay? Did drinkin' my blood affect you?"

185

"I'm happy to say that I'm feeling no ill after-effects," he said. "It must be because I didn't drink enough to counteract the antiserum."

"Thank goodness. We took a huge risk," she replied. She peered at him unsure but he seemed no different.

Étienne kissed her and propped himself up on one arm. He brushed a strand of hair from her face and she could sense he was struggling to say something.

Lexie stretched and snuggled closer not wanting to rouse from the sweet euphoria. "What is it E?"

He continued to gaze into her eyes, his silence unnerving. Curiosity won out and now fully alert, Lexie sat up to give him her full attention.

He took her hand and rubbed the palm. "The Book of the Originals has been handed down from generation to generation. It contains the only known recorded vampire lore. There is a legend that for every vampire there is an *Amant de Sang* or Bloodmate. *Amant de Sang* is the one male or female who, out of all vampires, completes the other, and destiny brings them together for eternity. When I'm near you I'm aroused all the time. You smell of lilacs in bloom. I believe you are my *Amant de Sang*."

"Give me a freakin' break."

"Let me finish, then we will discuss. The quandary is that nowhere in the history of vampires has there ever been a human *Amant de Sang*."

"I'm not all human."

He placed his fingers over her mouth his eyes tender and loving. "Now that we've made love, and I have tasted your blood, I am positive you are the one. The connection between us is undeniable, and that poses an obvious dilemma."

Lexie could only stare back, speechless. The ramifications of what he had told her chased away any vestiges of euphoria. He reached for her and she drew back, throwing her hands up to ward him off.

"Don't touch me right now." Visions of the recent massacre and Étienne forcing the children to drink his blood still haunted her. *How can this relationship possibly work?*

"I'll grow old and die and you won't," she said. *And I might have to kill you.* She kept that thought to herself.

"Yes, *ma petite* that is exactly what will happen," he replied. His gaze held all the love and desire that was in his heart and Lexie struggled to remain clear-headed.

"Shit Étienne, don't look at me like that. I can't think. This whole thing is crazy. What have we done?" She pulled on her T-shirt and began pacing. Étienne rose from the bed and tried to take her in his arms. She spun away and ran to the French doors.

"I've never felt about any man the way I feel about you. I'm pretty sure I'm fallin' in love with you and right now that seems like a really bad idea. If I'm your *Amant de Sang* how are we supposed to be together forever? I'm dyin' even as we speak." She turned and glared at him. "This is an impossible situation."

"No *ma petite*, it is not impossible. Difficult and unusual, yes, but workable." Étienne dressed quickly.

"Then what the hell are we supposed to do?" She walked towards him, hands on hips demanding an answer.

Étienne backed up to the bed sat down. "I do not know, *ma chère*. I'm as bewildered as you are. I only know that I love you and want to be with you forever. The rest we'll work out as we go." He opened his arms. "Please."

Lexie willed herself to stay and paced once more. Her heart pounded as the unthinkable rattled around her brain. *No way.* The situation they had created was hopeless, dangerous and, in her mind, unattainable. She halted and ran her hands over her face. The horrendous thought wouldn't go away. *Oh man, my Mom would have a cow.* Lexie gathered her courage and the words came tumbling out. "Has there ever been a vampire - Vampire Executioner?" *Hells bells, I can't believe I just said that.*

His face grew stern, his eyes cold.

"That will never happen." He rose and gripped her shoulders so hard she flinched. "Your humanity is too precious to me. To turn a Divinati descendant into a Strygoi would be an abomination and probably get me beheaded."

"It wouldn't be my first choice," she retorted, twisting in his grasp. Lexie tried to free her shoulders but his grip was too strong. She scowled at him. "Well has there ever been?" Shocked at the vehemence in her tone and that those words kept coming out of her mouth.

"No, *ma petite*, not that I know of. What am I saying? I will not even discuss the possibility of turning you. You don't know what you ask." He shook her to restore her sanity.

"It's too far-fetched to even consider, right?" She wrenched free of his grasp and continued pacing. *Crap, why does life have to be so damn hard?*

"Do you always pace when you're upset? There are things that complicate this situation even more," he continued. "First, you're a vampire executioner, sworn to hunt and kill vampires. If I hurt a human being, you would be forced to execute me."

"Don't go there," Lexie said, stopping in front of him. "And yes, I always pace when I am upset." She frowned. "I could never harm you. Didn't you hear me? I love you, you idiot."

"You have made me very happy." This time she relented as he gathered her into his arms "But no more talk of me turning you."

Despite their heated discussion, Étienne's body seemed to have a mind of its own and his cock hardened as Lexie slipped her arms around his neck and pressed her body against his. She took advantage of the moment. "Can't we at least discuss the consequences...other than the obvious ones?"

"Enough, I told you I would never consider it."

"Please darlin', humor me just a little."

He pulled away and shook his head said, "You won't let this go will you?"

"Nope."

"Shit! *Ma petite.* You are like a dog with a bone." He ran his hands down her arms and held her hands. "If, and that's a huge if, at some point I were the one to turn you, I would have to suck you dry. I would have to kill you, and that much human blood would throw me back to the dark side. I am unwilling to risk that darkness even if it means losing you."

She chose her next words carefully. "Then, when the time comes, we'll just have to figure out how to do that without turnin' you to the dark side."

Étienne held her kissing the top of her head.

"What if someone else turned me?"

Étienne shoved her away and she tumbled to the floor. "Fuck no!" he said. He stood over her his eyes black and his face veiny. His fangs protruded from his mouth "You're mine, now and forever. No other man will ever touch you."

Lexie sprang to her feet challenging him. "Who said anything about it bein' a man. It could be a woman. And, I'm not a piece of property. You don't own me."

Étienne whirled away, and slammed his fist against a wall. He stood with his back to her, hands planted shoulder width on the plaster and Lexie saw him shudder. "I'm sorry *ma petite,*" he murmured. "Of course I don't own you. But the thought of another man or woman tasting your sweet blood sends me into a frenzy."

"Are you jealous E?" Lexie said.

He faced her, all traces of his anger gone. "It's more than jealousy. You are my *Amant de Sang,* my life, my soul. For me we are one and there is no one else."

Lexie didn't understand his feelings, but the torture in his eyes was clear. "Forget I even mentioned it," she said, placing her hand on his cheek. He kissed her palm and nodded.

"But will you at least think about turnin' me?" she said.

"Alright, *ma petite,* I will think about it," he said.

She put her arms around his waist. "Thank you." His vanilla scent soothed her jangled nerves as she stood on tiptoe and kissed him.

"There's one last act we must perform to complete the circle of being Blood Mates. You must drink some of my blood so that we are bound together forever. We will always be able to feel each other. It will not turn you, but as you drink my blood through the years your life will extend beyond a normal human's."

"Ugh, E, that's disgustin'."

"Perhaps to you, *ma petite*; however, you must. I've already had the pleasure of tasting your sweetness." She heard the faint clicking sound of his fangs extending.

Étienne bit his wrist, and held it out to her. "Drink *ma petite*. Please."

Bile rose in her throat but she took his wrist and sniffed the blood before touching her tongue to the trickle oozing from the wound.

"I can't do this. I'm gonna be sick." She ran to the bathroom, and dry heaved into the toilet. Her breath came in painful gasps.

Étienne followed her into the bathroom and touched her back.

"Go away, I can't look at you right now," she moaned. "I need a minute alone. Please."

Étienne retreated to the bed. She heard the quiet squeak of the springs. Lexie rinsed her mouth and leaned against the doorway, her knees wobbly.

"Well that was way more than I can say grace over." She joined him, her breathing still rapid and uneven.

"I'm sorry *ma petite*. I shouldn't have been so insensitive." He took her hand and drew her down. "I've already overwhelmed you with information. I should have waited." He gazed at her, in deep sorrow at her disgust.

"It's okay sugar. I just wasn't ready for the whole meal deal. Now that I've had a minute, I can honestly say that your blood smells like vanilla. It's still gross, but at least it's a little more palatable."

"Nevertheless, I was wrong to force all this on you so soon. Now I must go."

"So soon? I hate the thought of you puttin' yourself in danger, and the possibility you might not return."

"The last thing I want to do is leave you," he said, buttoning his shirt. "The longer the 88P and formula are out there it increases the chance that François and Marielle might find them first."

"Oh, I get it. Love'em and leave'em," she teased, turning away pretending to be angry when her heart was aching.

He darted to her and grabbed her. "You are everything to me. I can't imagine life without you anymore."

She grinned at his reaction. "I was just teasing E. Don't be so dramatic."

He flipped her over his knee, and delivered a smart slap to her butt.

"Ow, that hurt," Lexie said, rubbing the hand print he'd left.

"You deserve worse," he said, kissing the red mark. "But it will have to wait 'til I return."

"With any luck, I will be back tomorrow night."

He leaned over and kissed her. "I will call you and Tom if I need help or if I've been successful in finding another clue." He kissed her again. "Don't worry, *chère*. Everything will be fine."

Lexie caught his hand halting him in mid-stride.

"Can we please try again? I promise to be better."

He touched her face. "Are you certain?"

"Hell no! I'm not certain but I love you enough to try again."

Étienne reopened the wound on his wrist. It began bleeding and the luscious vanilla scent wafted toward her. She took his arm, and touched her tongue to the blood. She placed her mouth around the tiny wound and drank.

Holy crap, I'm actually enjoyin' this. And, surrendering to the pleasure began sucking in earnest. He sighed at her eagerness, but after a couple of minutes he pulled his wrist from her mouth.

"That's enough for now. Too much of a good thing could be dangerous."

Lexie wiped her mouth with the back of her hand, and then licked the blood from it.

"Was that pleasurable for you?"

He kissed her thrusting his tongue between her lips. "You have no idea."

Her lips moved against his sensuous mouth. "Will you at least think about the possibility of turnin' me?"

"Vixen! We'll talk about it when I return from Germany."

"Thank you, sweetheart," she said, satisfied knowing she had won a small victory.

He went to the window and stepped out. He hovered there for a moment then disappeared into the night.

Lexie lay back on the bed, the taste of blood lingering on her tongue. She had never experienced such happiness or passion with a man. *Too good to be true?*

Now that he was gone, her blood pressure had returned to normal, and she realized she was hungry. She finished dressing in her jeans to raid the kitchen.

One of the stairs creaked as she climbed the stairs to her room. She glanced around and although she couldn't see anything she had the eerie sense she was being watched. She slipped back into her room, stoked the fire in the fireplace, and ate her picnic. She snuggled under the covers and shivered as she recalled their blood ritual. *I can still smell him.*

Chapter 20
Training Begins

Lexie heard a knock on her door, and woke disoriented. The morning had dawned bright and cold. *Étienne*. She could still smell him.

"It's Tom."

"Be there in a minute," she said, and hurried into her work-out clothes, looking forward to a day of strenuous training.

She greeted Tom with a dazzling "Good morning."

"What's good about it? It's 5:40 a.m., cold and dark, and we're about to do a full day of exercise. I'd rather be in my warm bed dreaming of beautiful women."

"You're just gettin' old," she teased and punched him on the shoulder.

"Ouch, that hurt. You're strong." He rubbed his shoulder and grinned at her. "This is gonna be fun."

"I didn't hear from Étienne last night, so I assume he found the Gunter's house and the hidin' place," she said on the way to the stables.

"If he has, then he should be back by this afternoon," Tom replied. They stopped briefly to say hello to Bella and Brute, each horse nuzzling and whinnying as if to say good morning. They entered the training room after passing through a deserted lab.

"Okay, Coach, what's first?"

"We warm up."

They completed a half hour of a bend and stretch routine. Lexie felt her unused muscles coming to life. Limbered up, they ran laps for an hour. Lexie not only kept up to Tom, at one point she was ahead by two laps. She took pity and slowed her pace, running alongside Tom.

"You're fast." Tom panted.

"As fast as a vampire?"

"Hardly, but you're much faster than me."

"I just hope I'm fast enough."

"It's time for yoga," he said as they rounded the last turn. "It's critical for core strength and flexibility, and it will be a part of your daily regimen."

"I've never practiced yoga. All my trainin' has been in self-defense," she replied, wiping the sweat from her face and neck. Tom's T-shirt was plastered to his body and Lexie couldn't help but appreciate his physique.

"Follow my lead," he said. He placed his hands on the matt and extended his backside upward. "This stretch is sometimes called Extended Mountain. It opens the spine and stretches tight chest muscles so your breathing becomes deeper. It fosters mental alertness and physical energy."

"It feels great." She extended her butt as far into the air as she could and glanced over her shoulder at him, grinning. "Are you starin' at my backside?"

"Can't fault a man for appreciating a nice ass." He grinned back at her. "Now we'll go through a series of fairly simple moves without stopping."

For the next hour, they practiced Mountain Pose, Extended Mountain Pose, Standing Forward Bend, Modified Long Staff, Upward Dog, Downward Dog, Knees to Chest, and Bridge, Tom talking her through every move.

"What's next coach?" she said as they lay on the mat to cool down.

"I think you're ready to learn Savate." He rose and approached the large screen TV that was located at one end of the gym. "This forty-five minute video will give you the history. After lunch, we'll begin with some basic moves. I suspect you to be way ahead of the game given your training in self-defense."

"I'm excited. I'd never heard of Savate until Étienne mentioned it."

She sat cross-legged and for the next forty-five minutes she was speechless watching the fighters punching and kicking their way through a bout of an old and deadly art.

"Well butter my butt and call me a biscuit. I had no idea!" Lexie said as the video ended. "I thought I was already well-trained, but that was extraordinary. How long do you think it'll take me to get good?"

"Not long," Tom replied. "You're already in great physical shape. Primarily it'll be teaching you the techniques."

"I want to begin now," she said, glancing at her watch. "It's only ten and we've got a good two hours before lunch. Can we start?"

"Now's as good a time as any." He tossed her a pair of boxing gloves and donned a pair himself. "The sooner you're up to speed, the better. At some point we'll outfit you with the traditional boots. Today we'll work in our bare feet to avoid injury."

"What, afraid I'll hurt you?"

"No, actually, I'm afraid I'll hurt you."

"Ha, that'll be a cold day in hell. Do your worst."

Tom delivered a quick blow to her chin. He followed with a roundhouse kick which deposited her on her butt.

"Hey, no fair, I wasn't ready!"

He smiled and pulled her to her feet.

"Now that we've established who's boss, we'll begin. The first move I want to teach you is the Fouette or whip kick. When this is executed properly it can not only break your opponent's nose it can drive the nose bone into the brain."

"And that does what?"

"It will kill a human and stun a vampire giving you an opportunity to kill." He shifted his weight and slowly but deliberately delivered a soft blow to her head with his leg.

"You try it. Remember it's one fluid movement."

Lexie shifted back and forth a couple of times to find her balance, and she executed the kick. Her leg connected with his shoulder missing his head. He reeled sideways catching himself just before hitting the mat.

"Sorry, I didn't mean to kick so hard."

He rubbed his shoulder where she had struck him. "No worries, you'll get the hang of it. Do it again."

For the next thirty minutes Lexie practiced the kick, each time with more accuracy. When she had executed the kick perfectly and gained control over her force, Tom stopped her.

"You're a quick study," he said, mopping his face with a towel.

She dried her face dripping with sweat. "What's next?"

"The Chas Bas and this one we must take slowly and softly as it can do serious and permanent damage to the leg or knee cap. I'll demonstrate first, and then you can practice."

He showed her where to position her hands to block the kick. He rocked back and struck at her leg with the heel of his foot. Although delivered gently, Lexie felt the force behind it that could fell an opponent and break bones. Tom executed the move several more times, increasing his force.

"Now it's your turn," he said.

The Chas Bas was easier for Lexie, and she mastered it quickly. On the last kick, Tom did a leg sweep that dumped them both on the floor with him on top.

"Ouch, that jarred my preserves," she said. "No fair. Now get off me you big lug."

"Sorry Lex, you're right, that wasn't fair. But I do like the way this feels."

She felt his cock growing hard against her belly.

"Hell's bells Tom. What the fuck are you doin'?" she wriggled away from him. His cheeks flamed red with embarrassment.

"Damn it Lex, haven't you guessed? I care for you. Why do you think I've been so disgruntled at your relationship with Étienne?"

She sprang to her feet and glared down at him as he scrambled to his feet. "You never said anything."

"Shit this is embarrassing." He grabbed a towel and covered his erection. "I probably never would've told you, but you felt so good underneath me, I blurted it out."

"Well, if this isn't a pig in a poke. Em and I often wondered why you never had a relationship. Em had a huge crush on you and we wondered why you never seemed interested."

He took a step toward her and she stepped back, keeping her distance.

"I think we both had a bit of a crush on you. Your timin' sucks."

He gave her a lopsided grin. "You had a crush on me? I never would have guessed. You were always so formal and stand-offish. Why didn't you say something or give me a clue?"

"Because, you idiot, you're my boss. It wasn't kosher. Besides it would have hurt Em."

He moved fast crushing her in his arms and kissing her. His lips felt warm and inviting. She struggled against him, her loyalty to Étienne overcoming lust. But as his tongue thrust into her mouth and his cock pushed against her body, feelings for him that had been suppressed for years betrayed her and she responded. His hand moved to her breast, teasing her taut nipple and Lexie whimpered against his lips.

Without warning images of the previous night with Étienne dominated her mind. She saw his face as clearly as if he was beside her. Stunned by the vividness of the images, and now uncomfortable and upset, she placed her hands on Tom's chest and shoved with all her might. He landed in a heap on the mat.

He scrambled to his feet. "What the hell Lex?"

"You butt-head, you know I have feelin's for Étienne and he has feelin's for me. Don't take advantage of what I once felt for you a long time ago." There was an awkward pause.

"How can you have feelings for him? He's a blood-sucking vampire, and you're a vampire executioner. How can that ever work?"

"Hell's bells, don't you think we've discussed that? We're tryin' to cross one bridge at a time." She paused. "Étienne is convinced I'm his *Amant de Sang*," She stopped herself from telling Tom about their blood-sharing. Nor was she ready to reveal their talk of him turning her. *He'd probably really have a cow over that one.*

"Talk about complicated and dangerous for all of us." Tom said. "At least with me you wouldn't have to worry about executing me someday."

"Is that why you called Cassie? To try and break us up?"

"Bugger! I hoped he would keep that to himself."

"No such luck, and I'm glad he had the sense to tell me. Thunder crap, what do we do now?"

Tom scowled at her "His *Amant de Sang*? Do you mean to tell me you might be his Bloodmate? I've heard the legend. I thought that could only happen between vampires."

"Apparently not. Étienne has suspected for some time, but last night when we...," she paused hesitating to continue, then went on. "You know, when we um made love, he said he was sure."

"You made love to him? Bollocks! This just gets better and better. Lex, even if you were his Amant de Sang, that doesn't change the way I feel."

"It doesn't matter," she said. "Despite the complications, I love him, and I'd appreciate you not throwin' a monkey wrench in the middle of that. You've always been a great friend and I don't want to lose you. Not to mention, Étienne depends on you to be at his side. Does he know how you feel?"

"Bloody hell, no! He thinks we're just good friends."

He waited and gave her his lopsided grin that used to make her heart skip a beat.

"Damn Lex, I want to go on record that I'm against it. It's a huge mistake. But I care for both of you and the dangers we're facing make it critical that nothing separates us. I promise he'll never know. You have my word as a gentleman and an Englishman."

She shook her head and looked him square in the eyes. "I think you have to tell him."

"You're joking right? He'd probably throw a wobbly if he knew."

She glared at him, hands on her hips.

"Bloody hell, you're serious," he said.

"Absofrigginlutely, we have to be able to trust each other completely."

"Bugger!" I'd rather not distract him right now. I'll tell him as soon as he gets back."

"Good, that's settled then," she sighed. *I doubt we've seen the end of this pickle.*

"What's settled?" Claudette asked, sauntering into the room.

Fuck, I hope she didn't overhear that.

"Tom was just givin' me the low down on our trainin' this afternoon," Lexie lied.

"She's a quick study, and her strength is developing nicely," Tom said.

"Ah, I see," Claudette replied. "Has the blind pig found the acorn?"

Lexie laughed at her Southernism pronounced with a French accent. "Are you teasing me?" She wondered if she and Claudette could be Best-Friends-Forever. Despite her mild distrust of the vampire, Lexie missed having a woman to talk to. *Wouldn't that be a trip.*

"Oui," Claudette replied. "I think your little phrases are très quaint."

"Stick with me, I have tons of them."

"And Tom is pushing you hard, *n'est-ce pas?*"

"Tom's a great teacher. I can't imagine a better one."

Tom grinned. "I've been taking it easy on you since this is your first day. That time is over. This afternoon we'll find out what you're made of. I predict that it's only going to take three or four weeks to fully train you."

"That's good news, right?"

"Very good news," he replied. "With François and Marielle escalating their attacks, having you ready will be a real asset for the Society."

Her stomach rumbled.

"I think we need to feed her," Claudette said.

He glanced at his watch. "Righty-oh – it's lunch time. Claudette will you be joining us?"

"Sure. I just need to check on a couple of things in case Étienne calls. He doesn't like it when I don't have answers."

The buffet was a healthy delight. Lexie helped herself to generous portions of salad, fruit, home-made yogurt and grilled chicken, and wolfed it down. Tom joined her and for several minutes they ate in silence, content to enjoy the meal.

"I wonder what's keepin' Claudette," Lexie said just as Claudette and André entered the room.

"There's word of another vampire attack in the town of Gap," Claudette said. "François and Marielle are ramping up."

Tom's cell rang preventing any further discussion, and Lexie held her breath hoping it was Étienne.

"Étienne, old man, how are you? We're just having lunch, and Claudette and André are here with us. How's the business going? That's too bad. We did start her training this morning and it's going smashingly. Do you want to speak to her?" Tom handed her his phone.

"I overheard Tom say that your business wasn't goin' as well as you'd hoped. You'll be gone another night? No worries. I love the trainin'. Okay, we'll see you tomorrow. Wait Claudette needs to speak with you."

Claudette grabbed the phone and stepped outside. Lexie heard her telling Étienne about the attack. She nodded a couple of times before disconnecting.

Claudette handed Tom his phone and he headed for the door with Lexie in tow. "Time to get back to work," he said. Tom glanced behind them.

"Étienne couldn't say much with Claudette and André in the room. We're still not sure who the traitor is," he whispered.

"I can't believe it could be Claudette or André. They both seem so trustworthy."

"We can't take chances. At this point it could be anyone. For all you know, it could be me."

Lexie punched him in the shoulder. "You ever say that again and I'll snatch you bald-headed. You're the one person I'm absolutely sure of."

Tom grinned at her outburst. "What the heck does that mean?"

"It's what we say in the South to someone when they say somethin' really stupid, or what a mom says to a child when they've said or done somethin' bad."

"Sometimes your 'Southernisms' confound me."

They walked in silence for a few minutes. "It's odd that Étienne hasn't found the next clue," Lexie said.

201

"I'm sure he'll find it and call us. Right now, we need to focus."

"What's first," Lexie asked as they walked through the lab. A few people waved at them, and Lexie felt the budding of a few new friendships.

"We'll warm up again, and then we'll continue with Savate. Later I have a surprise for you. A special exercise that will test your ability to sense vampires."

For the next hour, Tom pushed Lexie hard, making her practice certain moves and exercises until she could execute them automatically. She sweat profusely, and there were times when she was almost in tears from the pain in her muscles, but Tom never relented. He kept encouraging and working her, pushing her beyond her old limits. Several times she hated him and wanted to quit. Then, a voice in her head shouted, *Thunder crap girl! You're a vampire executioner.* You have no right to give up became her mantra.

Tom took a stop watch from one of the benches.

"What's that for?"

"We're going to do a nonstop round of fifteen minutes. It's time to test your stamina and see if you can put the kicks and punches together as if you were in a real fight."

"Am I ready for that? I'm just gettin' comfortable."

"I think so, and it's important for us to have an exact read on your stamina. Once I push the button and we start, there's no stopping until one of us is on the mat or the fifteen minutes is up. Ready? Go."

Tom feinted as she threw a Fouette to his head. He used her momentum against her and delivered a swift blow to her jaw, and she stumbled. She recovered and whirled so fast he was caught off guard as she delivered a Chasse Bas to his upper thigh. He barely had time to side-step as the blow could have broken his leg. He saw she was a little off balance and took advantage with a leg sweep which dumped her on her butt. She sprang to her feet without hesitation, and delivered a series of blows to Tom's head and midriff.

He struggled to protect himself. One punch caught him on the chin. Dazed, he didn't see the leg sweep coming and found himself on his back as the stopwatch dinged. She grinned down at him, her knee planted on his chest.

"I don't know about you, but I've had enough for today," he said. "You have incredible strength and speed, but you need Étienne's reflexes." He threw her a towel as he rubbed his sore chin. She noticed that the awkwardness and restraint that had been there earlier was gone. It made her happy. The door to the training room opened, and twenty of the château's staff walked in in single file, Claudette in the lead.

"Perfect timing," Tom said.

"What's goin' on?" Lexie asked.

"It's time for you to hone your vampire detection capability," he replied. The twenty or so staff had lined up along one wall of the room. "Étienne and I noticed that when you met André and the others, you had a definite reaction. Can you remember what happened?"

"Yep, my scalp itched like crazy. The same thing happened when I met Claudette for the first time and shook her hand."

"Good," he said. "What I want you to do is shake each person's hand, notice if your scalp itches. I want you to also notice if there's any reaction prior to touching them. Take your time, we're in no hurry."

She stood there for a minute, eying the staff, a little embarrassed.

"Come on Lex, this is a crucial part of your training and it could save your life, or mine or Étienne's in the future."

She walked up to the staff member at the head of the line. He was one of the scientists from the lab. He stuck out his hand she took it.

203

"Nothin'," she said. She moved to the next, one of the maids from the house. She took the outstretched hand and her scalp itched like crazy.

"She's a vampire."

"Did you notice or feel anything prior to touching her?" Tom asked.

"Nope, and I'm embarrassed at this whole process." She looked apologetically at the staff. "I'm sorry guys."

"Let that go," Tom said. "None of them object to this exercise. They are here to support you."

She nodded, and continued to move down the line, shaking each person's hand. Some elicited a reaction and others none. She felt more at ease with each person, and had just moved to the head cook when she noticed her heart rate accelerate. She took his hand, and her scalp itched.

"Thunder crap, this time I noticed that my heart rate accelerated before I touched him," she said.

"Good, Lex, good," Tom said. "Keep going."

As she progressed through the line she noticed her heart rate accelerated before each vampire so she was aware of their status, vampire or human.

"Oh man, this is freaky," she said, shaking Claudette's hand. "What a gift. Who would've thought that this would be part of being a vampire executioner?"

She found Tom, smiling from ear to ear. "Good work," he said. "Thanks everyone. We appreciate your participation in this exercise. Claudette, we need to find more staff, preferably one's Lexie is unfamiliar with as this will be part of her daily training. Can you see to that?"

"Of course," she replied.

"Wow, I feel like I've been given the keys to the kingdom," Lexie said. "Besides noticin' my negative reaction to André and a few others how did you and Étienne know?"

"Your Grandfather," he replied. "Jeremy had the same ability. His heart rate rose every time he was near a vampire, and after he touched them, his scalp itched. Your Dad didn't have the instinct but we were hoping that you would."

"Well, this is just gooder'n grits," she said. "What now coach?"

"I don't want you stiffening up between now and tomorrow when we start again. Time to hit the sauna and hot tub. Enjoy yourself. It's 4:30. Dinner's at seven. I'll see you then."

Lexie called over her shoulder as she jogged toward the ladies dressing room, "Come find me if Étienne calls. I'm anxious to hear from him."

"I will."

She changed into a bathing suit, headed for the hot tub and spent a half hour soaking in the heated water. The jets pounded on muscles beginning to stiffen. When the timer dinged, she entered the sauna and spent fifteen minutes luxuriating in the hot, dry air to relax her body and clear her head.

Lexie was fresh from the sauna when Tom stuck his head in the door of the dressing room.

"Are you decent? Étienne's on the phone, and he wants to talk to both of us."

"Come on in." Lexie motioned for Tom to join her. They retreated into the sauna as the thick cedar walls would protect their conversation from a vampire's acute hearing.

Tom punched the speaker button. "Can you hear us? We're in one of the sauna rooms. We can't be overheard in here."

"I can hear you clearly," Étienne said. "Is Lexie there with you?"

"I'm here E. Are you havin' any luck?"

"When I arrived in Kronberg early this morning, I went straight to the Gunter's home and then to the gazebo. I have been unsuccessful in finding the loose stone. I called hoping you and Tom were alone. Do you think you can walk me to the stone?"

"I think so. Start at the entrance," she instructed.

205

"I'm there now."

"Is there a picnic table and benches in the center of the floor?"

"Yes, I see them."

"Walk straight to the table until you just touch the end."

"Okay, I'm there."

"Perfect, now turn to your right, or maybe it's your left. No, I'm pretty sure it's your right. From the end of the table walk ahead five feet. The stone should be either directly under your feet, or slightly in front of you."

There was silence on the other end of the line as Étienne tapped on the stones.

"I haven't found any that are loose, and I've searched both under my feet and in a two-foot radius around me."

Lexie rubbed her forehead. "Rats. Go back to the spot at the end of the table, and try the other direction."

"I'm there now."

There was a minute of silence and more tapping.

"Shit!" came his frustrated voice. "There's none here either."

"That's impossible. I know it's there." Lexie looked at Tom. "Any ideas?"

"The variable is the table. Which direction did the table face when you were there?"

"I think the ends were facing each side of the gazebo. In other words, standing at the entrance or gate, the side of the table with the benches would be directly in front of you."

"It's not that way now. The table must have been turned around," Étienne said. "The end is now directly in front of the gate. Hang on a sec."

Lexie could hear the scraping of the table and benches as Étienne turned them around.

"I'm starting again."

Lexie and Tom were quiet as they listened to Étienne repeat his movements, and then the soft tapping as he checked the stones.

"I found it. And there's a box you mentioned. There's a note inside. It's another clue."

"Read it to us," Lexie said.

"Not over the phone. I should be back at the château later tonight. Be careful both of you."

"You be careful," she said.

"I wish I were there with him." Lexie said.

"Me too. But, we're not, and it's imperative that we act as normally as possible. We don't arouse any suspicion."

Lexie sighed. "I know, and actin' normally doesn't make it any easier. I'll meet you in the dining room at seven. I want to freshen up a little before dinner."

"See you in a bit," he replied, heading for the door.

Dinner passed with no sign of Claudette or André, and Tom was oddly silent and withdrawn. Too tired to care, Lexie fought against falling asleep at the table.

"You look exhausted." Tom observed.

A huge yawn caught her unawares and she covered her mouth in embarrassment. "I am. I think I'll hit the sack and get a good night's sleep. 5:30 will come soon enough."

"Are we good?" Tom said.

"What do you mean?"

"I mean are we good after our little incident earlier?"

"Absolutely. I've got nothin' goin' on about it. You?"

"My feelings haven't changed, but I'm okay with your and Étienne's relationship."

"I'm glad – you're important to both of us. Anything else?"

"Nope. I'll be at your door at 5:30 sharp."

"I can't wait to sink into those down pillows."

She left Tom at the table nursing a glass of wine. Back in her room, the fire needed stoking and she added logs so it would continue to burn a few more hours.

The night beckoned to her and she looked out thinking of Étienne. Soon they would be together. *I hope E's okay.* Lexie's heart rate sped up and a shadow flitted across her balcony. She stuck her head out and scanned both directions. Nothing.

"Hello? Is someone out there? Show yourself."

The only sound was the wind as it whistled through the trees. She locked the door and drew the drapes.

"I *am* paranoid," she muttered. She snuggled under the covers and her thoughts drifted back to Étienne. His voice, barely a whisper, came to her as she dozed.

"*Ma petite,* you are in danger."

"E?" She turned on the lamp and peered around the room hoping he had returned. No one was there.

I must have been dreamin'. She nestled under the covers, exhaustion forcing her to sleep.

Chapter 21
The Abduction

A coppery stench filled her nostrils. Lexie was colder than she'd ever been in her life. Her hands and arms were covered in blood. The more she struggled, the tighter a pair of arms held her in a vice-like grip. Her neck hurt and she could feel warm blood oozing down her chest dripping onto her arms and hands. She smelled vanilla – Étienne, he's changing me. Thunder crap, am I a vampire now? I can't be a vampire. I'm a vampire executioner. She gave a mighty shove and was free. She jerked a wooden stake from her boot and began to run blindly in the murky grey night. Her tongue felt slippery and thick. Am I drinking his blood? The vanilla scent grew stronger than ever.

She thought she saw François in the distance. I have to catch him. I have to kill the vampire. I have to kill. She ran, crashing through the underbrush, brambles and thorns catching at her clothes and skin. Her prey was slightly ahead. With a sudden burst of speed she caught him. Damn! It was a female. Marielle? Without hesitation Lexie drove a stake through her back, into her heart up to the hilt. The kill felt good. She thought vampires vaporized when stabbed, but Marielle collapsed face down, her long brown hair splayed out on the ground. She bent down, turned the body over and recognized her own face. Oh crap, I've killed myself.

Lexie woke with a start, dragging her consciousness back from her nightmare. Her heart pounded from leftover adrenalin, but now she remembered she'd heard a noise. Her scalp itched. *There's a vampire in here.*

209

She smelled vanilla and strong hands gripped her shoulders. "E?" she whispered. Her heart continued to race. She was flipped over and found herself staring into glittering blue eyes. *Not Étienne.* Before she could scream a cold hand clamped over her mouth and another clutched her throat.

"Do not scream, *ma chère*," said a deep voice reminiscent of Étienne's. "And don't bother to struggle. I'm much stronger than you and it will not go well."

Thunder crap, it's François. She struggled to free her mouth. Arms of steel encircled her legs, and the hand gripping her throat tightened restricting her air supply.

"She's a fighter, this one," François said, squeezing her esophagus.

"I warned you she was strong. Secure her tightly, or she'll cause problems," a familiar female voice said.

In that moment Lexie knew Claudette was the betrayer. She heard gun shots and shouting. *Tom, help. I need you.* Lexie renewed her efforts to break free. It was useless. Even with her superior strength, she was no match for two vampires. She stopped fighting. Her only hope was to wait for a chance to get away.

The hand gripping her throat relaxed, and without hesitation, Lexie bucked, freeing her arms and one of her legs. She punched hard with her free leg and felt it connect with a body. Claudette grunted in what Lexie hoped was pain. At the same time Lexie threw a right hook which landed solidly on François' chin and bit down on his hand. She broke skin and blood trickled onto her tongue. *Nasty.*

"*Merde*," François swore. "Get a rope around her legs!"

"I'm trying," Claudette shouted.

Lexie continued to swing hard with her free leg while attempting to land another punch to François' face. She was flat on her back under his weight, at a definite disadvantage. Astride her now, he grabbed her wrists with one hand and punched with the other. Lexie was temporarily stunned by a blow to her head.

She heard François' order. "Tie her now. The bitch bit me."

Biting wasn't the only thing Lexie wanted to inflict on François.

"Got her," Claudette confirmed. Lexie felt the pinch of a rope around her ankles. She fought off the effects of François' punch. Now that her legs were bound, she had no leverage and flopped about ineffectively as François bound her wrists to the rope at her feet.

"Can you handle her from here?" Claudette asked. "I need to go downstairs and see how the fight is going. Our men may need help."

"Go," François replied. "As soon as I've made sure her bindings are secure and shot her full of sedative, I'll be down." He yanked hard on the ropes, and Lexie felt the loss of circulation to her hands and feet.

"Ah *ma petite*, you are beautiful," he purred. "No wonder my father has fallen for you. Perhaps I should sample the goodies."

Hell's bells, he even uses E's pet name for me. "Pig! Touch me and you die," she snarled.

He chuckled, "You might enjoy what I have to offer."

His hands fondled her breasts, and to her dismay her nipples hardened. She felt herself moistening against her will. The vanilla scent lulling her mind. *This can't be happening.*

"Your Dad is gonna whup you like a rented mule if I don't get you first," she hissed. Her anger countered the lust. "You and that older-than-dirt-bitch killed Em. She was a sister to me, and as soon as I get the chance you are both goin' down."

"*Il n'a pas d'importance,*" François replied, scoffing at her threats. "My father is an old fool and not worth worrying about. And as for you, we will resume this pleasure later."

"You bet your evil patootie we'll resume this later. But it won't be pleasurable for either you or Marielle." A gag was shoved in her mouth.

He grabbed her arm, stuck her with a syringe and jammed the plunger. He tossed her over his shoulder like a sack of potatoes and headed down the staircase.

Fighting against the effects of the sedative and sick to her stomach from the ride slung over François' shoulder, it hurt when she was dumped on the floor. She could see Tom and Claudette fighting through blurred eyes. Tom seemed to be holding his own against the vampire's greater strength and speed.

"Tom," she cried. She shook her head to try and clear it, and with every fiber of her being strained against the ropes that bound her hands and feet. She saw the wooden stake in his hand, and rivulets of sweat ran down his face as he dodged and feinted. His T-shirt was soaked with perspiration from the battle. He was bloodied and weakening as he succumbed to Claudette's superior strength.

François joined Claudette in the fight against him. Lexie saw Tom redouble his efforts and he seemed to recover.

"Hang on Lex," Tom shouted, ducking as a crushing blow from François whizzed by his head.

She felt her ropes give a little, and concentrated on freeing her hands and feet. She pulled and strained trying to stretch the length between her wrists and ankles. She wriggled frantically, and managed to free her hands. Without wasting a precious second, Lexie tore at the rope binding her legs and leapt to her feet. She struck out at Claudette with her left leg. Still dizzy from the drug, what should have been a bone shattering blow, bounced harmlessly off the vampire's hip. Lexie landed off balance.

"Lex, look out," Tom shouted.

She turned in time to see François coming at her, his face no longer handsome but grotesque. *Hell's bells, I wish I was wearing boots.* Lexie's training kicked in. She shifted her weight back raised her balled fists, and upended François with a leg sweep, but he was up so fast she barely had time to blink. He caught her with a solid blow to her jaw. She feinted to soften the punch, and her eyes briefly caught Tom's. That was all François needed. He whacked Lexie on the back of the head with a vase and she dropped like a rock.

Lexie labored to get to her feet, her vision fuzzy, she watched in horror as Claudette grabbed Tom from behind. François lunged forward and sunk his fangs into Tom's neck. Lexie heard the gurgle as François pierced his jugular. Claudette released Tom, and he landed in a heap at Lexie's side. His eyes still held life as he struggled to say something. Blood gushed from the hole in his throat.

"Sorry, Lex, tell Étienne to…" His eyes glazed over, his body convulsed and was still.

She gathered him in her arms. "Oh, sweet Jesus, Tom."

He did not respond. She sat and rocked him with tears streaming down her cheeks, unable to comprehend what had happened.

"Give her more sedative and let's get out of here," Claudette snarled. She kicked viciously at Lexie with her foot. "We don't know how long our men can keep the château guards busy, and we don't need any more trouble from her. Besides, we need to find out what's happening with Marielle and Étienne. I'll take Tom."

"I'm injecting her neck this time. That should do the trick," François said.

Lexie felt the pin prick, and this time, she surrendered. Her last thoughts were of Tom, and then Étienne, and what would happen when he returned.

Chapter 22
Étienne and Kendrick MacDougal

Étienne flew over the snow-covered Italian Alps. Their craggy peaks sparkled in the bright moonlight like diamonds. Despite his eagerness to return to the château and Lexie, he reflected on their beauty. This was the part teleporting he loved, and although it somewhat weakened him, he took advantage of it whenever he could. It was much preferable to a plane, rewarded with sights like those ones below. He smelled the purity of fresh snow. The taste was crisp and clean. Suddenly his gut wrenched, and his mind opened. *Lexie's in danger and she's hurt.*

The strength of their blood bond pulled at him. He hovered over the mountains, distracted, and it took all his will power not to plummet to the earth. Something struck him in the head and he dropped several hundred feet. Étienne shook his head, turning just in time to dodge another crushing blow. *Merde who the…?* He ascended with a whoosh and saw a small blonde whirlwind heading towards him. *Marielle.*

Marielle's bell like voice rang out. "Hello Count. Your beloved is definitely in trouble. Our forces have attacked the Society, and Françoise has kidnapped her. She will be killed if you don't give me what I want. We know that Emma left you clues for the antiserum and its formula. If you don't hand them over, Lexie will die. "

"Even if I had it, I would never let it fall into your possession."

Étienne charged at Marielle with every intention to rip off her head. "If you harm one hair on her head, I will…"

"You'll do what?" she taunted dodging the impact.

He charged again. *Time to die.* This time he was quicker, and his blow to her head threw her a hundred feet away. He followed moving fast. He caught her before she could recover and delivered a killer blow to her stomach.

"You are much stronger than I thought you'd be," she gasped She darted away holding her stomach, avoiding a second devastating punch.

Driven by fury and his fear for Lexie, Étienne attacked viciously. The sound of their conflict echoed off the mountains as they charged and feinted leaving wisps of misplaced air in their wake. It was obvious Marielle used her size and speed to evade him, but Étienne was more adept and he delivered several blows to her tiny frame. She was tiring, bleeding from her head and mouth.

"You win for now Count," Marielle cried out. "But don't forget we have Lexie, and her life is in your hands. If we don't have what we want by tomorrow evening, she dies."

She darted off and Étienne watched her flee torn between pursuing his nemesis and hurrying to Lexie's side. Decision made, he soared toward Grignon and the château. He punched the speed dial for Tom's number. It went to voice mail.

"Shit, Tom, pick up!" He tried Lexie's number. Same result *Are they dead?* He left a message for Tom. "What's happening? Call me back as soon as you get this message."

The remainder of his journey seemed agonizingly long. The lights from the château appeared from miles away. Many bonfires burned. Étienne watched his men throwing bodies into them, and he feared the worst. This was the first time François and Marielle had attempted such a bold attack and he knew the damage would be devastating.

He found Claudette standing on the front porch giving orders, trying to maintain order.

"Thank goodness you're back. Something awful has happened," she cried, wringing her hands.

Étienne grabbed her by the arm. "Where's Lexie?"

Claudette jerked her arm away. "She's been kidnapped. And, Tom has been murdered."

"Then Marielle was telling the truth," he said.

"What do you mean?"

"She attacked me about an hour ago as I was traveling home. She said François had attacked the château and that Lexie had been kidnapped. I thought she might be lying to force me to give up the 88P and formula. I fought her off and she fled. What happened?"

"About three hours ago, André and the guards were patrolling the perimeter when they heard approaching vehicles. André sounded the alarm, but there wasn't time. Several helicopters flew overhead and about a hundred of François and Marielle's army descended. During the fight, someone managed to open the front gate and we were overrun. While our men fought them off, François must have slipped upstairs and taken her. We think Tom tried to stop him, but François killed him. I saw François teleport away Lexie over his shoulder. They headed west."

He grabbed Claudette's shoulders and shook her hard. "Why didn't you do something? Where were you? Where's André?"

Claudette wrenched free from his grasp. "I was busy fighting and so was André. We had our hands full. We're lucky we didn't suffer greater casualties."

Étienne's voice was husky with emotion. "Where's Tom? I want to see him."

"He's gone. André saw one of François' men load him into a helicopter and take off. We're assuming they've taken him to their stronghold."

Étienne brushed past her and entered the house. He paused at the carnage. More than twenty bodies lay strewn about the entry way. He smelled Tom's blood at the foot of the stairs.

"Where's André now?"

"He's with the men, tending to the injured."

"Bring me Brute, we're going after them." He ran for the stables, and Claudette scurried after him.

"Not a good idea," she said. We've no idea where their stronghold is. Our infiltrators, Jacques and Emile, informed us that they were moving a few days ago, but we haven't heard from them since.

"Brute can track them by the scent of Tom's blood."

Claudette blocked him. "Still a bad idea. Our forces have been depleted. Those who survived are tired and injured. It would be suicide to go after them now. We should wait until daylight when they are at their weakest to attack."

"I can't wait. Lexie's life is in danger. "

"They won't kill her until they have their hands on the 88P formula."

"And you know this how?"

"I don't *know* anything. It just makes sense. In the meantime, we can try to contact Jacques and Emile. Perhaps they can find out François and Marielle's plans."

Étienne grabbed her shoulders and stared into her eyes, sure she'd had a hand in the attack. She was shielding her thoughts from him and he knew. He struggled to compose himself. What she'd said made sense, even if it was further treachery.

"You're right," he said releasing her shoulders. "If the men are as exhausted as you say, they deserve a few hours to recuperate."

"What about the message to Emile and Jacques?"

"It's a good idea. I'll send it myself. Where is André?"

"He's with the men in the barracks."

"I'll join him. I need to assess the damage to our men. I want you to start the clean-up of the château." Claudette headed for the château and Étienne joined André and his men. He was appalled at their condition. All of them had multiple injuries.

"How many did we lose?" Étienne said.

"Ten, and as you can see the rest are sorely injured."

"What about François and Marielle's losses?"

"Even though they outnumbered us, their losses were much greater. We estimate fifty. We're burning the remains." André paused. "I'm sorry about Tom. And we did our best to protect Lexie."

"I have no doubt."

"There's something else," André said. "This was an inside job. They knew too much about our security system and the layout of the compound for it to be a blind attack. There's a traitor in our midst."

"Who?"

"I'd rather not say until I'm sure."

Étienne's head snapped around. "Name! Now!"

"It's hard to believe, but the evidence points to Claudette."

"Are you sure?"

"One of our men saw her hold Tom while François tore his throat open. He'd have no reason to lie."

Despite his own intuition confirming it was Claudette, Étienne was aware of a small doubt. *Is he throwing suspicion away from himself?*

"Which man? I want to talk to him personally."

"Unfortunately, he was killed as the rogue army retreated."

Convenient. "That bitch – time to kill," he said to assure André. His fangs descended as he turned to go. André caught his arm and stopped him.

"Wait, I think there's a chance we could use this to our advantage. We don't know where François and Marielle's compound is. Claudette must know and could lead us there."

Étienne decided to play along. He took a deep breath, and his fangs retracted as he calmed. "I won't kill her just yet. But when the time comes, she's mine. I want the satisfaction of ripping her head from her body."

"What about Lexie's rescue?" André asked. "I want to leave now, but the men..."

"Have them rest until sunrise," Étienne said. "We'll leave then."

Pain and love sent Étienne back to Lexie's room. He shut the door behind him and sniffed, her delicate fragrance permeating the air. He sat on the bed where they had made passionate love the night before. Flashes of their time together haunted his memory. He could still taste her blood, and despite his anger and grief, his cock hardened. All he wanted was to taste her and feel her beneath him.

He detected the distinct odors of François and Claudette. *Merde, it was Claudette all along.* He suppressed the urge to kill her and swore to the night.

"You will pay with your life along with that bitch Marielle. I don't care what it takes. I'll never stop until I send the two of you to Hell."

The crinkle of paper in his coat pocket, reminded him of the third clue. He read the lines several times.

Where the Picts and Celts once roamed,

A sea loch, remote and beautiful spreads before you.

There on the promontory, stands one of a kind,

Find what you are seeking in the gift.'

"I should ask Tom....." Tightness in his chest reminded him that his friend was gone. *I'm on my own.*

He read it again and this time his mind registered the last line. 'Find what you are seeking in the gift'. Must be the 88P and formula, but where? He read once more and the puzzle clicked into place. Sea loch and where the Picts and Celts once roamed.

That has to be the Highlands of Scotland. Kendrick. I must contact Kendrick.

Étienne pictured the handsome Scot, who served as his second-in-command. He reached for his phone and hesitated. His one-thousand-year-old friend had a strong penchant for human blood. In Kendrick's years before joining the Society he had been indiscriminate in his slaughter of humans until he had fallen in love with a human named Ariel. After she was murdered by Strygoi, Kendrick had almost lost his mind. His killing spree of vampires through Scotland was infamous and it was reported that he had done away with more than two hundred. Étienne had sought him out and persuaded him to join the Society. But his taste for human blood remained a concern and prevented Étienne from trusting him completely. He knew that Kendrick had refrained since he had begun to take 88P, but Étienne feared it wouldn't take much for him to revert to the dark side. *Do I dare risk letting him in on this?*

Étienne paced. He had no choice. He had to take the risk. He punched in Kendrick's speed dial number and heard the phone begin to ring. His mind reached out to his lieutenant hundreds of miles away. *Kendrick I need you. Calling now, please pick up.* Telepathy was risky. Other vampires had been known to intercept communications, his phone might also be vulnerable, but decided there was less risk. Kendrick's phone rang only once.

"What's up laddie, ye'r voice sounded urgent?" Kendrick asked in his thick Scottish brogue.

"The château's been breached and Lexie's been kidnapped. I have found what I think is Emma's final clue where the formula is hidden. But I need your expertise in deciphering it."

"Wait lad slow down; explain one thing at a time. What happened at the château?"

"François attacked the château tonight while I was in Germany finding the next clue."

"Bugger all, is everyone alright?"

"Tom's dead, and as I said, Lexie's been kidnapped."

"Bloody hell."

"I would have been back in time, but Marielle intercepted me on my way home. I wasted precious time driving her off and by the time I arrived, it was all over. They even took Tom's body. The only way François and his legion could have broken through our defenses is with an insider's help. It was Claudette. She helped François kidnap Lexie and kill Tom."

"So Claudette was the traitor and not André."

| Her smell was all over Lexie's room along with François'."

"Is Claudette still alive?"

"Yes, she's still here. I haven't let on that I know of her treachery.
"

"And what of Lexie?"

"She's still alive. I'd feel it if she was dead. "I'll send Jacques and Emile a message. We haven't heard from them in several days."

"Shit, I hope ye haven't lost them too." Kendrick said.

"François and Marielle are using Lexie as leverage to get the formula for 88P." Étienne said. "I don't think they'll kill her until I turn it over, which I will never do, but I have to find it first. I think the clue pertains to Scotland."

"Read it to me," Kendrick said.

"Too dangerous. It could be intercepted."

Étienne felt Kendrick push into his brain. "What are you doing?"

Accessing our blood bond. I've blocked our thoughts from other vampires. Read it.

'Where the Picts and Celts once roamed, a sea loch, remote and beautiful spreads before you, there on the promontory stands one of a kind, find what you are seeking in the gift.' I think the first line must mean the Highlands. I have no idea about the second. The part that reads 'find what you are seeking in the gift' is where I think Emma hid the antiserum and formula. Any ideas?"

221

Emma visited me here not long ago. She took a day trip to Loch Ewe, and a small town called Mellon Charles. The line that reads 'a sea loch, remote and beautiful spreads before you' could be describin' that loch. As I recall, she was completely taken with the Perfume Studio in Mellon Charles. The shop is perched on the edge of the loch. It's unique. She bought gifts for Lexie there. She couldn't stop talking about it. Do you think that could be it?

I think it's worth pursuing. I must go there immediately.

"Hold on. It's not far from Dunollie House and I can be there in minutes. It will take ya at least an hour. I know the proprietor of the shop and if I find something, I can meet ya halfway. I'll contact ya whether I find the formula and 88P or not, so keep ye'r mind focused."

"I'll leave now. Talk to ya in a wee bit."

Étienne sat down in the arm-chair by Lexie's window and stared out willing dawn to come. *Hold on ma petite. I'll be there soon.* His strategy for her rescue was too simple. Swoop in, kill anyone who got in his way, and then flee. It was full of unknowns. If Claudette had been drinking human blood, her strength and speed would be overwhelming. What if she'd given François and Marielle some of her antiserum? Their abilities would be equal to hers and the three of them could easily defeat him and his men. An unthinkable and dangerous idea began to formulate in his mind.

If he took an extra dose of the antiserum and drank human blood, he could gain the speed and strength that would make him virtually indestructible. François and Marielle would be no match for him. There was one ghastly consequence. By doing so, it would turn him back to the dark side, and as far as anyone knew, there was no antidote to this change. *Can I do this and give it up again?*

He reached out with his mind, *'Anastase I need to talk to you. Can you hear me?'*

The ancient Divinati answered so fast it seemed like he'd been waiting for Étienne's summons. *'I'm listening.'*

'We've had a breach here at the château. Tom's dead and Lexie's been kidnapped. I need your counsel.'

There was a long pause and Étienne wondered if Anastase was angry at his plea and had broken their connection. Then the old vampire spoke.

'Illumination is found by putting everything one has in jeopardy.'

Étienne felt more confused than ever. *'Merde, what does that mean?'*

'Figure it out. That's my counsel.'

Anastase broke their telepath connection and Étienne paced mulling over in his head what the Divinati had said. *Put everything I have in jeopardy.*

He fingered the last vial of antiserum remaining from Emma's supply. There was only half of the precious liquid left, but it was enough to accomplish his goal. The obvious question hammered at his brain. Is Lexie's life and the life of my son worth risking everything I've built and everything I've achieved over the last several centuries? He wasn't sure. But what if it was the only way to rescue Lexie and bring François to the light? I can't risk the lives of more of my people for my own interests. In addition, the human victims necessary for their blood would die. Would Lexie ever forgive him or would she kill him on sight?

Étienne's thoughts were interrupted by Kendrick. *Do ya call that keepin' ye'r mind clear? It's taken me precious minutes to intrude.*

Did you find it?

Did ya say that the clue says somethin' about a gift?"

"The exact wording is 'find what you are seeking in the gift'. Do you see anything that resembles a gift?"

Just let me compel the shop keeper.

It has your Emma's name on it lad. I'm openin' it now…

Étienne paced, his impatience increasing by the second.

I'm holding the 88P and the formula in my hands. Let me finish things here and I'm headed your way. Where shall we meet?

I'll meet you in Calais at Le Bar a Vins on the Places Armes in a half hour or so. Étienne was aware that Claudette watched him as he lifted off from Lexie's balcony. *If she tries to follow, I'll kill her.*

223

As Étienne soared over the French countryside his thoughts returned to his daring plan. Now that he and Kendrick had found the formula, he no longer needed to be concerned about supply and demand. But what if he couldn't come back from the dark side? Kendrick and his other lieutenants would rally and lead the Society against the dark side. Lexie was a whole other issue. He would be cut off from her forever. Should he harm a human being she would be forced to hunt and kill him. Could she handle that? He would be reunited with his son but condemned to an eternity of sadness and loneliness. If Lexie killed him, how could she recover?

Distracted, Étienne overshot the meeting place. He circled back and set down in the alley behind the bar and hurried inside. One glance around the crowded room found Kendrick. His honey-blond hair was easy to spot amongst the dark-haired French. The tavern boasted wood beamed ceilings, a long bar which gleamed in the soft lamplight, and oak furniture.

Kendrick sat in a corner, his back to a wall. A huge smile lit up his handsome face as he rose to greet Étienne. The French custom of briefly hugging and kissing a friend's cheeks would embarrass the Scotsman, so Étienne put out his hand and Kendrick gave it a good shake and a punch to his shoulder.

"It's good to see you laddie," Kendrick remarked motioning for another scotch. "Do ye want somethin'?"

Étienne shook his head.

"Sounds like ye'r having quite the time of it. Do ye need me to bring reinforcements?"

"Not yet, thanks," replied Étienne. "I heard you've been experiencing an unusual number of vampire raids in your area. You're needed there."

"Aye ye'r right. Ma hands are full at the moment keepin' peace in the Highlands. But remember, I'm only a thought away."

Étienne studied the ancient vampire, who like himself, had been Strygoi before he joined the Society. Étienne was fairly certain that Kendrick had not partaken of human blood since, but he wondered how Kendrick was faring with his bloodlust. He probed his mind gently and to his amazement, his friend opened up. Étienne scanned for violent thoughts but there was nothing but concern and love.

"Satisfied?" Kendrick said.

"I had to be sure."

"Rightly so, I would expect nothin' less."

The waitress arrived with Kendrick's MaCallan 25-year-old scotch, and he saluted Étienne before downing it in one gulp. "This helps most of the time, but the wantin' is always there beneath the surface."

Kendrick reached in his coat pocket and handed Étienne a gift box.

"We're going after Lexie as soon as the sun rises. François and Marielle will be sleeping, guarded only by their human minions. They will be at their most vulnerable. The only vampire we have to worry about is Claudette."

"Do ye know where their compound is?"

"I will force Claudette to tell us."

"And just how will ye do that?"

"By whatever means I have to."

"Do you want me to accompany you?" the Scot offered once again.

"Too dangerous. If something happens to me I'll need you to take over."

"I appreciate ye'r confidence. If and that's a big if something happens to you. Count on me."

The friends rose together. This time as they shook hands, Étienne couldn't resist. He pulled the Scot close and gave him a light kiss on each cheek. To his surprise, rather than withdrawing, Kendrick patted him on the back.

"Be careful my friend. We need you," Kendrick said as he teleported away.

"Always," Étienne called after him. He hated lying to his lieutenant. He was about to break a promise by taking the antiserum and drinking human blood.

All was quiet back at the château. Étienne returned to Lexie's room to wait for dawn and news from François and Marielle's stronghold. As he paced he remembered he hadn't contacted Jacques and Emile. A soft rap at the door roused him from his thoughts.

"Come in the door's open," he replied. It was André.

He handed Étienne a note. "More bad news."

Étienne opened the note and shouted, "Fuck!"

It read:

> *Dearest Étienne,*
>
> *You know by now that I have been secretly working with François and Marielle. Too bad for you. I hope it galls you to know I have been doing it right under your nose. It makes me sad (but only a little) our relationship had to end this way, but then it has been over for a long time.*
>
> *If you want Lexie to live you must give us the formula. Choose. Jacques and Emile have been eliminated, so don't expect any help from them. Knowing how stubborn you are, I'm sure that very shortly I'll have the gratification of taking your pretty little vampire executioner's life. You will experience pain and suffering.*
>
> *Until we meet again,*
>
> *C*

"Why didn't you stop her?" Étienne said.

"She was too fast. I think she's turned to the dark side. I tried to follow but I couldn't keep up."

"Leave me."

André didn't quibble.

Étienne saw red. He felt he was going crazy. Tom's death, Lexie's abduction, Claudette's treachery came crashing in. How was he going to find Lexie without Claudette? Tracking was one option, but could be time consuming and time was one thing he didn't have. His path became clear. He would do the unthinkable and hope he could maintain enough of his humanity to rescue Lexie before succumbing to the dark side. *Put everything I have in jeopardy – here goes.*

He drank the rest of the 88P and left Lexie's room as if chased by the devil.

"André, where are you?" he shouted.

"I'm here." André's voice called from the bottom of the staircase. Étienne reached out to André searching his mind. The big Moor surrendered and Étienne read nothing but concern and anger. He had not helped Claudette leave, but had done everything in his power to stop and track her. He had been out maneuvered.

"You can trust me," André said.

"I had to be sure my friend. There is too much at stake."

Étienne handed him the small box with the 88P and formula. "Take this and hide it. Never, and I mean never tell me where it is. Even if I command you as your maker, you must refuse. Tell only Lexie or Kendrick."

"Why...?"

"Don't argue and don't ask questions, just do it."

André nodded and hurried off.

Now to find human blood.

227

He flew up the stairs toward the fourth floor, a blur in the shadows. He opened the first door he came to and stood in the opening disgusted at what he was about to do. It was worth it. He moved to the first bed and baring the sleeping maid's carotid sunk his fangs into her neck. She struggled for a moment but as the pheromones from his saliva entered her system she became pliant and willing. He sucked her dry, his cock stiffening from the rush of blood and lust. He left her in a heap and moved to the second bed. He felt the 88P and human blood rushing through his body. He had to act quickly.

He teleported out the window and sniffed the air in an attempt to capture Claudette's scent. But it evaded him. *Brute.* His horse's nose was infallible. He had often helped Étienne track rogue vampires. He hovered outside Claudette's room. She had fled in a hurry and she was certain to have left clothes behind. He entered and grabbed the first item he encountered – a Hermes scarf that reeked of her. He wrinkled his nose in disgust and wondered how he had ever been attracted to her. *Never mind that.*

As the eastern sky began to brighten, Étienne led Brute from his stall. Brute seemed to sense his master's distress and pawed at the ground Étienne held Claudette's scarf against Brute's nose. The sniff was long and deep and the horse nodded his head as if to say "I got it, let's go." He leaped into the saddle, but standing in his way was André, bigger than life, hands on his hips.

"Where do you think you're going?"

"Get out of my way. I'm going to get Lexie."

"Not without back up you're not."

"I don't need back up and I don't want to risk anyone's life. I've taken the last of my antiserum and consumed human blood. I must get to her before I turn to the dark side. I don't have time to wait."

"*Fils de pute*! Have you lost your mind? Please tell me you're joking. How the hell will we get you back?"

"This is no joke. I couldn't think of any other way. We'll worry about getting me back once Lexie is safe. Now step aside or I'll run you down."

The big Moor didn't budge and Étienne spurred Brute who lunged forward. André dove to the side, but not before Brute's shoulder slammed into him knocking him against the wall of the barn. Étienne heard bones breaking.

He heard André calling after him. "Étienne wait! Don't do this!"

He gave Brute his head and spurred him viciously in the sides. Brute responded. The horse had Claudette's scent and Étienne heard him snorting from time to time but he never wavered or faltered.

Étienne felt the inescapable beginnings of his turning, and he prayed that he would get to Lexie in time. *Hang on ma petite.*

Chapter 23
The Rescue

Fuzzy, my brain feels fuzzy. Cotton mouth. Lexie awakened, to a prescient thirst. Her mind worked its way back to consciousness. Slowly she remembered the horrors of the previous night, hoping it had been a nightmare. Tom was murdered! The triumphant look on Claudette's face as she held Tom captive haunted her. *That bitch.* The awful gurgling when François sucked Tom's throat. She allowed her grief to overflow and tears streamed down her face. *Not a nightmare.* Her next thought was of Étienne. He would be moving heaven and hell to get to her and must be devastated at the loss of his good friend. *He'll come.*

She forced her eyes open and experienced a moment of panic. She couldn't see. *Am I blind?* She reached up and felt a blindfold, and slipped it off her head. Her eyes adjusted to the darkness of the room. She could just make out a sliver of light filtering under a door.

She stretched her cramped arms and legs, and realized she was no longer tied up. She lay on a soft bed that smelled old and musty. *Where am I?* A wave of dizziness and nausea swept over her as she sat up. She dropped her head between her knees and the sensations eased.

She could see the room clearly. She turned on the lamp that sat on a bedside table. Lexie stood next to a king size bed covered in an opulent but frayed blue satin duvet. Black velvet draperies covered the windows and she drew a section back. It was still dark outside. She opened the window and stuck her head out. She was at least a hundred feet above the ground. *Too far to jump.* The door was locked from the outside. She paced, frustrated at her predicament. *I need a plan.* She stopped at the open window and looked longingly at freedom. She flopped down on the bed to think, but her situation was hopeless. *Someone's coming.* Footsteps stopped outside the door and a key turned in the lock.

"Wakey, wakey," a high-pitched female voice said. "Time to play." The door swung open to François and Marielle looking so innocent and young.

"If it isn't the evil frick and frack. What do you want?"

"Tell us everything you know about the antiserum's whereabouts," Marielle said.

"Even if I knew, I wouldn't tell you."

"Foolish girl," François said, sitting beside her. He grabbed her hair and pulled, hard. Lexie felt hair rip out. "You will tell us everything or I will do things to you from which you'll never recover."

Lexie froze. He gazed into her eyes attempting to compel her.

"I love it when you talk like that," Marielle said to François. She joined him on the other side of Lexie. Marielle reached out and stroked Lexie's throat. "Do you taste as good as you smell?" Marielle's hand wandered down Lexie's chest and caressed her breast.

"Take your hands off me, you evil cow!"

"Don't be rude," Marielle pouted. "Perhaps you prefer François' touch? Chèr, why don't you show our little mouse."

François grabbed Lexie's breast, He squeezed until her eyes watered, but she remained silent. He grabbed the nipple and she nearly passed out from the pain.

Marielle watched his cruelty, giggling. "Look at you getting hard," she said, leaning over to stroke the front of his pants. Lexie saw the huge bulge of François' cock.

"If you don't tell us what we want to know you will experience the full power of that," he said. He gave Lexie's nipple another cruel twist and scraped his fangs down her throat, whispering in her ear. "Where is the formula?"

"I don't know."

Marielle slapped Lexie and her lip bled. "Don't lie to us!"

That did it. Lexie leaped from the bed, pulling François with her, his hand still tangled in her hair. She kicked out and caught Marielle on the side of the head, flinging her into the wall. Using the momentum of her kick Lexie swiveled and concentrated her strength into a kick meant to do serious damage to François' groin. He was too fast. Using her hair as leverage he side-stepped and she lost her balance. She crashed to the floor. François kicked her in the stomach and the breath left her body. He sat on her chest and slapped her face repeatedly.

Lexie struggled to remain conscious.

"Enough! If you kill her we'll have no hostage." Marielle said. "Lay her on the bed and let's continue with our interrogation. She should be ready to talk by now."

François lifted Lexie from the floor and placed her on the bed. His smell was so like Étienne's she nestled into his chest seeking comfort. He flung her on the bed and bent over her. "Time to talk." He grabbed her other nipple and twisted. The pain cut through the fog of the beating and she jerked away.

"I don't care what you do to me, I'll never tell you anything."

François chuckled. Lexie felt his hand move down her body to her crotch. Marielle held her arms as he began to massage. At first he was gentle. "C'mon chère, tell us."

"No way."

He sighed and gripped her so hard Lexie was sure she would suffer permanent damage. "Tell us," he growled.

The pain was so intense she could barely breathe. Tears trickled down her cheeks. She shook her head.

"This is useless," Marielle said. "It's dawn and we have to go underground. I already feel the effects of the rising sun."

"But she hasn't told us anything," François said. "I think I should give her a taste of what a real man feels like." He rose and unbuttoned his trousers. His penis was huge and engorged. Lexie gasped, in too much pain to move. *He'll tear me apart.*

"She will tell us *mon amour*. Save that for me," Marielle said. "We'll chain her to the dungeon wall while we sleep. The drugs will weaken her without food or water." François stroked himself and Lexie saw he wanted to rape her.

"You would be such a treat…" he began.

"Étienne will come. And when he does — " Lexie said.

"Not likely," François hissed. He shoved his penis back in his pants. "My father has no idea where our compound is."

"Doesn't matter," Lexie said. "He will come and you will die."

"We must go," Marielle said. She walked to the door, and barked orders to someone Lexie couldn't see. "Take her to the dungeon and chain her. No food or water and inject her with this." A huge man appeared in the doorway and took the syringe from Marielle.

"M'lady," he said bowing to Marielle. He walked to Lexie and grabbed her by the arm forcing her to her feet.

"Be careful with her Claude," François said. "She's stronger than she looks."

Claude nodded and without hesitation socked her in the jaw. Lexie was dazed and sagged against him. He picked her up and threw her over his shoulder.

"Tell the other human servants that we have gone to sleep and that Claudette will be here soon." François said to Claude.

"Oui, M'sieur," Claude said.

Lexie bounced along on the man's shoulder until she was sure they weren't being followed. "Please put me down, I'm gonna to throw up. I won't give you any problems." Claude wasn't a vampire. His touch hadn't made her scalp itch. *I just need a second.*

"You better not. You won't like the consequences." He set Lexie on her feet pulling her hands behind her back he clasped them in one of his huge hands. Claude removed his belt and secured it around her wrists, cutting off the circulation. He shoved her ahead of him.

They descended several flights of stairs and arrived at what Lexie assumed was the dungeon. Claude halted her in front of a cage and fumbled for keys, taking his attention off Lexie. It was all she needed. She was too close for leverage but Claude's chin was directly above her head. *This is gonna hurt.* She bent her knees and jumped up in one movement. She heard his teeth rattle as her head connected with his throat and chin. Claude's grip loosened on her hands. She wrenched free and hit him on the bridge of his nose. Claude staggered backwards and she whirled, landing a hard kick to the side of his knee. Claude toppled over and hit the floor head first with a loud crack. Blood oozed from his temple. She kicked him in the head once more for good measure and his breathing stopped. *Thunder crap I've killed him.*

Lexie's head throbbed where she had connected with his chin, but she ignored it. She grasped the belt in her teeth and opened the buckle, freeing her hands. They tingled as circulation was restored. She scanned the room looking for an exit. There were several empty cages in the cavernous room, their floors bloodstained. Heavy chains hung from the walls. She grimaced imagining what they were used for. She took the time to go through Claude's pockets, and found the syringe filled with the drug they'd planned to use on her. She slipped it in her back pocket. *Might come in handy.*

Going back up the stairs was a bad idea. Human servants would be roaming the castle and she might not be so lucky next time. She searched for another exit and spotted a small wooden door and felt a surge of relief when it was unlocked. It was pitch black inside. She felt fresh air wafting through the opening. She had to go for it. *Flashlight would be good.*

Lexie hated dark places. They reminded her of childhood punishments. Whenever she rebelled against her mom's religious beliefs, Cassie locked her in a closet for hours.

She had to stoop to enter the space. As she felt her way along she figured she was in a tunnel about four feet in diameter. She was able to touch both sides of the stone walls. Her eyes adjusted to the darkness and she could see quite far down the tunnel. *Another perk of being a vampire executioner.* She heard the squeal of rats, and she shivered in disgust.

Soon the man she had killed would be missed. She picked up her pace, scrabbling along like a crab. The breeze got stronger and she smelled pine trees. Intent on getting out of the dark, she plunged ahead and ran headlong into an iron grate barring her exit to the outside. *Give me a break.* She turned sideways and kicked with everything she had. The grate didn't open, but she felt it move. She kicked again and the bolts rusted from years of exposure popped. She was free!

Lexie stood upright and stretched. She was in a dense forest. The first rays of sunlight peeked through the trees. As she moved away from the opening she thought she heard a sound behind her. Before she could react, she was struck on the side of the head and sent crashing into a tree. She recovered, in time to jump aside as the man she thought she'd killed charged. She pulled out the syringe and as Claude passed she jabbed him in the neck and squeezed the plunger. He staggered with the empty syringe hanging from his neck. Claude growled, took two steps before crumpling at her feet. This time she made sure. She picked up a nearby rock and bashed her assailant's head with it. For good measure she continued to hit him until she saw brain matter. She searched for a pulse and found none. He definitely wasn't breathing. She sank to her knees in shock and waited until the waves of nausea passed. *Gotta get going.*

She had no idea where she was but her intuition urged her to head east. She began to run. The forest floor was covered with pine needles, slippery from the morning dew and it slowed her down. All she could think about was getting back to Étienne. Her legs pumped harder, eating up the ground with every step.

She wasn't sure how long she'd been running when she heard a twig snap. Her left leg was jerked painfully in the air and flipped her upside down. Her finger tips hung three feet off the ground. *Shit, booby trap.* She swayed back and forth with the blood rushing to her head. She waited until the swaying stopped and craned her neck to see that a rope, two inches thick, held her suspended. She strained to grab the rope, but failed. Her muscles screamed in protest. She relaxed before trying again.

Shit. Someone's coming. François and Marielle's people had discovered her escape. She stretched with all her might. She couldn't quite reach the rope, but she didn't give up. Her fingertips brushed the rope, but never enough to grasp it. She heard the pounding of hoof beats. She flung her body upward, but she didn't make it. A huge black horse broke through the underbrush. *I'm caught.*

"*Ma petite* what are you doing hanging upside down?" Étienne's silky voice was music to her ears.

He's here. Her heart leapt. The black horse was Brute. "Don't be an ass. Get me down from here."

He chuckled as he lifted her free. He stood her upright and enveloped her in his arms.

"Are you hurt?" He held her so tight she could barely breathe. "How did you escape? What did they do to you?"

"Wait. One question at a time. I'm fine, but Tom… Claudette…"

"I know *ma petite*. André told me what happened."

"That bitch is the traitor. She held Tom while François drained him."

Étienne's arms tightened even more. "One more reason for me to put her down."

"E, I can't breathe."

His mouth captured hers and he murmured against her lips. "I just want to hold you closer and closer."

His hug eased and she sighed as his tongue thrust into her mouth. She wound her arms around his neck and matched his urgency with her own tongue. She felt his cock harden and he groaned, pressing her against him. "I love you. No matter what happens, remember that always."

"I love you too," she said, as his kisses became less urgent.

Étienne held her away from him "How *did* you escape?"

"I killed one of François and Marielle's human servants."

"Did they torture you?"

"They interrogated me and François was a little harsh. Nothing I couldn't handle. What about the formula, did you find it?"

"Kendrick helped me decipher the clue and recovered the 88P and formula from a small shop on the Scottish coast near his home. Kendrick and I met in Calais and when I returned to the château I gave it to André for safe-keeping. He knows there they are hidden."

"I remember you mentioned Kendrick as your second in command. But wasn't there something about uncontrollable bloodlust? Are you sure you can trust him?"

"I'm sure. He's in line to take over should anything happen to me. And, André knows…. It's just a precaution in case—"

Lexie felt her heart constrict in fear. "E, you're scarin' me. What's goin' on?"

"Now is not the time to discuss this. We must get you to safety."

"But E."

He ignored her and mounted Brute. He stretched out his hand. "Get on."

"Will it be okay?"

"I don't know but we have no choice."

Lexie approached Brute. He sniffed her without moving. She took Étienne's hand and swung into the saddle. Brute danced for a minute and settled down. Étienne urged him in the direction he'd come. Lexie hung on marveling at the horse's speed and strength. Her extra weight didn't seem to faze him. Emerging from the protective cover of the forest, they thundered through the pastures toward the château. Étienne pulled Brute up hard.

Lexie peered over Étienne's shoulder. "What's wrong?"

"Horses approaching fast."

"Yes, I heard them before. I forgot to mention them."

"We may have to run."

She grabbed Étienne around the waist fearful that if he had to move fast she would be unseated.

"It's André." Étienne said, urging Brute forward. Minutes later they were surrounded by André and his men.

Étienne lowered Lexie to the ground and dismounted. He turned to André and Lexie noticed that the big Moor was watching Étienne cautiously. A moment later André's eyes flicked to her, but not before she noticed his anxiety. "Are you okay?" he asked.

"I'm fine. Just a little bruised."

Lexie turned to Étienne. "Let's keep going. I'm sure François and Marielle's servants are searching for us." She noticed that Étienne trembled and his eyes flickered from black to green.

"E, what's wrong with your eyes?"

"What do you mean?"

"They're flashin' black and green. Not only that but you're shakin'."

"It's nothing *ma petite*. I'm just angry. It's time for you to go." He shoved her toward André and turned to mount Brute.

"Wait, you're not comin' with us?"

"This is the closest I've been to François and Marielle in five-hundred-years. I'm going on to their compound."

"You can't, it's too dangerous."

"I can and I will. My son's life is on the line, not to mention I have an opportunity to kill Marielle and Claudette."

Oh hell no. "Then I'll go with you."

"Out of the question, you would only get in my way."

That hurt. Lexie looked to André for support and found none. She wouldn't win this argument. "Promise me you'll come back."

Étienne gathered her in his arms. "You are my *Amant de Sang*. I must come back to you. Now get on the horse and go."

She kissed him hard. "E, you smell funny. What's goin' on?"

"No more questions. André take her."

André reached down and lifted her up behind him. "How will you find your way?"

"Brute has Claudette's scent. He will take me to her."

"I hate this. At least take some of the men with you." Lexie said.

Étienne pulled her head down and kissed her. *He doesn't just smell, he stinks.* "They are needed at the château." He mounted Brute, and as he rode away he yelled, "Take care of her. She's my life," before disappearing into the trees.

"Come we must go," André said, turning his horse toward the château.

"How can you say that? He's ridin' to his death. We have to go after him." Lexie said.

"Your safety is paramount. Besides you would be a distraction. He's better off on his own."

"But—"

"No more argument. Étienne needs to know that you're safe. It's my job to make sure of that. Hang on to me." André motioned to his men, spurred his horse, before Lexie could protest further.

She held tight to André, and focused on staying on the horse's back. Yet, she couldn't ignore the thought running through her mind. *He'll be okay. He has to be.*

Chapter 24
The Change

Étienne's clothes were drenched in sweat. It took all his concentration to remain in the saddle. He felt the dark side gaining strength and power. His body trembled at the changes. At times the pain was excruciating but sometimes the sense of euphoria was the most pleasant he'd ever experienced.

He urged Brute onward anxious to complete his mission. Brute stopped sniffing as if he'd lost the scent. Étienne shoved Claudette's scarf near Brute's nose. The horse flared his nostrils reacting to the urgency in his master's voice and he surged forward. His powerful stride told Étienne Brute knew where he was going.

Pain gripped Étienne and he doubled over, tumbling to the ground. A series of violent convulsions ripped through him and he lost consciousness. When he woke, they had subsided. Étienne stretched out his hand for the reins but Brute shied away blowing through his nostrils and pawing the ground. *Interesting, I must smell different.*

"Easy boy, it's still me." Étienne whispered, and the sound of his master's voice calmed him and Brute stood firm. Étienne hauled himself into the saddle, and gave Brute a last sniff of Claudette's scent. Brute sprang forward as if pursued by the devil.

Étienne's senses were on overload. He heard fish breathing through their gills as he splashed through a small river. The sound of a woodpecker tapping assaulted his ears and made him wince. He noticed ants crawling through a rotted log several-hundred-feet away. And the smell emanating from his skin was

…he stank like rotten meat. He knew his time on the light side was over and he prayed that his love for Lexie could pull him back. But as he rode on, that thought seemed less important. *My son, I get to see my son.*

As Étienne broke free of the forest, Brute stopped so abruptly that Étienne was almost thrown over his head. He recovered as Brute reared and then danced around snorting and shaking his head.

"Doucement mon garçon, what's wrong?" Étienne patted Brute on the neck to settle him. Brute blew out through his nose, hard. *Can he smell them?*

At Étienne's touch, Brute stood still, but every muscle in his body quivered. Étienne surveyed his surroundings. In the distance he could see the town of St. Jalle with its cobblestone streets and a medieval castle that dominated the tiny village. Small stone houses dotted the landscape and Étienne could make out people moving about the streets. *Human servants?*

In his excitement at being reunited with his son, he forgot to be cautious. This was François and Marielle's stronghold.

"*On y va,*" he shouted. Brute sprang forward and within minutes Étienne faced the stone archway leading into the town. He eased Brute to a walk and as they stepped through, Claudette appeared with several human servants flanking her.

"So you have found us," she snarled. "It doesn't matter. You will be dead in a minute." She rose in the air, and charged Étienne, brandishing a wicked looking blade. Étienne levitated from the saddle to avoid the killer blow.

"Brute, go," he commanded as Claudette charged again. She pulled up short of swinging the sword and a look of confusion crossed her face.

"What have you done? You look odd, your face… and your eyes." Étienne saw her struggling to understand.

"I have consumed the rest of the antiserum and taken human blood. It has sent me to the dark side. I am full Strygoi." For a moment he felt a pang of sorrow, but it passed and he felt nothing. *Have I lost my humanity?*

Claudette edged closer. "I can smell you."

"Rather like stale blood, right?" She nodded and eased to the ground and Étienne followed.

"You smell too." He said, sniffing at her. "Have you taken human blood?"

"I have," she said.

"We're both virtually indestructible," she said.

"What about François and Marielle?"

"I have been giving them a little of the antiserum. But my supply was minimal. I was afraid I would run out and you would suspect something. The only thing we've noticed is they can rise earlier. The setting sun doesn't burn them." She replied. "Lexie's escaped. Do you know where she is?"

An image of Lexie's beautiful face flashed through his mind. "She's safe. I sent her back to the Society with André." Sadness punched him in the chest so hard, he winced. As it dissipated, he strained to bring the image back. It appeared but had turned murky. He struggled to pull it into focus and gave up. It was too much effort. As he let it go Lexie became a distant pleasant memory. Her blood, he craved her blood, sweet, rich and effervescent. *One day I shall drink her dry.* For a moment he was repulsed by the thought but the bloodlust won and his fangs extended in anticipation.

Without warning his past surfaced. His anger flared and he snarled. "I should kill you for being a traitor and what you did to Tom."

"Tom's fine. He's here with us now. François is in the process of turning him."

Étienne lunged for her throat intent on killing her. "He'll hate that."

She side-stepped, evading his grasp. "Always the noble one," she sneered.

"I trusted you, cared for you, and you betrayed us all." He slumped, the torment leaving his body. "But somehow it seems unimportant." *That's odd, I feel nothing.*

"Welcome to the dark side. It suits you." Claudette reached out to touch him and he pulled away.

"Keep your distance, I haven't forgiven you."

"What a shame. We could be so good together. Perhaps with time…"

"Don't hold your breath. You have a lot to make up for."

"How did you find us?" Claudette said. "We've been moving every couple of days."

"Brute followed your scent." At the mention of his name, Brute came and stood behind Étienne.

"Clever horse. Did anyone follow you?"

"André may have tried, but he had no idea where I was going. He's not a concern."

"And the formula?"

"I gave them to André before I left. Only he knows where they're hidden." *Merde, I shouldn't have revealed that.* He had just put André in harm's way.

"Asshole, your last valiant deed. Why are you here?"

"It seemed like the right thing to do at the time. I'm here, to see my son."

"After all the centuries of you trying to kill him and Marielle. Do you really think he's just going to forgive and forget?"

"I was only going to kill Marielle. It may take some time to win him over, but I'm hopeful."

"Good luck with that. He and Marielle won't rise for a couple hours. Let's find you a place to rest and a human donor. You must be hungry."

His stomach grumbled and he noticed his hands were trembling. Side effects of being turned to the dark side.

"*Oui*, I believe ravenous is the appropriate word." His need for human blood overrode any remaining essence of his humanity. He salivated at the thought of warm, fresh, red blood. *No more animal blood for him.*

Claudette motioned him to follow her, and linked her arm through his as if they were old friends. This time her touch didn't bother him. He gathered up Brute's reins and walked with her toward the stone castle. "Where are all the people?" There were no cars to be seen, and the few humans walking about were pale and thin.

"We've turned most of them to Strygoi. The rest we're using as a blood source or human servants by feeding them small amounts of our blood. The human servants are trained to watch over us during the daylight. But once we have the antiserum we'll no longer require their service. They'll be used as a blood source or turned to Strygoi."

"How many people are we talking about?" Étienne asked.

"Worldwide about three million turned in the last century. That doesn't include the six million who had already been turned."

Étienne couldn't believe it. His humanity haunted him and for a moment he felt panic. *We're going to need a bigger army.* The tug of war between his dark side and the light made him feel like he was being pulled apart by wild horses. He stopped and fell to his knees as the conflict raged inside him.

From a distance he heard Claudette's voice. "Étienne, can you hear me, what's happening?"

She touched his shoulder and he snapped at her. "What the...?"

"Give me a minute, it's passing." The trembling subsided and he stood. "That was unpleasant."

"I remember that," Claudette said.

"The Society has no idea of the size and strength of your resources."

"It wouldn't matter if they did. We're going to win this war. We already have farms where humans mate and breed to provide our food source. It's only a matter of time."

That information was inconsequential. He shrugged. *C'est la vie.*

As they entered the castle grounds, a human servant approached to take Brute to the stables. "Cool him down and give him a bath before you feed and water him," Étienne said. He patted Brute on the neck before handing the servant the reins. As Brute was led away, the bond he felt with the horse surprised him, and he chalked it up to their long partnership.

Claudette led him into the castle. Although dark and gloomy, there were antique tapestries decorating the walls. In the main hall, a fire burned in a walk-in fireplace. Red velvet upholstered settees were place strategically around the hearth giving the room a sense of elegance.

They climbed two sets of circular stone stairs and proceeded down a long balcony. One side was open to the main hall below. The other had doorways every twelve feet which Étienne surmised were sleeping quarters. Claudette stopped in front of one motioned him inside.

He was pleasantly surprised. A king-size bed filled one wall, its red silk duvet and black sheets were in keeping with the opulence Étienne had already seen. The lighting was muted and the tiny slits in the outer walls had shades that could be lowered to filter out any daylight that strayed through.

"This will be your room for now," Claudette said. "Make yourself at home and I will send someone to take care of your hunger. Get some rest. I have a feeling you're going to need it."

"You are too kind," Étienne responded. "How will I know when François has risen?"

"I wouldn't worry about that. I'd worry about what he and Marielle are going to do to you. They'll smell you even before they're fully awake. Maybe they won't kill you before you can plead your case." She left, her laughter echoing in the large chamber.

Étienne reclined on the bed to wait for his blood meal. Inevitably his thoughts turned to Lexie. *Do I still love her?* He knew he must. She was his *Amant de Sang.* Without warning her face appeared in his mind crystal clear and disturbing. Her mouth moved as if she were trying to speak to him. He strained to read her lips. It looked like she was saying *"Amant de Sang."* He tried harder but the image faded. The harder he tried to control it the faster it disappeared. *What is happening?*

A knock at the door interrupted his efforts. *I smell blood.* "Enter," he called out. The door opened and a young woman walked toward him. "I am here to serve you," she said. Claudette followed her inside.

"You're staying?" Étienne said.

"I wouldn't miss this for the world. I've been waiting for over a hundred years for you to finally succumb to your natural instincts."

"I certainly wouldn't want to deprive you of that privilege." He took the young woman's hand, and for the first time noticed her beauty. Her eyes were a deep blue, her hair long and blond, and her skin was translucent. She wore a white shift made of gauzy material. The outline of her nipples and their aureoles caused Étienne's cock to twitch.

"What is your name?" he asked.

"Yvette *Monsieur.* I'm to give you my blood." With those words, she burst into tears and hid her face.

Merde, I didn't expect her to cry. Étienne placed his hands on her shoulders and Yvette's tears subsided. "Hush, *ma petite." That sounds familiar.* She faced him and he placed his arms around her. His intention was to soothe her fear. Instead his bloodlust thundered forward and unable to control his urge he threw her on the bed. Étienne covered her body with his, sank his fangs into her jugular, and began to suck. His cock thickened and out of control he ripped her panties away and plunged into her. He rode her hard and fast his thrusts matching the rhythm of his sucking.

"Please *Monsieur* no more!" Yvette said, as she struggled to push Étienne away.

Lost in his own pleasure he didn't heed her and continued thrusting and drinking. His climax had him screaming and left him spent. He rolled to the side and waited for his heartbeat to calm.

"I had no idea what I've been missing," he said. Yvette didn't respond. He raised his head to look at her and her sightless eyes unnerved him. "Shit. Have I killed you?" He felt for a pulse. There was none.

Claudette appeared at the side of the bed, her hand stroked between her legs. She was clearly aroused. "*That* was even better than I'd imagined."

"I killed her."

"It's not important, but I doubt your precious Lexie would want you now."

"And that's a problem because? Who cares about Lexie when I am about to be reunited with my son and join his quest."

"Aren't you just the Mr. Dark Side. I find it hard to believe you have given Lexie up so easily."

"Believe what you will. She's no longer important to me."

"Such determination…how about relieving this itch between my legs?" she waved her hand under his nose and he caught a whiff of her juices. It disgusted him.

"Leave me," he said.

Claudette sashayed to the door. "Until later," she said and slammed the door.

His emotions were erratic. He felt nauseous at what he'd done to Yvette, and he knew that Claudette was right about Lexie. *How can I ever face her?* At the same time, he felt no remorse or regret. There was only the euphoria of being satisfied and fulfilled. *I could get used to this.* He was bloody and sticky. He stared at Yvette's body and smiled at the carnage he had caused. He wanted a shower.

He allowed the hot water to pound his neck and shoulders. He liked the smell of the soap, a mixture of lavender and verbena. He soaped himself and as he massaged his genitals his cock throbbed for attention. *Need more.* He stroked penis and Lexie's face ebbed in and out of his mind. *She's haunting me.* But the vision was mixed up with Yvette and what he had experienced with her. His fangs extended. He was as turned on as he had been when he was sinking them into Yvette's artery and pounding his cock into her tight cunt. He stroked faster, massaging his scrotum as it tightened. He came three more times, shouting as he erupted.

His lust eased, he wrapped a towel around his waist re-entered the bedroom. It was clean. Yvette and all signs of what had occurred were gone. The red duvet and been replaced with a black one, and the sheets had been refreshed with red ones. Even the silk smoking jacket was new. He was impressed. There was still time before François and Marielle rose and he settled back on the down pillows to rest. *I've made the right decision.* His eyelids grew heavy and for the first time in centuries felt the pull of sleep and he surrendered.

Chapter 25
The Darkness

Lexie and André pulled up in front of the château stables. The men and women who had ridden with André surrounded the two, alert to any danger. The château bustled with activity. Every window in the house was open, and the faint smell of bleach wafted through them. Armed men with dogs were stationed at twenty foot intervals completely encompassing the château, and Lexie could see others off in the distance patrolling the grounds.

Lexie dismounted. What's goin' on?"

"The château staff is busy cleaning up the mess from last night's attack." André said. "We have doubled the guard while we repair the damage done to the security system."

"How long will that take?"

"I estimate before nightfall. We're re-programming all the codes and scanners just in case…"

"In case of what?"

"Now isn't the time to discuss that."

Lexie glared at André. "I'm so tired of everyone tellin' me now isn't the time to discuss stuff. Tell me what's goin' on?" She addressed the others. "Well…? Anybody?"

"Come with me," André said, taking her arm. He led her towards the house.

Lexie protested but the look on André's face changed her mind. Sure enough, the staff worked diligently to restore order. Some were scrubbing the floor and walls, while others sponged blood off the furniture. Still silent, André escorted her to the second floor and into Étienne's office. He locked the door.

"I've never seen you look so grim," she said.

"It's for a good reason." He sat next to Lexie and she could tell he tried to mask his upset.

"Out with it André. The suspense is killin' me."

"It's Étienne—"

"Thunder crap, I knew it. What's he done?" Lexie jumped up and began pacing.

"Not until you calm down."

Lexie took a couple of deep breaths and resumed her place next to him. "It's bad isn't it?"

"It's the worst. He's taken the rest of his antiserum and consumed human blood. He is my maker and my boss, but if he were here right now I would be tempted to throttle him."

Lexie couldn't believe what she was hearing and a wave of washed over her. "Why would he do such a thing? He knows what will happen to him. I don't believe it!"

"He thought it was his only choice. Claudette had betrayed him, Tom was dead as well as Jacques and Emile, and you'd been taken. He was willing to risk everything to bring you back. . "

"Okay, but once he saw I was safe, why didn't he... Does this mean he's Strygoi?"

"He was turning when he found you and I suspect the full transformation to Strygoi has happened."

"Shit, shit, shit how do we get him back?"

"We don't. We can't. There's no antidote when a vampire on the light side takes the antiserum and drinks human blood. The transformation is permanent."

"I will not accept that and I don't understand how you can be so calm."

"Believe me I'm anything but calm. But panic isn't the answer. As Étienne's progeny this action is the ultimate betrayal and I still love him." André leaned back in his chair and closed his eyes.

"We can't just sit here. We have to do somethin'!"

"There's nothing to be done. He believed that his love for you would be strong enough to pull him back. But, meanwhile, he is now Strygoi and perhaps the most powerful Strygoi in the world. We have to protect ourselves."

"I'm gonna knock him into next week when I see him. This is insane." Tears threatened to spill as she processed the truth. "What if our love isn't enough? That means we've lost him forever. I'm his *Amant de Sang*. I can't believe he would do this not only to me, but to you, the Society, and to himself."

"How can you be his *Amant de Sang*? This never happens with humans."

"I don't know how and I don't care. He was sure. He wouldn't throw that away. Besides, we exchanged blood. That has to mean something."

"*Merde*. Now I understand why he thought he could return. I'm sorry Lexie. He thought it was the only way to save you."

"I saved myself... almost." She thought of her last exchange with him. *I have to save him.* "Where is the antiserum and the formula?"

"Before he started to turn he told me he was afraid that he would be tempted to steal it and give it to François and Marielle. It's well-hidden."

"This can't be happenin'. I understand why, but I still can't believe he would take the risk. He must have been out of his mind with grief and worry."

"Étienne's love for his son has been a driving force in his life for centuries." André said. "I suspect that the transformation to the dark side has caused him to join François and Marielle. Even his blood tie to you may not be strong enough to pull him back. You must accept that and let him go."

Lexie slumped over engulfed in grief. It was hopeless. Her stomach heaved and she retched into the office wastebasket. She wiped her mouth. "Shit." Her mind raced with memories of their last night together. The joy they had experienced as their love blossomed into something real.

André handed her a moist towel. She tried to smile, but her mouth refused to cooperate. "This sucks," she said. "What do we do now?"

André took her hand. "We go on. We keep fighting the good fight."

The phone rang and André grabbed the receiver on the first ring. "*Oui, c'est* André," he said.

"It's Kendrick," he mouthed. "Hold on I'm putting you on speaker. Lexie's here with me."

"Thank the Druids you're okay. I'm Étienne's — "

"I know who you are." Lexie said. Kendrick's calm voice gave her a sense hope. "Thank God you called."

"What's happened lassie? Where's Étienne?"

"He's turned Strygoi."

"Bloody hell! No wonder he hasn't been respondin' te ma thoughts. He must've been desperate."

"He didn't know I'd escaped on my own. He found me in the forest. We were headed back here when we met up with André. He made me go with André and went on alone to find his son and kill Claudette and Marielle."

"The last time I spoke with him he told me everything that had happened at the château." Kendrick said. "I got the feeling he was close te the breaking point. I'm nay surprised he's gone after Claudette and Marielle. Suckin' them dry would go a long way to avenge Tom. I would do the same."

Étienne's concerns regarding Kendrick's bloodlust silenced her. *Thunder crap, can I trust him?*

252

"What can we do now? I want to go after him and André insists I have to let him go. I don't want to let him go. Did he tell you I'm his *Amant de Sang*?"

"Ye must put that aside. He's no longer the vampire—"

"Don't tell me that 'I must' anything. I love him. I won't accept there's nothing we can do."

"Are you daft? Even with an army, he's stronger than anything we could throw at him. Ye ken I'm a thousand years old, right? And under normal circumstances I would be able to best him in a fight. But, now that he's Strygoi there's little in this world that can kill him. I'm tellin' ye there's nothin' te be done."

"If I hear that one more time I'm gonna—"

"Hold on te your knickers lass, I'll be there as quick as I can. In the meantime, you and André must get the word out te the rest of the Society's branches. Everyone needs te be on the alert."

Further argument was useless. Lexie felt deflated. Hopelessness returned.

"Please hurry," Lexie whimpered. "We need you."

"Do what I said, I'll be there shortly."

The receiver clicked. He was gone. "Let's get started," she said. "Where are the phone numbers for the other branches?"

"No need for that," André replied. "Geneviève is connected by computer to every branch. We'll send out an urgent message. Everyone will have it within the hour."

"I thought she only responded to Étienne's voice."

"He reprogrammed her to recognize mine as well as Claudette's a couple of months ago. After he rode off to rescue you I blocked both of them. Let's go to Étienne's private office. I feel safer in there than I do here."

253

When André and Lexie entered the stables Bella nickered, recognizing Lexie's scent. Lexie felt Brute's absence like a physical blow. The lab was empty. Lexie was puzzled. "Where is everybody?"

"Either working on the security system, cleaning up the house or tending to the injured."

"Why aren't they makin' 88P? I thought that was top priority."

"I haven't had a chance to contact Heinrick. I'll do that once we're secured in Étienne's office."

"Why Heinrick?"

"He worked with Emma to perfect the 88P and can read her formula better than anyone."

They paused in front of the eye-scanner's key pad and André punched in a code. Three beeps sounded and he motioned Lexie to subject her eyes to be recorded. A red light blinked in sequence and three more beeps sounded. The door opened with a loud click.

"I've programmed the scanner to recognize only my eyes and yours. Neither Claudette or Étienne can enter. If they try, a signal sounds high alert and a message sweeps the Society."

Étienne was now considered the enemy. His office screamed Étienne everywhere she looked. His loss made it painful to breathe. "I need to call my Mom."

André handed her the phone. "You can do that while I am working with Geneviève." Lexie moved away for privacy. Cassie's phone rang and Lexie experienced a moment of panic. *Who knew how Cassie would react. This could get ugly.*

"Sweetie pie is that you?" Cassie's soft Southern drawl left Lexie struggling to hold back the tears. She had to swallow a couple of times before she could respond.

"It's me. How are you?"

"I'm fine honey, but your voice sounds funny. Are you okay?"

"I'm okay…but somethin' awful has happened." She rushed on before she could be interrupted. She spilled everything. Her kidnapping, Tom's murder, Claudette's treachery, and Étienne turning to the dark side in his desperation to save her. There was silence on the other end. "Momma are you there? Say somethin'."

"I knew that no good would come of this…I told you—"

"Not now, please. It's bad enough without you sayin' I told you so. All the branches are on alert."

"Damn vampires, can't trust any of'em."

"I'm surrounded by vampires. I have no choice but to trust'em."

"You could come home. Forget all this nonsense."

"You know I can't do that. Besides if there's any chance to bring Étienne back…."

Lexie heard her mother pacing as her slippers swished on the hardwood floors. "You know, I always hoped that you and Tom would hook up. He would've made a great husband."

"Not now Momma, please."

"I'm just sayin'…"

It took a lot for Lexie to swallow her pride. "Momma, can you come? I feel so alone and I need your support right now."

Cassie didn't respond right away and Lexie heard the continued pacing. "Of course I'll come. I need to make arrangements for someone to look in on Bessie. Her mind isn't what it used to be. It's five a.m. here. I think there's a flight to Paris at eleven this mornin'. I'll text you with the particulars. With the time difference, I should be in Paris by midnight tonight."

"You'll have to spend the night there. It's too late to catch the train to Valence."

"Not a problem. I'll call you when I arrive in Paris and catch the first train in the mornin'."

"I'll have someone meet you at the station. Just let me know when."

"Darlin', I want you to know that I am sorry this happened. You must be so frightened. What's gonna happen to the Society?"

"Do you know who Kendrick is?"

"I've heard Tom talk about him. He's Étienne's second in command."

"He's on his way. I'm sure he'll know what to do."

"Maybe, but don't forget he's another vampire. He could be another Étienne."

"I have to trust somebody. Étienne trusted him." *Not a good reason. He also trusted Claudette.*

"...Just be careful."

"I promise. Give my love to Bessie."

"I will sweetheart. You just hang on."

"And Momma, I'm really glad you're comin'."

"I love you sweetie pie. See you soon. Bye now."

"Bye."

André was watching her. "She doesn't trust any of us does she?"

"Cassie can be difficult at times, and her suspicion of vampires runs deep. Can't say as I blame her. She's lost a lot to them and so have I. Did you send the message out?" She steered the conversation away from the trust issue.

"All done. And Heinrick will be here in the morning."

"What do we do now?"

"We wait."

"I can't just sit here and wait. Isn't there something else I can do?"

"Let's go back to the château. Perhaps there's news."

"I feel like I'm in the middle of a nightmare and any moment I'll wake up and everything will be okay."

Silence. Lexie followed André from the lab.

At the château, all evidence of the previous night's attack had been scoured or thrown out. The foyer was adorned with fresh flowers.

"It's as if nothin' happened," Lexie said. "I can almost imagine Étienne comin' down the stairs."

"It's a nice fantasy," André said. "But it's just that – a fantasy."

"You could have gone at least 24 hours without sayin' that." It felt like a knife in her gut and she struggled to hold back her tears. Her stomach grumbled. *I can't believe I'm hungry at a time like this.*

"I'm starvin'. I haven't eaten anything since dinner last night. If you need me for somethin', I'll be in the kitchen."

"*Bon Appétit.* I'm going to the office. There may be news from the other branches."

"Come get me if there's any word from Étienne."

Chapter 26
The Reunion

Étienne was jarred from sleep by a high pitched female voice that shrieked into his ears, coming from another part of the château.

"What do you mean he's here? Why haven't you killed him?"

Marielle, my son. He bolted from the bed, and quickly donned his clothes.

He was tucking his silk shirt into his black riding breeches when the door burst open and a small blond whirlwind launched herself at him. His fangs descended. Étienne snarled and back-handed Marielle. She smashed into the wall and crumpled to the floor.

François walked to Marielle and helped her stand. "Is that any way to treat your daughter-in-law?" The tiny vampire was dazed but unhurt. She ran her fingers through her hair and smoothed her leather skirt before turning her blue eyes on Étienne.

Étienne was speechless. The timbre of François' voice evoked memories of happy times, and he appeared exactly as Étienne remembered his son from centuries ago. His lustrous brown hair was pulled back in a pony-tail at the nape of his neck. Handsome and winsome in life as a vampire François was beautiful. His eyes, which were glued to his father, were the same startling blue Étienne recalled but rather than sparkling with fun, they were icy and distant. Hatred and distrust stared back at him. As a young man, François had never cared about fashion. Now he was the dandy, clad in a charcoal grey designer suit, blue silk shirt, matching cravat with a diamond tie pin and handmade leather loafers. Étienne inhaled and found François' odor musty but pleasant. He gently probed his son's mind, but it was closed to him.

"My son, you're just as I remember you." Without thinking, he held out his arms.

"Really father? It's a little late for that," François said.

"Just kill him and get it over with," Marielle hissed. "I can't believe he's stupid enough to enter our nest alone."

"Give him a chance," Claudette said. "I told you he's transformed." She stood in the doorway, resplendent in a bright green dress, cut low to hug her svelte body. Her long red hair swayed about her shoulders. She smiled and Étienne wondered if she was really on his side. His lust stirred by her full breasts exposed by the plunging neckline. *Did you dress for me?*

"How can we be sure?" Marielle said. "For all we know he's come to kill us all. How he plans to do that alone I have no idea, but I don't trust him, and you shouldn't either. Maybe he has an army waiting in the forest for his signal to attack."

"Silence," François said. "Your chatter is giving me a headache." He took a step toward Étienne and stopped. "What's happened to your eyes? They used to be green and now they're black."

"It's part of the transformation," Étienne responded, holding his ground as François advanced.

François wrinkled his nose and sniffed. "Marielle, he smells just like Claudette did when she changed. A blend of human blood and pheromones."

"I don't care if he smells like lilies. Kill him now and be done with it."

François circled Étienne sizing him up. "Why now after all these years? For centuries you've done nothing but pursue us, torment us, and kill us."

"I am here to join your cause, not harm you." Étienne said. He watched his son, alert to any change of aggression. "You should know that I'm rather difficult to kill which makes me a powerful ally. Plus I've developed a strong taste for human blood."

"Believe him." Claudette said. "I've seen proof."

"What proof? A little bloodsucking and murder? That's nothing. It's all a trick to gain our trust," Marielle said. "I can't believe you're falling for his lies." She cuffed François on the back of the head. "Kill him or I will do it myself."

"I *almost* believe him," François said. His arm blurred and he lunged at Étienne with a dagger aimed at his heart. Étienne stepped aside effortlessly and grabbed François who tried to twist away. But Étienne held him fast, rendering the younger man helpless. "*Merde*, you are strong!" François shouted.

Étienne loosened his grip and pushed his son away. François whirled and landed a killer blow to Étienne's jaw with no effect. François lunged, again, the blade aiming toward Étienne's throat.

Fangs bared, Étienne threw François to the floor and stomped on his back. There was a sharp crack as François' back broke. François screamed and lay still.

"What have you done?" Marielle shouted. She dropped to her knees beside François, but Étienne shoved her aside and gathered his son into his arms.

He smoothed François' hair back from his forehead. "I had no choice, he meant to kill me."

Étienne kissed François on the forehead. "This is not how I wanted our reunion to go. I can't kill you, you're my son. We have wasted so much time...."

François' eyes fluttered open. "That hurt." Étienne helped him to his feet. "It's a good thing I heal quickly." He twisted back and forth and Étienne heard his vertebra pop back into place.

Étienne reached out to touch him and François pulled back. "I'm sorry that I hurt you. It seems I've acquired killer instincts, but I can't kill you."

"I heard you before. But after centuries of being enemies you suddenly appear and claim you want to join us? Why should I believe you?"

"I know it will take time, but give me a chance. You are my son and now that I am Strygoi I see how foolish I've been to fight against you. We are family and bound by blood. I promise you won't regret it."

"Lies, it's all lies," Marielle said. "Don't listen to him. He will betray us."

"Enough! Your nagging is annoying," François said. "What if he's telling us the truth? Despite our differences we are still blood."

"You idiot, we've done just fine without him for centuries, don't get sucked in to his lies. If you won't kill him because you love me than as your maker, I order you to kill him."

François grappled with Marielle's order. As her progeny it, was almost impossible to refuse any order she gave him. Painful to watch, Étienne wished he could do something to ease his son's torment.

"I've made my decision. He is welcome here until he proves otherwise." François held out his hand and Étienne clasped it. For a few moments he knew joy as centuries of hate and distrust fell away.

"You've no idea how much this means to me," Étienne said. *I'm treading on thin ice but he's chosen me over Marielle.* He was surprised at the amount of emotion that welled inside. *Un petite victoire.*

"I will not allow this." Marielle lunged toward Étienne. In her hand was the dagger which she plunged into Étienne's heart. It sank up to the hilt and blood spurted from the wound.

Claudette screamed.

François tossed Marielle across the room. "You bitch, if he dies…"

Marielle hit the wall and landed and crouched ready to fight. "I hope he does!"

"Father…" François clasped the dagger and withdrew it from Étienne's chest. He put his arm around him and eased him to the bed.

261

Étienne sank back dizzy from the blood loss. *Can't die now.*

François pressed his hand to the wound. "Get me a towel!" He stretched his hand out and Claudette shoved a large bath sheet in his hand.

"He won't die. He's been taking the formula and consumed human blood. The only way to kill him is to behead and burn him."

François pressed the towel to the wound and Étienne felt the blood flow lessen. "I'm okay," he said rising.

"Father wait, the wound is deep and the knife has pierced your heart."

Étienne pushed his son's hand aside and François gasped. The wound had healed. All that remained was a faint red line and that was fading.

"I've never seen a mortal wound heal so fast," François said, backing away.

Marielle peered over François shoulder. "Neither have I," she said.

François seized Marielle by the throat, lifting her until her feet dangled. "What the hell were you trying to prove," he growled. She beat at his chest and gurgled as she tried to breathe.

Claudette stepped up beside them. "Don't kill her. We need her."

François released Marielle. "And I still love her. Even if she weren't my maker I could never kill her. But watch her."

François grasped Étienne's shoulder. "Are you really turned to the dark side?"

"I am fully Strygoi. In fact, I am stronger, faster and harder to kill than any other except for the Originals."

"What about the Society and Lexie?"

"I no longer care about either. Theirs's is a lost cause. I am ready to join the Strygoi in the quest to subjugate humanity. Lexie was a pleasant diversion." As he said this Lexie's face swam into his vision. It startled him and he shook his head to clear the image. "I am only interested in drinking her blood until she's dead."

"Don't believe him," Marielle said. "It's treachery."

"Are you afraid Étienne will take over your power, Marielle?" Claudette said, her tone nasty and taunting. "You've always been a power hungry twit."

Marielle launched herself at Claudette, fangs bared. "That has nothing to do with it."

Claudette laughed and swatted Marielle aside as easily as an annoying mosquito. "You forget, I'm ten times stronger than you."

Marielle rose from the floor, anger and hatred distorting her features. "You're just on Étienne's side because you still love him."

"Enough! Both of you," François shouted. "We're not going to kill him. Not yet. If he's as he says, he's a valuable asset and we need him."

"You're a fool," Marielle said. "He's been trying to kill us both for centuries and now you're willing to forgive and forget. How can you be certain?"

"We will test him, François said. If he has turned to the dark side, he will not be able to resist human blood. If he's still even slightly on the light side, he won't drink."

"I already told you he drank from a human and killed her." Claudette said. "After all these years —"

"I want to see it with my own eyes. It's not personal. I don't trust anyone."

"Especially not him," Marielle said. She inched closer towards Étienne and Claudette glanced at him to assess reaction.

"It's okay, she can't hurt me." Étienne said.

Claudette allowed Marielle to lean in and sniff.

"He does smell like Claudette. It's pleasant, but I'm not wholly convinced. I know, bring us a human," she said to Claudette.

"I'm your progeny not your servant! Get one yourself."

"Don't be so touchy. You've been well taken care of."

François touched Claudette's shoulder. "Bring us a couple of humans. It's time for Marielle and me to feed as well." Claudette didn't answer and slammed the door behind her.

"She can be such a bitch." Marielle said "If your father fails this test I want the pleasure of killing him. Torture would be fun."

Étienne ignored her comment, more interested in François' feelings. "We've been at war for centuries. I hope we can put that behind us." He glanced at Marielle and whose eyes were filled with hatred and distrust. *She could be a problem.*

"Patience, both of you. Let's see how he does with the tests." François said.

Claudette entered the room with three humans in tow. "Dinner is served."

Étienne didn't hesitate. The smell of human blood had him salivating. His fangs elongated and he grabbed a female sinking to the floor with her. He twisted her head to the side and his fangs penetrated her carotid. A blast of lust swept over him. Claudette joined him on the other side of the victim's neck.

Claudette's scent was too enticing to ignore. Étienne pulled her to him. She knew what he wanted. She straddled him and spread her legs. Silk panties ripped away easily and her fingers were swift as she freed his cock.

Étienne plunged into her and continued drinking from the young woman's neck.

His lust threw Claudette into spasms of pleasure mingled with moans of pain as he pounded her harder and harder. He felt her clitoris contract and increased his rhythm. He exploded and at the same time he felt Claudette's climax surge and grip him in a vice.

Satiated and panting, he shoved Claudette off him and withdrew his incisors from the female's throat. She was dead and he pushed her away. He glanced up. François and Marielle had finished drinking from their respective donors and had been watching him and Claudette. It made him happy. *Family. This is how it should be.*

Étienne stood and zipped his pants He wiped his mouth with the back of his sleeve. "Satisfied?"

"It's a good start," François said.

"You're a fool," Marielle said to François. "I'm going to summon my maker. He's one of the Originals and can prove whether or not Étienne's a Strygoi."

"I don't think that's necessary." François said.

"I don't care what you think. Your brain is addled by his lies and the fact that he's your father. He's still our enemy and I don't trust him."

"Do what you must, but in my book his actions speak well enough."

Marielle sped from the room and François shrugged. "She's always been cranky."

"It's not a problem. I have nothing to hide or fear," Étienne said.

"Pretty sure of yourself aren't you."

Étienne smiled. "Do we need her? It seems she's more trouble than she's worth."

"Unfortunately we do," Claudette said. "She's first generation Strygoi and among only a handful who can turn humans."

"Not to mention that she and I have been together for centuries. We love each other in our own way." François said.

Étienne hoped he hadn't overstepped his place. "*C'est la vie.* It was just a thought. Where do we go from here?"

"I want to hear you break the news of your defection to Lexie," François replied. "I'm sure her reaction will be amusing."

"Another test?"

"Call it what you will. Remember, you're still suspect."

Étienne dialed the Society's number. François and Claudette watched him for any sign of betrayal.

"Relax, this will be entertaining and the chaos caused by my betrayal will be doubly-diverting even if it is from a distance." He put the phone to his ear and waited.

"*Bonne nuit*, André, I wish to speak with Lexie. I don't care whether or not you think it is a good idea. Put her on the phone!"

Chapter 27
Kendrick and Lexie

Lexie heard André calling her name. His voice sounded urgent. *What now?* She shoved the last bite of the sandwich in her mouth and hurried from the kitchen. She met him descending the stairs from the offices.

"What's up?"

"Étienne's on the office phone and he wants to talk to you. I don't think you should. It could be some sort of trap, but it's your decision."

"It is my decision, and I want to talk to him."

Lexie followed André into Étienne's private office and closed the door. She grabbed the receiver. *He's comin' home.*

"Étienne?"

"Ah *ma petite*, it's good to hear your voice." Lexie felt relief rush towards her, hearing his words. *Everything's gonna to be okay.*

"Are you hurt? Have you killed Marielle and Claudette? When are you coming home?" The questions tumbled from her mouth and she paused to catch her breath.

"I am wonderful. It is good to be with my son."

"I've been so worried —"

"I find it amusing that you've been concerned. But there's no need. I'm where I belong."

Lexie had trouble speaking. "What are you sayin'?"

"I will not be returning. I'm Strygoi now. You and the Society are the enemy. The next time we meet will be in battle. I look forward to that day. Your blood will be the sweetest prize of all."

All hope crumbled as her throat constricted. Her anger took precedence.

"No, damn it, I will NOT allow this to happen. You can't just throw away five hundred years of work. And, I'm your *Amant de Sang*. We belong together. I love you!"

"But I no longer love you. And, five-hundred years is nothing next to eternity. Good bye *ma petite*. Until we meet again."

The phone clicked and she threw the receiver across the room where it smashed a hole in the wall.

"Shit, shit, shit! How can this be happening? André do somethin'."

"What would you like me to do? He's gone ma chère *fille*. He has made his choice."

"You make it sound so hopeless. I love him and I know that somewhere deep inside he still loves me. We're blood mates. There has to be a way."

"There's no known antidote once a vampire has been turned Strygoi. As Kendrick said, Étienne is not the same vampire you fell in love with."

"Don't say that. He's in there somewhere."

"No he's not. Get it through your thick head that he's gone."

"Étienne would never give up on me." Lexie sobbed. Let's call Heinrick. Maybe he knows…" She stopped, realizing how desperate she sounded.

"Don't cry," André murmured, patting her shoulder. "We'll talk with Kendrick when he gets here. He may know something we don't."

Except, it did seem hopeless, and if she got really straight with herself, it felt like Étienne was lost forever. He was as good as dead. *I will not give up.*

There was nothing to do but wait for Kendrick and the other members of the Society who said they would come. Aching to be close to some part of Étienne, Lexie collected the pieces of her shattered phone, and gave André a halfhearted smile.

She left Étienne's office and went to her bedroom on the third floor.

Étienne's unique scent met her as she entered. Haunting memories of their love making excited and depressed her. She ached for his touch and her lips tingled as she recalled his passionate kisses.

Too restless to sleep, she sat in the chair by the window reliving her last conversation with Étienne. She couldn't believe he'd meant what he said about no longer loving her. Maybe he was being tested and had said it to convince François and Marielle he'd turned. But he sounded so cold and cruel about them meeting in battle and that he couldn't wait to drink her blood. *Could I kill him?* Never in her life had she felt so alone. *He has to come back.*

She tried lying down but as she buried her face in the pillow, Étienne's scent made her crazy with longing. She paced. She felt their blood tie calling to her just as Étienne said it would. She had to do something even if it was fool hardy. *I'm goin' after him.* It would be tricky getting past André and the others but she had to try.

She grabbed a jacket and opened her door listening for any telltale sounds. All was quiet. She reached the staircase and tiptoed down. The front door was just ahead. She waited for a moment to be sure no one was about and scurried ahead. *Please don't squeak.* The door opened silently and she eased it shut behind her.

Her dash to the stables went unnoticed and she ran directly to Bella's stall. "C'mon girl, we have work to do." Bella nickered as if she understood and stood still while Lexie slipped on a halter.

It would take too long to bridle and saddle her. A halter would have to do. The thought of riding over fields, streams and fences was a little daunting as Lexie hadn't ridden bareback for a while. She'd have to manage. She led Bella from the stables and leaped on her back. Responsive as always, Bella waited until Lexie was settled. She sprang forward from Lexie's soft kick and Lexie gave Bella her head. *I wonder if she misses Brute.*

Lexie quickly adjusted to Bella's smooth pace. Thick clouds covered the moon. *Thunder crap, nothin' looks familiar.* She hoped her night vision was good enough to lead her to Étienne.

She and Bella entered the forest and Lexie felt confident she was on the right track. She urged Bella to go faster and hunkered down as low branches threatened to dismount her. Bella jumped a log and went to her knees, throwing Lexie over her head. Lexie landed hard and gasped struggling to breathe. She lay still waiting for her lungs to work. She heard the mare groaning. *Oh God, Bella.* Still winded, Lexie managed to crawl to Bella's side and explored her front legs. The right foreleg was broken with the bone protruding through the skin. It was too much. Lexie burst into tears as she stroked the mare, trying to soothe her.

"I'm so sorry. This is my fault. If I hadn't been so hell bent on findin' Étienne…"

Her voice faded away as she sobbed harder. Bella nuzzled her hand and Lexie cradled her head in her lap. Her sadness subsided as anger replaced sorrow. With no one else to talk to, she talked to Bella.

"Damn him. How could he do such a thing and he was so happy about it. I have to let him go, but he's not gonna win this war. He'll regret this decision as long as he lives. Or whatever vampires do."

She dropped her head to Bella's and continued to stroke her neck. Bella's breathing was more labored, indicating she was in terrible pain. Lexie was not about to leave her there alone and settled in, hoping that someone would find them. She had just changed positions to ease the cramps in her legs when she heard a whoosh and a rustle. She looked up. The second most beautiful man she had ever seen touched down on the ground. Her heartbeat doubled. *Crap, a vampire.*

Lexie was not afraid. Something about him exuded safety. "Who the hell are you?" she asked. He grinned and the whole world seemed to light up when he did.

"Seems like ye'r in no position te ask questions. A better question might be who the bloody hell are you? And what are ye doin' in the forest in the middle of the night? Let alone sittin' with a horse's head in ye'r lap."

"I'm Lexie Miles and this is Bella. We've had an accident and she's broken her leg. Not that it's any of your business."

"Actually it is. I'm Kendrick MacDougal, at your service." He knelt beside Lexie and examined Bella's leg. "That's a bad break lassie, we need te put her out of her misery."

Blood thirsty Kendrick MacDougal. Great. Lexie shoved that thought away. "How did you find us?"

"I heard you talkin' and the horse's breathin'. You both sounded distressed and I landed to see what was happenin'."

Bella grunted and Lexie stroked her head, murmuring softly to her.

"She's in agony," Kendrick said.

"I know. I just don't have anything…"

"It's alright Lass. You go stand over there and I'll handle it."

"What are you—?"

"Better ye don't ask. What's her name?"

"Bella." Lexie stroked the mare's neck. "This is my fault. If I hadn't been so stubborn this wouldn't have happened." She leaned over and kissed Bella on the cheek.

Strong hands lifted her from behind and she didn't fight. "Go on lassie, let me take care of her."

Lexie limped a few paces away and clung to a tree for support. She heard Kendrick say something to the mare and then a sharp crack. She sank to her knees the sense of loss and guilt making her legs weak. She hugged her legs and wept.

Lexie heard the click of fangs extending and then the light pop of skin being punctured and she scrabbled to Kendrick's side. "What are you doin'?"

Kendrick had his wrist between Bella's lips and she was gently licking his blood. "I'm givin' her a bit of me blood te heal her."

"You can do that?"

Kendrick chuckled. "I'm a thousand-year-old vampire. I can do lots of things." Lexie watched in awe as Bella's breathing became strong and the light in her eyes returned. Kendrick removed his wrist and patted Bella on the neck. "It's alright she's out of pain now."

Lexie couldn't help herself. She hugged Kendrick tight. "How can I ever thank you? You saved Bella's life."

Kendrick lifted her chin. "Étienne told me about ye and that ye are his *Amant de Sang*. I know his betrayal must hurt and the blood tie will n'er be denied. But where were ye goin'?"

"I was goin' after him."

"Are ye daft? I know you're a vampire executioner, but ye don't stand a chance against François and Marielle. Not to mention Étienne. If he's turned Strygoi he'd chew ye up and spit ye out. We can't afford to lose ye too."

"But..."

"No buts, he's gone lassie. There's nay 'gettin' him back'."

"What about an antidote? You're older than dirt, you must know somethin'."

Kendrick's laugh rumbled through the night, but he ignored her question. "Cheeky lass. I like ye. Enough of this gabbing, we need to get back to the château."

"It's a long way to walk."

"Who said anythin' about walkin'? Close your eyes so you don't get nauseated." He put his arms around her and lifted off. The world tilted. It was dizzying. She took his advice and squeezed her eyes shut.

"Wait, what about Bella?"

Kendrick's arms tightened. "Her leg will mend in a couple of hours and she'll find her way home."

Lexie felt relief at his words and allowed herself to relax a little.

"That's right lass, calm yourself you're safe with me."

She felt a twinge of guilt as she realized she *did* feel safe.

Am I crazy? I just met him.

People scurried everywhere as Lexie and Kendrick touched down in front of the château. She opened her eyes and bent over as waves of vertigo washed over her.

André appeared out of nowhere, grabbed her arm and swung her around. "*Merde*, where have you been?" Lexie pulled away, fighting the temptation to drop him on his ass.

"I went after Étienne. But Bella stepped in a hole and broke a front leg." Tears threatened to spill over and she brushed at her eyes. She hated appearing weak in front of vampires. "Kendrick found us and brought me back."

"And Bella?"

"I gave her blood. She'll be fine and on her way home shortly." Kendrick said.

"*Idiote*, whatever possessed you?"

"I know it was irresponsible. And anything else you want to add. I know I have to let Étienne go. But another part of me screams to go after him."

"It'll get easier," Kendrick said. "Focus on your role in the present conflict."

"Keep tellin' me that. Right now it hurts so much I can hardly stand it. I won't be so stupid again. I promise."

"Good," André said. "That makes my job protecting you much easier."

A crowd had gathered around them and Lexie saw the relief on their faces. She didn't have a come-back for André. She knew she'd been selfish and if Bella had died she'd have never gotten over it.

It started to rain and it matched her mood. "I don't know about y'all, but I'm gettin' soaked. Can we take this inside?" Without waiting for a response, André and Kendrick followed her.

"Have any of the other Society leaders arrived?" Kendrick asked.

"Paris, Rome, Madrid, London, Edinburgh, Bucharest and Berlin are here. The others should be here by dawn." André replied.

Lexie stopped at the bottom of the stairs. "Any word from my Mom?"

"She called when she arrived in Paris. She's spending what's left of the night there and catching the first train here in the morning."

Hurry Mom, I need you. "I hope you had the good sense not to tell her I was missin'. She'd be frantic."

"I told her you were sleeping and she said not to wake you."

"Thank God for small favors."

"She's got her phone in case you want to talk to her."

The three reached Étienne's office on the second floor, and Kendrick closed the door.

"Have you heard from Étienne?" Kendrick asked, directing the question to Lexie.

"He called earlier this evenin'. It was pretty simple. He said he's fully Strygoi and isn't comin' back. He's where he wants to be with his son and he doesn't love me anymore." She shrugged. "The next time we meet he's gonna suck me dry."

274

"What a numptie, I don't mind sayin'," Kendrick said. "It's gonna be hard te adjust te him bein' the enemy. Not te mention he'll be the devil to kill."

Lexie cringed at the thought and took a good look at Kendrick. About the same height as Étienne, he was the opposite in every other way. Silky blond hair was tied back in a ponytail and his blue eyes had a mischievous glint. A plaid shirt was tucked neatly into wool trousers and a tweed jacket hung perfectly from his broad shoulders. *A thousand years old?*

Earlier I asked you about an antidote and you didn't answer." Lexie said.

"As far as anyone on this planet knows, none exists."

"What about our blood tie? The last time we were together we exchanged blood. Could that be somethin' we could—"

"What's it going to take to convince you he's a lost cause?" André shouted. His eyes turned black with anger. "You're stubborn as a mule."

"It's better than bein' a giver upper," she retorted. "Y'all are actin' like it's all over. I'm doin' my best to come to terms with his loss, but he's not dead… well technically he is, but you know what I mean. He wouldn't give up on me and I'm not givin' up on him."

André looked as if he was going to throw a punch and Lexie stiffened ready to fight back. Kendrick placed his arm around her shoulders, giving her a squeeze.

"Easy you two. We're all on edge. Right now we need te focus on gettin' ye trained, gettin' ye and your ma to safety, and makin' sure we're less vulnerable."

Lexie leaned into Kendrick's embrace, sensing an ally. She caught a whiff of his scent. *He smells like the forest.*

"God I'm tired, and I miss him," Lexie said

"I know lassie," Kendrick replied. His eyes softened in understanding. Her heart did a flip flop, and she felt guilty at her reaction. *What's that about?*

"Étienne is ma dearest friend in the world and it pains me deeply that he's turned."

"Why don't you get some rest," André suggested. His expression softened. "It'll be morning soon and your mom will be here."

"Shit, you should call her right away and tell her to wait for us in Paris." Kendrick said.

"Why?"

"I've decided te take ye both to Castle Dunollie. We'll leave for Paris first thing. "

"Wait, what?" Lexie asked. The thought of leaving the château without Étienne pierced her heart like a knife.

"Ye'll be safer there. The castle is impenetrable and I have more people to protect you."

"But…"

"It's a good idea," André said. "That will leave me free to work with the other Society leaders."

Arguing was an exercise in futility. Lexie had learned her lesson. And, it might make it easier to accept Étienne's loss if she wasn't in his home.

Cassie picked up on the first ring. "Darlin' are you okay?"

"I'm okay. Don't leave Paris. Kendrick is takin' us to his castle in Scotland tomorrow. We'll be on the first train to you in the morning."

"Why on earth…?"

"He thinks it's safer for us there. Where are you stayin'?"

For the first time in her life Cassie didn't argue. "I'm stayin' at Ritz Carlton, 15 Place Vendome."

"I'll call you when we arrive in Paris and we'll come pick you up." Lexie said. "I can't wait to see you."

"Me too sweetie."

"Get some rest and I'll see you tomorrow. Bye."

"Anything else I need to do?"

"Nothing right this minute." André said. "Go rest. You look like you need it. Kendrick and I will wait for the leaders."

She was too tired to answer and concentrated on putting one foot in front of the other until she reached her room. She flopped across the bed, dressed. Sleep didn't come right away, her thoughts jumbled and sad. *E how will I go on without you? Maybe I should join you.*

She shoved that thought away as Emma's face drifted through her mind. Her best friend had died to protect what she believed in. Lexie felt she had to honor Emma's sacrifice and avenge her death. That day in the church after Emma's funeral she'd killed a man and she figured her destiny had been sealed in that moment. Anger returned remembering the night the château was attacked. She'd watched Tom, her next best friend, brutally murdered. Étienne's betrayal forced her to admit her mom might be right. Perhaps one could never trust vampires. Yet, she was going to be holed up in a castle with several soon enough. *Should Cassie and I just go back home?*

She punched a pillow and paced. And Bella had almost been sacrificed in Lexie's impulsive attempt to reach Étienne. And for what? He no longer loved her or wanted her. *I might just love killin' him.* She knew she didn't mean that. Her heart ached for him in spite of everything.

A soft knock startled her. "Lexie, it's Kendrick. May I come in?"

Thunder crap. What now?

"Just a sec."

She opened the door and stepped back quickly, uncomfortable with her reaction to his masculinity. She felt vulnerable and in need of a male protector.

"What's up?"

"I've dispatched a couple of our best men in Paris to watch over ye'r mother. I thought ye might be concerned for her safety."

"Quite frankly with everything else that's goin' on I hadn't thought about it. Thank you, anything else?"

"If it's okay I'd like to come in and talk for a wee bit."

Not a good idea.

"I'm really tired…"

"This will only take a minute."

She nodded, motioning for Kendrick to enter.

His energy filled the room and for a heartbeat she felt a wave of panic. *Alone – with a vampire who craves human blood.* She shook off the fear. "Take a seat."

"I came te ken how ye'r doin'. It's up te me now to get ye trained and ready for battle. Ye've been through a lot in a very short period of time. It would be a normal reaction te cut and run."

"The thought had occurred to me."

Kendrick smiled. "I appreciate your honesty. However — "

"Stop. You don't need to worry about me. I'm hurt, confused, alone, but above all, I'm pissed off." She paced. "Étienne sold us down the river and I don't think I'll ever forgive him for that. Cassie was right when she said I shouldn't trust him. I don't know if I can trust any vampire. I'm beginnin' to understand what it's gonna to take to be a vampire executioner."

"Lassie…"

"Don't interrupt. I'm on a roll. I can't believe I'm sayin' this but Étienne is no different than François or Marielle. As much as I love him, right now I hate him too. *Amant de Sang* or not, if push comes to shove I *will* kill him." Her tears surfaced. She swiped at her cheeks angry that it hurt so much.

Kendrick was silent while she struggled with her emotions.

Lexie grabbed a Kleenex off the nightstand and blew her nose. "So here's what I see. I can either feel sorry for myself or I can go kick butt. I prefer to be a bitch on steroids. I'm not gonna let those assholes win. They've taken enough from us." She glared at Kendrick, "Well, say somethin'."

Kendrick stood and hugged her, then stepped back. His eyes held hers for a long moment.

"Ye'r gonna be a great vampire executioner."

"No, I'm gonna be the greatest vampire executioner ever."

He chuckled. "I believe ye. Ye'r anger is powerful. Use it."

"That's what Étienne said." The pain in her chest flared and she covered her face.

"Shit lass, I'm sorry—"

"There's nothin' to apologize for. Right now everything reminds me of him. I wish you could compel me and take away my memories and love. God, that sounds so cowardly." She sat on the bed and curled into a ball. "I'm a mess."

"Ye have a right te be."

The bed moved and strong arms embraced her.

"Maybe, but feeling sorry for myself isn't goin' to make any difference. It's gettin' in the way. He's gone and that's reality."

Kendrick patted her back and stood up. "I can see why Étienne fell in love with ye. Get some rest. We leave at seven in the morning. We have a lot of work to do." He didn't wait for her reply.

Lexie wondered if she'd ever get used to how fast vampires could evaporate. Her feet were heavy as she plodded to the bathroom. The woman who stared back at her in the mirror was a disheveled imitation of the vibrant woman of two nights ago.

"E, I'm so mad I could throttle you with my bare hands." Lexie poked her tongue out at the reflection. She laughed hysterically. The more she thought about the absurdity of her situation, the funnier it seemed. In the space of a week she'd lost her best friend, found out that vampires are real, learned that she's a super being called a vampire executioner and lost Tom. She'd fallen in love with a vampire, become his *Amant de Sang*. No sooner realized than he had been ripped away in a crazy moment, his love lost to her forever.

Her laughter turned to sobs that wracked her body. She sat on the edge of the bathtub and gave in to the grief. Minutes later, the anger stormed back in. She blew her nose, wiped her eyes and checked her reflection. She looked worse than ever. Puffy and red eyed. She didn't care.

"Look out world, I'm one pissed off super hero." The Strygoi were gunnin' for a fight and she was gonna give them one. She would find a way to bring Étienne back even if it took the rest of her life. That is, if she didn't have to kill him first. Or worse that he would kill her. *When Hell freezes over. Not gonna happen.*

Acknowledgements

To Kathrin Lake, my writing coach and without whom none of this would be possible. To Martin Crosbie who is so generous in sharing his wealth of knowledge regarding self-publishing. To Kevin Mosley, screen writer extraordinaire and someone who always trues me up. To Veronica Knox, my editor, who added humor and fun to the tedious and demanded my best. To my Beta Readers who gave me honest feedback and praise when it was warranted. To all wonderful authors, Anne Rice, Charlaine Harris, Laurell K. Hamilton, etc. who inspired me to delve into this fantasy world. And, last but not least my amazing friends and family who cheered me on despite my moods, my solitude and my crankiness – you loved me through it all.

I love each and every one of you.

About the Author

Ellen Chauvet with Author Anne Rice

Ellen Chauvet lives in Vancouver, British Columbia and finds the months of rain and gloom particularly conducive to creating in this genre. Ellen's love for reading and writing developed at an early age and she wrote several short stories and plays which were lost over the years and many moves.

In 2003 a friend introduced her to *Buffy the Vampire Slayer*, and Ellen was fascinated by the idea of good and evil vampires. At that point she started reading every vampire novel she could find, particularly loving Anne Rice, Charlaine Harris and Laurell K. Hamilton.

When Darkness Falls is the first in a series of adult fiction books called *The Vampire Redemption Series*.

About Relentlessly Creative Books

Relentlessly Creative Books™ offers an exciting new publishing option for authors. Our "middle path publishing" approach includes many of the advantages of both traditional publishing and self-publishing without the drawbacks. For more information and a complete online catalog of our books, please visit us online.

For readers, join our Readers Group. Register online and enjoy free eBooks, sneak previews on new releases, book sales, author interviews, book reviews, reader surveys and online events with Authors.

RelentlesslyCreativeBooks.com
books@relentlesslycreative.com

Made in the USA
Columbia, SC
10 September 2017